Alice-Miranda
to the Rescue

Books by Jacqueline Harvey

Alice-Miranda at School
Alice-Miranda on Holiday
Alice-Miranda Takes the Lead
Alice-Miranda at Sea
Alice-Miranda in New York
Alice-Miranda Shows the Way
Alice-Miranda in Paris
Alice-Miranda Shines Bright
Alice-Miranda in Japan
Alice-Miranda at Camp
Alice-Miranda at the Palace
Alice-Miranda in the Alps

Clementine Rose and the Surprise Visitor
Clementine Rose and the Pet Day Disaster
Clementine Rose and the Perfect Present
Clementine Rose and the Farm Fiasco
Clementine Rose and the Seaside Escape
Clementine Rose and the Treasure Box
Clementine Rose and the Famous Friend
Clementine Rose and the Ballet Break-In
Clementine Rose and the Movie Magic
Clementine Rose and the Birthday Emergency
Clementine Rose and the Special Promise

Alice-Miranda to the Rescue

Jacqueline Harvey

RANDOM HOUSE AUSTRALIA

A Random House book
Published by Random House Australia Pty Ltd
Level 3, 100 Pacific Highway, North Sydney NSW 2060
www.randomhouse.com.au

Penguin
Random House
Australia

First published by Random House Australia in 2016

Random House Books is part of the Penguin Random House group of companies
whose addresses can be found at global.penguinrandomhouse.com/offices.

National Library of Australia
Cataloguing-in-Publication Entry

Creator: Harvey, Jacqueline
Title: Alice-Miranda to the rescue/Jacqueline Harvey
ISBN: 978 0 85798 522 4 (paperback)
Series: Harvey, Jacqueline. Alice-Miranda; 13
Target audience: For primary school age
Subjects: Dogs – Juvenile fiction
            Dog shows – Juvenile fiction
            Friendship – Juvenile fiction
            Detective and mystery stories
Dewey number: A823.4

Cover and internal illustrations by J.Yi
Cover design by Mathematics www.xy-1.com
Internal design by Midland Typesetters, Australia
Typeset in 13/18 pt Adobe Garamond by Midland Typesetters, Australia
Printed in Australia by Griffin Press, an accredited ISO AS/NZS 14001:2004
Environmental Management System printer

Random House Australia uses papers that are natural, renewable and recyclable
products and made from wood grown in sustainable forests. The logging
and manufacturing processes are expected to conform to the environmental
regulations of the country of origin.

For Ian and Sandy, and Suzie the wonder dog,
biter of meter men, collector of rubbish,
swimmer extraordinaire and faithful family pet

Prologue

The tiny pup struggled to free himself from beneath his mother's matted fur. She growled softly as he grazed a raw patch of her flea-bitten skin. In the corner of the enclosure, his six siblings lay entangled, shivering to keep warm. A sliver of light grew larger as the shed door scraped open and the silhouettes of two men appeared. One was tall and heavy-set, the other slightly built and rangy.

Tails whumped on the bare concrete. Several of the creatures struggled to their feet, an as-yetunextinguished hope in their eyes. The taller figure walked to a plastic tub at the end of the shed and prised open the lid. 'Hurry up,' he muttered, 'we haven't got all day.'

'Why do I always have to get the bowls?' the other lad griped.

'Because I said, and I'm the oldest.'

'You're not the boss of me.' The words flew out of the younger lad's mouth before he had time to wish they hadn't. Within seconds his brother was upon him, pummelling his ears before a swift kick to the shin sent him hopping about and moaning in pain. 'I hate you,' he hissed under his breath.

The older fellow laughed and walked back to snatch up a small measuring cup. A few of the animals began to bark, their sharp hacks drowning out the high-pitched whimpers of many more. 'Quiet down, you lot!' he yelled.

His brother limped along the row of cages, opening and closing the wire doors and piling putrid plastic dishes into a tower. At the far end, the curly caramel pup pushed his paw against the door. It opened just enough to get his foreleg through and then his head. He wriggled and squeezed and eventually tumbled out.

He padded towards the open door, then stopped to glance back at his sleeping brothers and sisters, their barrel-like chests rising and falling with each breath. One of them flinched as if in the middle of a terrible dream. His mother mustered the energy to raise her head and looked at him with sad brown eyes. The pup let out a whine and turned back to the shed door. The canine chorus drowned out the sound of his skittering claws as he raced across the concrete to freedom.

Chapter 1

Alice-Miranda and Sloane waved goodbye to Millie as girls charged off all over the place to their second lesson of the day.

'See you at morning tea,' Millie shouted. 'And good luck with the experiment. Don't let Plumpy blow up the Science lab again.' She jogged away in her PE kit, wielding a hockey stick by her side.

Neither Alice-Miranda nor Sloane noticed the group of students walking just ahead of them and they certainly didn't see the smile which had lit up one of the girls' faces.

Sloane groaned. 'It's probably about time, you know. Plumpy hasn't blown anything up for ages.'

'I think Mr Plumpton's reputation for explosions has always been much worse than the reality,' Alice-Miranda said as she bounced along beside her friend. 'And you know it's always an accident. He never *means* to.'

'Good morning, you two,' Miss Reedy greeted the pair as she caught up to them on the path. 'Beautiful day, isn't it?'

A grey dawn had cleared to a dazzling blue sky with just the slightest breath of wind. The temperature was crisp but there was a promise of warmth in the day ahead.

'It's gorgeous,' Alice-Miranda agreed.

'Where are you both heading?' the teacher asked.

'I've got Maths and we're doing *really* long division,' Sloane said with a sigh.

Miss Reedy frowned. 'I hadn't realised there was anything more complicated than ordinary long division.'

'There's not,' Sloane said, grinning. 'I'm just not a fan of any sort of division. Isn't that what calculators were invented for?'

Alice-Miranda giggled. 'It's Science for me and we're doing an experiment but it's a surprise.'

The corners of Miss Reedy's eyes crinkled into a smile and she glanced at the oval diamond on her left hand.

Alice-Miranda noticed immediately what she was looking at. 'It's a stunning ring.'

'Yes, it is,' the woman said, her cheeks rising red. 'I was beginning to wonder if Mr Plumpton was ever going to ask me. And then the ring almost went over the side of the hot-air balloon, and Josiah with it – I thought my heart was going to stop.'

The child smiled. 'Thankfully, it didn't and Mr Plumpton's safe and now you have the most exciting engagement story I've ever heard.'

Livinia Reedy beamed. 'That's true. I can only hope the wedding is less eventful.'

'How come it's so soon?' Sloane asked. 'I thought weddings took ages to organise.'

Miss Reedy nodded. 'Mr Plumpton has a surprise arranged for our honeymoon and we have to go away on a particular date or we'll miss it. He says it's a once-in-a-lifetime event, so Miss Grimm has granted us special leave during term.'

'I wonder what it is.' Sloane wrinkled her nose and thought for a moment. 'Probably some boring Science thing.'

Alice-Miranda nudged her friend. 'It sounds like it will be unforgettable.'

'No offence, Miss Reedy,' Sloane said quickly. 'It's just that seeing the migration of the bandy-footed bongo bird isn't what I'd want to be doing on my honeymoon.'

Livinia Reedy's smile faltered slightly. 'Has Mr Plumpton said something to you?' she asked the girl.

'I'm sure Sloane just made that up,' Alice-Miranda giggled.

Sloane grinned and shrugged. 'I was only guessing. I'm sure it will be way more exciting than that, like swimming with giant snapping turtles or –'

'Is everything organised, Miss Reedy?' Alice-Miranda asked, thinking it best to step in.

'Almost.' The woman bit her lip. 'I think Mrs Smith has the menu in hand and I've booked the minister and the school chapel. But I've still got to sort out the cake and the decorations for the dining room and the chapel, not to mention the flowers – heavens, now that I think about it, there's still plenty to do.'

The woman's breathing had become shallow and she seemed to be gasping for air.

'Are you all right, Miss Reedy?' Alice-Miranda asked.

The teacher clutched the folder she was carrying to her chest and exhaled. 'Yes, I'm fine,' she replied unconvincingly.

'What about your dress?' Sloane asked.

'Oh, I've had that for over a year now,' Miss Reedy replied.

Sloane did the calculations in her head. 'But you didn't even know that Mr P liked you until we went to Paris,' she pointed out.

The woman blushed. 'Did I say a year? I meant a month, silly me. Oh dear, look at the time. Must be off.' Livinia Reedy raced down the path towards the main building.

Sloane chuckled. 'She's *so* had that dress for a year.'

'Well, I don't care if she's had it for ten years, I'm just glad they finally realised how much they love each other. It's going to be a beautiful wedding,'

Alice-Miranda said. She held open the door as they filed into a long corridor teeming with girls rushing to their lessons.

'I'll see you at morning tea,' Sloane said, turning in to her classroom.

Alice-Miranda gave her a wave and walked to the end of the hall, where she could see Mr Plumpton through the laboratory windows. Half-a-dozen large red balloons bobbed against the ceiling while the man was busy filling another from a gas cylinder. The girls had all retrieved their white lab coats and protective glasses from the storeroom next door and were patiently waiting for their teacher. He looked up and beckoned for them to enter.

'Hello everyone, I'm just about ready,' Mr Plumpton said as he tied off the last balloon and released it into the air. As always, he was wearing his white lab coat over the top of his short-sleeved shirt and tie, shorts and long socks. He had his safety glasses on too.

'Is it your birthday, sir?' one of the girls called out.

'Not today, Paige, but I think you're going to find our lesson very exciting nonetheless.' He clapped his hands together. 'Now, who can tell me which gas is lighter than air?'

Hands shot up around the room. The teacher pointed at a girl in the back row.

'Helium. That's why the balloons are floating,' she said confidently.

'Yes, Mimi, that's true, but there's another gas that's even lighter than helium,' the man replied.

Alice-Miranda raised her hand and he pointed her way. 'Hydrogen,' she said. 'It's far more dangerous too. In the early twentieth century, inventors built huge airships and they used hydrogen to power them until there was a terrible tragedy involving a ship called the *Hindenburg*. It was coming in to land in New Jersey all the way from Germany when it caught fire and lots of people died. And that's why they stopped using hydrogen in airships.'

'My goodness, Alice-Miranda, that's an excellent account of what happened. Now, girls, I thought you might like to see for yourselves the dangers of hydrogen gases.' The teacher picked up a long taper, like the sort used to light a barbecue or a gas cooker. 'Who wants to come up and help?'

There was a chorus of shouts and a sea of waving hands. The teacher selected seven girls, who quickly made their way to the front and collected their tapers.

'Isn't it a bit dangerous, sir?' a small girl called from the middle of the room.

'No, it's *exciting*!' Mr Plumpton fizzed. 'On the count of three, light your tapers. 'One, two, three!'

The girls ignited their flames and reached them up to a balloon. There was a series of explosions followed by a shower of sticky red powder. Several of the girls screamed in horror while others stood rooted to the spot, wondering whether the red shower was intentional or not.

Mr Plumpton wiped the top of his head and stared at his blood-red palms. 'That wasn't meant to happen,' he muttered.

There was a hiss as the overhead fire sprinklers sputtered to life, spraying water across the room and sending rivers of red trickling all over the girls and the classroom.

'Everyone out!' the man shouted.

Teachers and students who had heard the commotion spilled from their classrooms and into the corridor, eager to see what was going on.

'It looks like a crime scene, sir!' a girl exclaimed.

Mr Plumpton raced to a control panel and turned the sprinklers off before staggering outside. 'Calm down, everyone, we're all right,' he shouted, unaware that he resembled an axe murderer. He tried to wipe the paint from his safety goggles, which only made it worse. 'Go back inside, the rest of you. There's nothing to see here.'

Mimi examined her hands. 'What is it?'

'It looks like powdered dye,' Alice-Miranda said, rubbing the substance between her fingers. 'When it gets wet it stains everything.'

One of the girls glanced around at the streaky crew. 'I think we might need new lab coats, Mr Plumpton.'

The teacher grimaced. Mrs Howard was going to have a fit. She complained enough as it was about having to wash their lab coats every couple of weeks. 'Whoever thought this was funny is going to be very sorry.' The man rubbed his brow, smearing red all over the front of his bald head. 'Come along, girls. We need to get this place cleaned up.'

The children followed him back inside. Alice-Miranda grabbed a roll of paper towels and began to distribute sheets to the girls. She glanced up and saw Caprice Radford standing in the hallway, staring into the room. The smile on her face was troubling, to say the least.

Chapter 2

Sloane Sykes slid into the chair beside Millie and placed a steaming mug of hot chocolate on the table. 'I just heard what happened in Science,' she said, looking at Alice-Miranda gleefully.

'You mean Plumpy's modern art lesson,' Millie said. Judging from the whispers and giggles around the room, everyone else was talking about it as well.

Alice-Miranda's face was blotted with red, which no amount of scrubbing had been able to remove.

'I told you it was about time he blew something up again, but he's outdone himself today,' Sloane said, rubbing her hands together.

Millie nodded towards the doorway. 'Look, here he comes.'

Mr Plumpton entered the dining room with Miss Grimm by his side. He was still wearing his lab coat and his entire head was now stained red. The headmistress's high heels tapped across the timber floor as she marched to the podium at the end of the room. Mr Plumpton followed her onto the stage. From the shocked expression on Miss Reedy's face, she hadn't yet seen the results of the prank on her fiancé, either.

'I give you Detective Grimm and Exhibit A,' Millie whispered in a deep voice. Sloane giggled.

Ophelia Grimm switched on the microphone, which emitted a high-pitched screech. Everyone in the room winced. 'Good morning, girls and staff. I hope you've all enjoyed Mrs Smith's delicious carrot cake this morning.' Ophelia looked over and nodded at the cook, who was standing at the servery. 'Because I can tell you I think it is definitely one of her best.'

Doreen Smith smiled at the headmistress uncertainly, wondering exactly what she'd done to deserve this morning's accolades.

'I think we should all stand and give Mrs Smith a huge round of applause.' Ophelia Grimm began to clap as chairs scraped on the floor and the girls rose to their feet. It wasn't long before they were stamping and cheering, and Mrs Smith's nervous smile grew into a wide grin. 'Thank you, girls, please sit down,' Miss Grimm directed.

'What was that for?' Millie eyed the headmistress suspiciously. 'And why is she just leaving Mr Plumpton standing there like some creepy art exhibit?'

The girls exchanged quizzical looks.

'I suspect that by now most of you will have heard about the unfortunate incident in the Science laboratory during our second lesson this morning. It seems that someone thought it funny to fill the balloons Mr Plumpton was using for an experiment with red dye, which is now all over Mr Plumpton, the lab and every girl in the class. I don't know why anyone would do such a thing, but they are very fortunate that no one was injured.' Ophelia Grimm was curious as to why the man had thought it was a good idea to simultaneously light up seven hydrogen balloons in the first place, but she decided to speak to him about that later.

Mr Plumpton pirouetted so that the girls could see every inch of the damage.

Alice-Miranda glanced across the dining room at Caprice, who was sitting with the Head Prefect, Sofia Ridout, and blinking innocently.

Ophelia Grimm paused for a moment, then turned her attention back to the cook. 'Excuse me, Mrs Smith, what have you got on the menu for lunch today?'

Doreen Smith frowned. 'Lasagne and salad with treacle pudding for dessert, which reminds me, I'd best pop out and get the pudding started.'

Miss Grimm smiled sweetly. 'Yes, don't let me keep you.'

'She's up to something,' Millie whispered. 'The lunch menu's over there on the wall. Everyone can see it.'

'Unless, of course, we give you the rest of the day off,' Miss Grimm said.

Doreen Smith stopped in her tracks and turned around. 'I'm sorry, ma'am, but I don't think that's possible. There's no one else to do the cooking.'

Miss Grimm smiled. 'Oh, it's possible. In fact, it's going to happen if the person responsible doesn't come forward right now.'

'I knew it!' Millie hissed. 'She's going to starve us until she finds the culprit.'

'That's not fair,' Sloane griped loudly. 'I'm always dying of hunger by lunchtime.'

Miss Grimm shot the girl a look that would bring the most determined of toddler tantrums to an abrupt end. 'Let's talk about fair, Sloane. Do you think it's fair that girls have missed their lessons and have had to spend the entire time cleaning the Science lab, which will need many more hours of attention? Do you think it's fair that Mr Plumpton and the girls in his class now look as if they're accident victims because that dye takes hours to scrub off? Do you think it's fair that girls at this school behave in a manner that brings the *entire* student body into disrepute?'

Sloane gulped and shook her head.

The headmistress arched an eyebrow at her. 'No, I didn't think so.'

From the table closest to the servery, Caprice raised her hand in the air. A rustle of whispers ricocheted around the room.

Sloane nudged Millie. 'I don't believe it.'

Miss Grimm stared at the girl. She wondered if Caprice was about to confess, although from past experience that didn't seem likely. 'Yes, Caprice?'

The girl pushed back her chair and got to her feet. 'I know who did it,' she said confidently as she tossed her copper tresses over her shoulder.

'Do you think she's about to own up?' Sloane whispered.

Millie shook her head. 'You've got to be kidding.'

'It was . . .' Caprice unfurled her pointer finger and directed it across the dining room. 'Millie.'

The whole room gasped.

Millie looked at the girl, her mouth gaping. 'Me?!' she yelled, jumping to her feet. 'No, I didn't!'

'That's a very serious allegation, Caprice. I hope you have your facts in order,' the headmistress boomed.

Caprice nodded. 'Of course, Miss Grimm.'

'She's lying. I didn't do anything,' Millie protested, her voice quivering with rage.

'I heard her telling Alice-Miranda and Sloane on the way to class that she hoped there weren't any explosions at Science and the three of them were laughing,' Caprice said.

Miss Grimm eyeballed the girl. 'That hardly proves anything. We all know that Mr Plumpton has a bit of a reputation.'

Josiah's cheeks burned. If it weren't for the red dye, everyone would have seen he was blushing from head to toe.

'Check her fingernails, Miss Grimm,' Caprice said, folding her arms across her chest. 'I think you'll find all the proof you need.'

Millie's whole body was quaking. 'You're lying again!' she yelled at the girl.

'If you have nothing to hide, just come up and prove it,' the headmistress urged.

Millie gulped. She glanced down at her fingers, then clenched her fists into two tight balls.

Alice-Miranda put a hand on her friend's arm. 'What's the matter?' she asked.

Millie shook her head and shuffled out from the table. She walked up to the podium, her footfalls echoing around the room. Miss Grimm beckoned for Millie to come forward and looked at her expectantly. The girl took a deep breath and laid her palms flat. 'I can explain,' she said softly.

A veil of disappointment dropped across Miss Grimm's face.

'Caprice tricked me when we were in Art this morning,' the child blurted. 'She told me Miss Tweedle needed help putting the dyes into smaller containers.'

'Now who's lying?' Caprice said, stalking towards the podium. 'Why would I do that?'

Ophelia Grimm glanced around the room, searching for the Art teacher. A tiny woman, both in height and scale, Verity Tweedle had recently joined the school. Despite her diminutive size, she was already proving to be a forthright member of staff and the girls had quickly learned that she wasn't to be messed with. Miss Grimm located Miss Tweedle, who was sitting at the back of the room with Miss Wall, the PE teacher.

'Miss Tweedle, could you tell me what activity you had the girls doing in the first lesson today?' the headmistress asked.

'They were working on linocuts,' Miss Tweedle replied. There was a murmur from the rest of the girls. 'And no dye was involved whatsoever.'

The students gasped again.

Millie swallowed hard. Miss Tweedle had made her sound like a liar too. It all made sense now – Caprice had tricked her while the teacher was faffing about with Constance Biggins's cut finger. Caprice had told Millie, who had come in late from her piano lesson, that Miss Tweedle needed assistance sorting out some dyes in the prep room for her next class. She'd wondered why there was no one else helping but she'd already finished her linocut and didn't feel like starting another one. Caprice had just bossed her around and done none of the work.

'I think you'd better come with me, Millie, and we can discuss this further in my office. You too, Caprice,' Miss Grimm said. She turned to Cook. 'In light of all this, Mrs Smith, you'd better get on with that pudding.'

'Of course,' the woman replied. She scuttled into the kitchen, mumbling something about running late.

Chatter erupted as the girls began to speculate about what had really happened and whether or not Millie was guilty. Miss Grimm strode out of the dining room with Millie and Caprice in tow. Caprice turned and smiled at Alice-Miranda as she went out the door.

'Did you see that?' Sloane said, outraged.

Alice-Miranda nodded. She wondered what Millie had done to be on the receiving end of Caprice's wrath this time.

But Alice-Miranda and Sloane weren't the only ones to spot the girl's contemptuous grin. Josiah Plumpton had witnessed it too.

'Excuse me, Livinia,' he said to his fiancée, who had just brought him a cup of tea and a slice of cake. 'I need to speak with the headmistress right away.'

Chapter 3

Myrtle Parker's feather duster danced along the skirting boards of the sitting room. As she neared the front window, she stood up and pulled aside the sheer curtain. Her eyes scanned up and down the empty street, but there was nothing out of the ordinary. She glanced around at her beloved Newton, who these days sat pride of place in the centre of the mantelpiece. He hadn't been allowed outside once since he'd returned from his year away. Myrtle clicked her tongue. 'There's something going on today,' she said to him. 'I can feel it.'

As always, the garden gnome declined to reply. Myrtle resumed her dusting. She was a proud housekeeper and, now that the sitting room was back to its best, minus the industrial-sized hospital bed where her husband had lain in a coma for over three years, she found the task immeasurably easier. Fortunately, Reginald Parker had woken up some months ago and proved to be in near-perfect health.

Somewhere in the distance, a clattering diesel engine grew louder. Myrtle scurried back to the window just as a convoy of removal vans roared past. They were followed by a silver four-wheel drive towing the longest dog trailer she had ever seen.

'I knew it!' Myrtle muttered, dropping her duster to the floor. 'Reginald!' she called. 'Someone's moving into the house at the end of the road. And they've got *dogs*!'

Her husband was, at that minute, sitting in the kitchen enjoying a quiet cup of tea. He paused as he raised the teacup to his mouth and wondered what he was supposed to say.

'Did you hear me?' Myrtle screeched. 'Reginald!'

The old man sighed. He stood up and tipped the last of his tea into the sink, then ambled down the hallway. 'Yes, dear,' he answered. 'What would you like me to do about it?'

The woman let go of the curtain and turned to face her husband. 'We need to find out about them, of course. We can't be too careful when it comes to who's living in the village, and you know I'm not especially partial to dogs.' Myrtle picked up her feather duster.

'I think the feeling's mutual,' the man replied.

'What was that?' she demanded.

'Nothing, dear.' Reginald Parker took a deep breath. He thought he might as well tell her and get it over with, although he was surprised she hadn't heard all about the newcomers on the village grapevine. 'They're breeders.'

Myrtle frowned. 'I didn't see any children in the car.'

Reginald chuckled. 'Dog breeders, Myrtle.'

'Oh, how do you know that?' the woman asked.

'I saw a sign for their kennel go up yesterday when I went for my walk.'

'What sort of dogs do they have? Not those savage bull pits, I hope.' The woman blanched at the thought. 'Or rottweilers. We can't have any dangerous dogs in the village. I won't allow it.'

Reg ignored his wife's histrionics. As far as he knew, he lived with the only rottweiler in the village. 'No need to worry yourself, dear. They breed Afghan hounds.'

'But they're *huge*!'

'They're lovely dogs,' Reg said. 'At least they are to look at.'

Myrtle set aside the feather duster and picked up a can of furniture polish. 'They'd better not be barkers,' she blustered. She sprayed the sideboard and rubbed it vigorously with a cloth. 'We can't be woken at all hours by constant yapping.'

'No, dear.' Reg doubted the dogs could be any worse than his wife's constant yapping. As for being woken in the middle of the night, Myrtle, who had been a stickler for her eight hours' sleep prior to his accident – not a minute more or less – now woke every hour on the hour. These days they slept in separate beds in the same room. Her waking wouldn't have worried Reg except that the woman had taken to prodding him with an old telescopic television aerial she kept by the side of her bed to make sure that he was still breathing. He supposed, after having been in a coma for the better part of three and a half years, he couldn't really blame her, although there were some days he wondered if he mightn't have had a more peaceful existence if he'd stayed asleep.

'Here, you finish the polishing and I'll get started on a cake,' she said, handing her husband the cloth and can of spray.

'Don't you think you should give them a day or two to unpack and settle in?' he asked.

Myrtle looked at him as if he were mad. 'Absolutely not. I don't want them to think they've moved into a snooty village,' she replied. 'Everyone is welcome in Winchesterfield, even if they do breed overly large dogs. Besides, I have to make sure they will be properly contained.'

Reg raised an eyebrow. 'Everyone's welcome, are they? I didn't see you rushing off to welcome the Singhs when they arrived.'

'Oh, that was years ago. You know I love a curry as much as the next person,' Myrtle said. 'Except vindaloo – there should be a law against that.'

The man stifled a grin as he recalled his wife's petition to close down the new curry house in the village before it had even opened. Myrtle had argued that the smell of the curries would overpower the fresh air that their little pocket of countryside was renowned for, but Reg suspected it had as much to do with her fear of the unfamiliar as anything else. To everyone's great surprise, Indira Singh and Myrtle Parker had bonded over a mutual love of organising. Indira went on to become head of the local garden club and often asked for Myrtle's help with planning events. Myrtle had just invited her onto the Show Society Committee too.

'Well, don't just stand there,' Myrtle said, eyeballing her husband. 'We've got work to do.'

Chapter 4

Myrtle Parker pinned a pillbox hat onto her helmet of brunette curls before wrestling into a bold floral coat that matched her dress. She applied her favourite coral-coloured lipstick and smacked her lips together, then hurried to the kitchen to pick up the cake.

Reginald met his wife at the front door.

'What in heaven's name are you wearing?' she said, looking him up and down.

Without a word, the man walked back down the hall and changed out of his favourite brown cardigan and into the checked sports jacket his wife had bought for him.

Myrtle smiled her approval and gave him a peck on the cheek. 'Much better. You look very handsome.'

Reg didn't agree. He'd always thought the jacket looked like it had been made from one of Myrtle's tablecloths. Her own ensemble could have been sewn from the lounge-room curtains, but at this stage in life there was no point arguing. It would only upset her.

The mismatched pair walked down the front steps and onto the driveway. Myrtle glanced over at Ambrosia Headlington-Bear's front garden and tutted. 'Ever since that woman got herself a job, that garden has been in sharp decline. She really should do something about it.'

'I'll pop over and mow the lawn this afternoon,' Reg said, glad for the excuse to escape.

'Good, but she'll have to find a more permanent arrangement. We can't have Wisteria Cottage letting the street down, can we?' Myrtle nodded, apparently forgetting that her own weed-infested garden had blighted the landscape until Ambrosia had set to and performed nothing short of a miracle makeover.

Rosebud Lane ended in a cul-de-sac just over the rise from the Parkers' plain bungalow on one side and pretty Wisteria Cottage on the other. The house on the curve of the road was a rambling affair with a thick hedge shielding it from the neighbours. The previous owners had extensively remodelled and updated the house but had only ever used it as a weekend retreat. Myrtle had hoped that Mr Cutmore and his wife would become more involved in village life, but her entreaties were always met with a curled lip and protestations that Mr Cutmore was far too busy with his work commitments. The man was a barrister of some repute and Myrtle would love to have had him on the Show Society Committee. In the end, she wasn't terribly disappointed when the 'For Sale' sign had gone up, although the prospect of new neighbours always set her teeth on edge.

One large removal van was still parked in the driveway and another on the street but the four-wheel drive and trailer were nowhere to be seen. Outside the front gate was the sign Reginald had told her about. Written in swirly script were the words '*Nobel Kennels, Breeders of Exquisite Afghan Hounds*' beside a painting of a regal-looking dog. Myrtle squinted at the name. Surely it was a spelling mistake, she thought to herself.

A spotty young fellow in a blue singlet walked down a ramp at the back of the truck balancing a large armchair above his head. Myrtle and Reg followed him up the path to the front door.

'Excuse me, can you tell me where the owners of the house are?' Myrtle asked.

'Last I saw, Mr Dankworth was in the sitting room,' the man replied. He shifted from one leg to the other, his muscles straining under the weight of the chair.

'And what about the dogs?' she asked, peering into the hallway. 'Are there any dogs in the house?'

'No, they're in the palace up the back,' the fellow replied, as a trickle of perspiration snaked down his left temple.

'Thank you.' Myrtle nodded at the man, wondering what on earth he was talking about. A palace – what nonsense! The fellow grunted as he repositioned the chair and continued down the hallway.

'I think we should come back tomorrow,' Reg murmured as several burly removalists barrelled towards them on their way back to the truck.

'We're here now,' Myrtle insisted. 'I'm sure they'll be glad of a cup of tea and a slice of cake.' With a look of determination, Myrtle set foot into the house. 'Hello! Hello!' she called in a singsong voice. 'Are you there, Mr Dankworth?'

She manoeuvred around a huge pile of boxes and walked through the door at the end of the passage. It opened into a large kitchen and dining room on the left and a sitting room to the right, with a grand central fireplace dividing the spaces. A man was up a ladder, hammering a picture hook into the wall. Standing beside him was a thin woman wearing a black velour tracksuit with the letters HH in swirly silver script across her bottom. Her long blonde hair was pulled back into a ponytail and she wore a full face of make-up, including glossy pink lipstick and eyelashes that would have made a Jersey cow weep with envy. A large picture frame was resting on her leg.

'Hello there, neighbours, welcome to Winchesterfield,' Myrtle sang out just as the man swung the hammer. Startled, he missed and hit his finger.

'Ow!' The man jammed his thumb into his mouth and looked over at Myrtle and Reg.

'Be careful, Barry,' the woman chided. She leaned the picture against the wall and walked over to the visitors. 'Oh my, we weren't expecting anyone today. I must look an awful mess.'

'You're fine, dear,' Myrtle said. She eyed the woman, who appeared to have applied her make-up with a trowel. 'Are you all right, Mr Dankworth?'

'Don't mind Barry,' the woman said. 'It's not the first time he's hit his thumb this morning and I dare say it won't be the last.'

'I'm all right,' the man mumbled and stepped down from the ladder.

'My name's Myrtle Parker and this is my husband, Reginald. We thought we'd welcome you to Winchesterfield and especially to Rosebud Lane,' Myrtle said. 'You must be Mr and Mrs Dankworth?'

'We prefer Barry and Roberta,' the woman replied.

'I've brought you a hummingbird cake,' Myrtle said, thrusting the cake box into Roberta's hands. 'It's home-made. I think you'll find we're very good at that sort of thing around here.'

'Thank you.' The woman smiled, revealing the whitest teeth Myrtle had ever seen. It was as if the lighting in the room had suddenly been turned up a notch.

Reg walked over to shake Barry Dankworth's hand. He was a handsome fellow with dark hair and warm brown eyes. 'Sorry to land on you today,'

Reg said quietly, 'but once Myrtle has it in her mind to do something, I'm afraid there's no getting around it.'

'Nonsense,' Myrtle scoffed. 'I think Mr and Mrs Dankworth look as though they need a break. Why don't I put the kettle on?'

Roberta glanced over at the half-empty boxes in the kitchen. She doubted whether she'd be able to find the kettle let alone the crockery, but Myrtle Parker was on a mission. The woman was digging about in the kitchen before Roberta had time to object. Within ten minutes Myrtle had located the silver kettle as well as plates, forks and some rather unusually wide mugs (she had searched in vain for china teacups and saucers) and, to Roberta's great surprise, she had even unearthed a tablecloth.

Meanwhile, Reginald had busied himself by holding the spirit level for Barry, who was hammering another picture hook into the wall. 'I thought most people only got around to hanging the artwork weeks after they'd unpacked everything else,' Reg said, picking up the heavy frame. He spun the picture around and came face to face with the head of a very large dog.

'Not in our house,' Roberta replied. 'My babies are the first things to go up.'

'How lovely,' Myrtle said as she set about clearing some space on the dining table. She looked up just as Reginald passed the painting to Barry. 'That's not a baby!' she blurted.

Roberta laughed. 'Of course she is. That's my Emerald,' the woman said. 'She was my first champion, God rest her soul.'

'Do you have other . . . *children*?' Myrtle asked.

'Oh, yes,' Roberta replied with a smile. 'They're in the Poochie Palace. Except for Farrah Fawcett – she's hiding.'

'Where?' Myrtle gasped, her eyes darting about.

'Under the covers in our bed. She's been very anxious about the move, the poor princess. The vet said I should just let her find a warm spot where she feels safe, and eventually she'll come out when she's ready.' Roberta hurried over to another large framed picture and picked it up. 'I just love this shot of me and Farrah. Isn't she divine?'

Myrtle Parker flinched at the sight of Roberta Dankworth nose to nose with what appeared to be some sort of miniature poodle. 'So that one's not an Afghan?' she squeaked.

'No, Farrah Fawcett's my little bubba. We always do our hair the same way. Well, I do hers *and* mine because, of course, she can't manage a hair dryer, although given half a chance I think she'd try. You should see her with the curlers in – she's adorable.' Roberta could have prattled on for days. 'And don't you love that outfit? I had her blouse made exactly the same as mine and it got *so* many compliments – it's part of our Haute Hound Spring/Summer collection.'

Myrtle stared and shook her head. 'And where is this Poochic Palace?' she asked.

'Out the back. We had it built before we moved in,' Roberta said. 'Would you like to see it? I can take you to meet the family.'

'Perhaps later,' Myrtle replied quickly. She wasn't especially keen to meet the beasts, though she did want to find out just how many there were.

'At least come and have a peek through the curtains,' Roberta pressed. 'They won't bite you from here.'

'They'd better not bite me from anywhere!' Myrtle put down the cake knife and followed Roberta Dankworth to the back of the house, where she pulled the drapes aside. 'Good grief!' Myrtle reeled. 'Reginald, you must come and see this!'

In the back garden was a house, about half the size of the Parkers' bungalow but much prettier. It was almost like a slightly smaller version of the Dankworths's main house with its own picket fence too.

Her husband padded over to the window. 'Now, *that's* what I call a doghouse,' he said, his eyes sparkling.

Roberta smiled. 'I'm going to be featured on *Dog Days* – they're coming to film me and my babies. Barry's company sponsors the show.'

'What sort of business are you in, Barry?' Reg asked.

'Accessories for dogs,' the man said. 'We sell everything from puppy ponchos to hound haircare. Designer clothes, shoes, collars, beauty products – you name it, we've got it.'

'Ah, Haute Hound – Couture for Designer Dogs. Is that you?' Reg said. He'd seen it advertised on the telly the other night after the movie had finished.

'That's us!' Roberta beamed, all teeth and lips. She wiggled her bottom with the HH logo on it in Reg's direction.

'It gave me a laugh seeing all those dogs on the runway,' Reg said. 'Beautiful creatures, they were.'

Myrtle rolled her eyes.

'Two of them were my big girls and Farrah Fawcett, of course. She's a natural when it comes to modelling – you've never seen a dog with a more effortless twirl,' Roberta said proudly, pushing her shoulders back and her bosoms forward.

'Do you really mean to tell me that's where your hounds live?' Myrtle asked. 'That's preposterous!'

Over on the ladder, Barry Dankworth winced. He wished Myrtle hadn't said that. Roberta never took kindly to criticism when it came to her beloved dogs.

'No, it's not!' Roberta snapped. 'My babies deserve only the very best.'

Myrtle snorted. 'Next you'll be telling me it has central heating and a swimming pool out the back.'

Roberta glared at the woman. 'Well, for your information –'

'Perhaps we should let you get on with moving in,' Reg interjected. 'I think we've intruded for far too long, Myrtle.'

'We haven't had our tea yet,' the woman bristled and hurried back to the kitchen.

There was a stony silence as Roberta stalked along behind Myrtle and picked up the cake knife.

'How many hounds do you have?' Myrtle asked.

'Six,' the woman replied curtly, 'including the current Chudleigh's Grand Champion.'

Myrtle poured water into the teapot. 'Are they barkers?'

'I can assure you they are *not*, and even if they were, you wouldn't hear them anyway. We had the Poochie Palace fully insulated, double-glazed and soundproofed,' Roberta replied tartly.

Myrtle had never heard anything so ridiculous – a double-glazed doghouse! She and Reginald only had their windows upgraded a few years back. 'Oh, I've just remembered I have some urgent things to attend to before the Show Society meeting tomorrow,' Myrtle said. 'I'm the president, you know.'

A thin smile perched on Roberta's otherwise extremely full lips. 'Never mind then.'

Reg Parker shook Barry's hand and nodded at Roberta. 'It was lovely to meet you,' he said, apologising with his eyes.

Myrtle was already halfway down the hall when she called out her goodbyes. 'Well, that was disappointing,' she sniffed as her husband caught up to her on the garden path.

'It was kind of you to make the cake but, really, I'm sure it would have been better received if we'd waited another day or two,' Reg said, gently touching his wife's arm.

Myrtle flinched. 'She didn't even say thank you. Did you see that, Reginald? Not a word of thanks from that woman's overblown lips.'

Meanwhile, back at the Dankworth residence, Roberta's mood was similarly glum.

'Who's she to tell me what my babies should and shouldn't have?' Roberta huffed as she put away Farrah's tea set.

'She's probably just never seen anyone as dedicated as you are,' Barry said, trying to placate her as he popped a piece of cake into his mouth. 'Mmm, this is delicious.'

'Make sure you enjoy it because you won't be having another one ever again,' Roberta said. 'I can assure you Myrtle Parker and I are *not* going to be friends.'

Chapter 5

Millie picked at the coloured skin around her finger-nails as she and Caprice waited outside Miss Grimm's study. The headmistress's secretary was nowhere to be seen, leaving Millie to surmise that she was probably still in the dining room enjoying her morning tea. Millie had been enjoying hers too until Caprice had ruined everything. Now it felt like there was a great lump of carrot cake sitting in her stomach hardening into a rock.

Millie looked over at Caprice, who was sitting on the other side of the room. 'Why did you do it?' she asked.

The girl turned her head ever so slightly and smirked. 'I don't know what you're talking about,' she replied.

Millie could feel the heat rising to her cheeks. She clenched her fists and breathed in deeply. 'You're unbelievable.'

The girls couldn't help but overhear snatches of conversation coming from inside the study. Mr Plumpton had caught up to them in the corridor and had insisted on having a word to the headmistress right away. Millie's ears pricked up when she heard the man say her name.

'I really don't believe that Millie had anything to do with the paint bombs,' the man said. 'We all know that Caprice tells lies, and if Millie says that she was set up, then it's more than likely to be the truth.'

Caprice glared at the door.

'Josiah, my instinct is telling me you're probably right but the evidence points to Millie,' the headmistress replied. 'Plus, I don't understand why Caprice would do this to her.'

'I can't believe you're going to get away with it,' Millie whispered.

Caprice blinked her big blue eyes. 'Get away with what? You're the one with the paint under your nails.'

'You know, I was actually starting to like you when we were ice-skating in Zermatt – and now you've gone and done this. Was it about me or has Plumpy done something to get up your nose?' Millie fumed.

Caprice shrugged. 'Sorry, did you say something?'

The door opened and Mr Plumpton strode out. He looked at Millie and smiled tightly.

'Girls, Miss Grimm would like to see you now,' the man said. Millie pushed herself up off the chair and walked towards the door. Mr Plumpton gave her a reassuring pat on the shoulder as Caprice stalked past.

'Thanks for trying, Mr Plumpton,' Millie said quietly before following the girl inside to meet her fate.

★

Millie slammed the door and hurled herself onto her bed. 'She's a monster!' the girl bellowed, burying her head under the pile of pillows.

Alice-Miranda jumped up from her desk, where she'd just started her homework. She hadn't seen Millie since morning tea and had been worried all day. She sat on the edge of the bed and rested her hand gently on her friend's shoulder. 'What happened?' she asked.

Millie rolled over, her face streaked with tears. 'I'm on gardening duties with Charlie for the whole weekend and I have to clean the Science lab tonight after dinner.' Fresh tears sprouted from Millie's eyes and she hastily brushed them away.

'That's it, I'm going to talk to her,' Alice-Miranda said, sliding off the bed.

'Don't bother,' Millie whispered. 'She's a psychopath.'

'I just don't understand why she'd do it,' Alice-Miranda said.

Millie grabbed a cushion and hugged it. 'Who knows? But I'm sure she's not going to tell you.'

'Don't worry. I'll help you clean the lab and I'll see if Sloane can come too,' Alice-Miranda said. She pulled on a cream cardigan and slipped her feet into a pair of pale pink ballet slippers. 'I'll be back soon.'

'You're wasting your time,' Millie called, but Alice-Miranda had already gone.

Alice-Miranda knocked on the door next to their own and poked her head in to find Sloane reading at her desk. 'Hi. May I come in?'

Sloane turned and smiled, setting her book aside. 'Of course. Is Millie back?' she asked.

Alice-Miranda nodded and closed the door behind her, then relayed the story about Millie's punishment.

Sloane shook her head. 'I can't believe Caprice set her up again – and after you practically saved her life when we were in Zermatt. I just don't get her at all.'

'Do you know where she is?' Alice-Miranda asked.

'At some singing lesson with Mr Trout and Mr Lipp,' Sloane said, rolling her eyes. 'I'm surprised you haven't heard all about the extra rehearsals she has to attend for the National Eisteddfod at the end of the term. She's talked about it non-stop since we came back to school.'

'I'm going to help Millie clean the lab after dinner,' Alice-Miranda said. 'Do you want to give us a hand?'

'I'd love to, but if I don't finish this book Miss Reedy will have me in detention for the rest of the term. It's the class novel and I should have read it over the break. Sorry,' Sloane said, frowning. 'I know you don't believe in revenge, Alice-Miranda, but we have to do something about Caprice. The more she gets away with things the worse she behaves,' Sloane said, swivelling her chair.

Alice-Miranda sighed. 'I don't know what it is with her and Millie.'

'She's jealous,' Sloane said. 'I was the same when I first arrived. You and Millie are so close and I'd never had that sort of friendship with anyone.'

'But now you do and Caprice could too,' Alice-Miranda said, her brow wrinkling.

'That's true, but not everyone is as kind as you are, Alice-Miranda, and not everyone is willing to share their friends, either,' Sloane said.

Alice-Miranda bit her lip. 'I just don't know what more we can do. She was at the palace and she was skiing with us.'

Sloane stood up and walked to the window. She stared into the garden, deep in thought. 'All that happened by accident. Caprice wasn't really invited, so she knows that we just put up with her and that's why she's so mean to us and especially to Millie. And remember, it was really you she was after at camp because she thought you were going to win the medal. She used Millie to try to get to you, which was pretty evil, and I suppose when her plan didn't work, Millie became her target. Deep down I'm sure she knows we'd rather she wasn't here,' Sloane said. The girl spun around to face Alice-Miranda, her eyes wide. 'Wow! Did I actually work all that out?'

Alice-Miranda grinned at the girl. 'Sloane Sykes, I think that you just might be the smartest one of all of us.'

Chapter 6

Becca Finchley sat at the kitchen table sipping tea from a china mug. She tapped her pen on the page and stared at the rosettes that papered the walls. The dog on her lap stirred and sighed deeply before falling back to sleep. Becca began to fill out the form. Could she really do it without him? He'd want her to – that much she was sure of – but the thought of being there without him made the ache in her chest worse. She wondered if seeing everyone would just make things harder. They'd be lovely, of course, and sympathetic, but that wouldn't bring her husband back.

The paperwork was due on Friday, along with the hefty entrance fee. But this was Chudleigh's and maybe her last hurrah. As Becca signed her name on the bottom of the page, she heard the gate followed by the sound of running feet. The front door slammed as Daniel arrived home from school.

'Mum!' he shouted. 'Where are you?'

'In here,' Becca called, and waited for the hurricane to reach the kitchen. Sure enough, seconds later, her only child flew into the room, his face shiny and red. He poured a glass of water and grabbed an apple from the fruit bowl before walking over to give her a kiss.

'How was your day?' he asked.

Becca grabbed him around the middle and pressed his face against hers. 'All the better now that you're here. What about yours?'

He shrugged and took a bite of the apple. 'I came first in the Maths test.'

'Well done. See, I told you studying would pay off.' Becca raised her eyebrows at the boy as he walked to the pantry and opened the door.

Daniel grinned. 'Yeah, but I wouldn't want to make a habit of it,' he teased.

He was a smart boy. They both knew it, but he'd changed since the accident. His teachers said that he was handling things well and making good progress but Becca worried that he was keeping up appearances for her sake. Some days he'd go for a run and disappear for hours. He'd come home exhausted and flop into bed, where he'd sleep fitfully. There were nights she would hear him crying. By the time she'd manoeuvre herself out of bed and into his room, he'd have stopped. It frightened her that he was bottling things up. The counsellor said it was just his way of dealing with what had happened and that he'd talk about it when he was ready, but it didn't do much to put Becca's mind at ease.

'Did you walk up from the bus stop?' she asked.

Daniel closed the pantry door and leaned against it, looking at her. 'Mrs Bird gave me a lift.'

'I hope you said thank you.' Becca pushed the wheels of her chair backwards and swivelled around. The cavalier King Charles spaniel on her lap woke up with a start and jumped onto the floor, headed straight for the utility room. Becca wheeled herself to the stove and lifted the kettle.

'I'll do that.' Daniel stuffed the apple into his mouth and took the kettle from her hands. He flipped open the lid and began to fill it.

'Sweetheart, it's okay,' she said softly. 'I have to do things for myself. I made a cup of tea at lunchtime and didn't spill a drop.'

'I don't want you to,' Daniel said. 'What if Siggy knocks into you and you get burned? Or you fall out of the wheelchair? I don't see why I can't just stay at home and do my lessons with you.'

'You're already smarter than I am, Daniel. Anyway, you don't want to be cooped up here with your boring old mother every day for the rest of your life.'

'Don't say that!' Daniel snapped. He turned away from her and brushed angrily at his face.

Becca reached out and placed a hand on his arm. 'Oh, honey, I didn't mean to upset you. But you have to go to school – we can't change how things are.'

Daniel stared out of the kitchen window. 'I could have,' he whispered. 'I could have changed everything.'

Becca winced. 'You know that's not true.'

'Yes, it is!' Daniel said, shaking off her hand. 'If I hadn't gone to Grandpa's, Dad would still be alive and you wouldn't be in that stupid chair and we'd still have the dogs.'

'Daniel, it's not your fault. Come and sit down and we can talk about things.'

'I don't want to,' he said, sucking in a deep breath. He could feel the anger surging. 'I'm going for a run.'

'Please, just stay here with me,' Becca called after him, but Daniel was already gone.

She watched through the glass door as he jumped the low stone wall that separated their farmhouse garden from the open field and jogged off into the distance.

Chapter 7

Mr Trout's fingers ran along the piano keys as he ended the accompaniment with a flourish. He closed his eyes and meditated on the last note before speaking. 'Caprice, that was astonishing!'

Harold Lipp nodded. 'I have a good feeling about you retaining that crown at the National Eisteddfod, my dear.'

Caprice Radford smiled sweetly and flounced her copper curls over her shoulder. 'I love that song. Do you really think it suits my voice?'

'It's perfect and you can thank Mr Lipp for that,' Cornelius Trout replied as his colleague gathered his musical scores together and placed them into a briefcase.

'I just knew it would be right.' Harold smiled, then glanced at his watch. 'Oh dear, I must get going or I'll be in trouble with Professor Winterbottom. We've got a late staff meeting. I'll see you again soon.' And with that he hurried out the door.

Cornelius Trout stood up and closed the piano lid. 'You must be exhausted, Caprice. I'll walk you back to the boarding house.'

Although Mr Trout and Mr Lipp had expressed their disappointment with the girl's behaviour at the school camp, both men seemed to get over it very quickly – unlike horrible Mr Plumpton. Caprice couldn't believe he wouldn't allow her to miss a few silly Science lessons so she could fit in extra singing rehearsals. His classes were mind-numbing anyway and she could already recite the periodic table off by heart.

Her thoughts wandered to the uncomfortable conversation she and Millie had overheard in Miss Grimm's study that morning. Plumpton was definitely out to get her. There was no reason why he should think the paint bombs were her doing when all the evidence pointed straight at Millie. The girl's mind raced as she tried to think of what lesson she could teach the man for being so mean.

'Come along,' Mr Trout said, ushering her from the room.

As they reached the entrance to the building, Miss Grimm appeared. 'Oh, good, you're still here,' she said. 'Mr Trout, could we have a quick chat about the music for this week's assembly?' the woman said.

'I was just about to walk Caprice back to the boarding house,' Cornelius replied.

Ophelia didn't want to miss her favourite television show that was due to start in half an hour and she knew that conversations with Mr Trout tended to be longer rather than shorter. 'I'm sure Caprice is more than capable of getting herself back to the house.' The headmistress looked at the girl. 'Aren't you?'

Caprice nodded. 'Of course, Miss Grimm.'

She said goodnight and walked down the path and across the quadrangle. Lights shone in the kitchen window and she could see Mrs Smith's silhouette at the sink. Caprice was lost in her thoughts when she rounded the corner, past the newly planted flowerbeds, and heard a plaintive cry. She stopped and glanced around. 'Hello?' she said softly. 'Who's there?'

A mournful squeak replied.

Caprice crouched down and peered through the flowers. She parted some spindly chrysanthemums and saw a puppy with huge eyes and a wagging tail sitting in the garden. She knelt down and held out her hand. 'Aren't you cute,' she said.

The puppy took a couple of tentative steps forward, then retreated underneath a large leaf.

'Are you hungry?' Caprice asked. She felt around in her pocket to see if she had anything to eat, but all she found was an empty lolly wrapper.

The pup began to cry again.

'Stay there and I'll get you something,' Caprice instructed.

She fled across the quadrangle and around the back of the kitchen to the garbage bins. As much as Caprice loathed the idea of rummaging around in the rubbish, the puppy needed food and this was the best place to find it. She lifted the lid and reached for a couple of slices of meat, gagging at the smell.

'He'd better appreciate this,' Caprice muttered, cringing at the touch. A slimy splodge of gravy fell onto her shoe. 'Gross!'

Caprice carried the leftovers back to the garden and was glad to find the puppy hadn't moved. She knelt down and offered him a scrap of that night's roast beef. The pup's nose twitched and its body shook as it rushed forward only to retreat again. But the lure of the food was too great. The little creature eventually snatched the piece of meat from Caprice's hand and chewed as if there was no tomorrow. She grinned and waited until he'd finished before offering the second piece. When he was done, Caprice leaned in and picked up the tiny pup.

'Pooh, you stink,' she said, screwing up her nose. Despite his offensive odour, Caprice giggled when his tongue shot out and licked her on the cheek.

She paused to consider what to do next. Miss Grimm would probably call the dog catcher, who'd take the puppy to the pound. It didn't even cross the girl's mind that someone might be missing him. Caprice had always wanted a dog of her own but she'd *always* had to share her pets with her brothers. The little puppy looked at her; his big brown eyes were just about the saddest thing she'd ever seen.

'I could look after you,' she whispered. 'You could be *all* mine.'

Caprice pondered where to hide him. As a whinny sounded in the distance, the perfect spot sprang to mind. It was warm and dry and she would even be able to give him a bath to get rid of that stink. She could take him food every morning before the girls were awake. This was going to be the best secret ever. Caprice cradled the pup against her chest and made a beeline for the stables.

Chapter 8

Alice-Miranda was up early, determined to have a word with Caprice before they left for breakfast. Last night she'd helped Millie clean the Science lab — they'd been up to their elbows in rubber gloves and bleach, donning face masks to avoid the fumes. Mr Plumpton and Charlie Weatherly had helped too, which Alice-Miranda and Millie both agreed was very kind. The two girls had got back to the boarding house in time for showers and bed. Caprice hadn't returned from her rehearsal, which Alice-Miranda had thought a bit odd, as she'd spotted Mr Lipp's car roaring off down the driveway while they were walking back to Grimthorpe House.

Millie rolled over and stretched her arms up above her. 'Where are you going?' she asked.

'To talk to Caprice,' Alice-Miranda replied, tying the laces of her school shoes.

'She's never going to confess, you know,' Millie said. 'She'll just come up with some evil plan to get you too.'

'We'll see.' Alice-Miranda gave Millie a wave and almost bumped into Sloane, who walked out of her bedroom door at the same time, yawning loudly. The girl had a towel slung over her shoulder and a shower cap perched on her head. 'Good morning,' Alice-Miranda sparkled.

'Ohhh, I hate Howie's stupid bell,' Sloane griped. 'Jacinta says that the housemistress at Caledonia Manor doesn't even own one. Sounds like heaven.'

Alice-Miranda chuckled. 'Did you get your reading done?' she asked.

Sloane nodded. 'Nearly. I fell asleep and woke up at half past two with the book over my face. It's a miracle I didn't suffocate. Imagine the obituary: *Death by Dickens.*'

Alice-Miranda grinned. 'Is Caprice in your room?'

Sloane shook her head and rubbed her sleepy eyes. 'I think she's having one of her extra-long showers.'

'She wasn't in the bathroom,' Alice-Miranda replied, frowning. 'I'll check the sitting room.'

'See you at breakfast,' Sloane said.

Alice-Miranda scurried along the hallway to the back room, where Mrs Howard was busy sewing a button onto one of the girls' blazers.

The woman looked up from her needlework. 'Good morning, dear. You're up bright and early.'

'Good morning, Mrs Howard. Have you seen Caprice?' Alice-Miranda asked.

'I'm afraid not. She was late in last night, but I haven't spotted her this morning.' The woman finished her last stitch and cut the cotton thread, yawning widely.

'Did you sleep well?'

'Like a stone, which is just as well because I am getting far too old for all this,' the housemistress sighed.

Alice-Miranda smiled. 'You always say that, but you still come back every term.'

'Well, you know I would have thought seriously about retiring if things had worked out with Ursula, but now that the woman has decided to become a teacher, I can't leave you lot to your own devices, can I?' Mrs Howard said. 'Not until I find a suitable replacement.'

'It wouldn't be the same without you,' Alice-Miranda said.

Mrs Howard scoffed. 'You'd get used to it.'

'Will Ursula still come on the weekends when Mrs Shakeshaft isn't available?' Alice-Miranda asked. The girls had enjoyed having someone a bit younger taking care of them. Ursula Frost had recently quit her job working for Silas Wiley, the Mayor of Downsfordvale, and had taken up some casual employment at the school. Alice-Miranda had helped the woman reunite with her father, Stan Frost, who lived in a pretty cottage called Wood End, hidden deep in the woods a few miles from the school. Mrs Howard, who liked the young woman immensely in spite of the fact that she was Myrtle Parker's niece, had been truly hopeful that house-mistressing might have suited her as a permanent career change but, alas, that wasn't to be.

'Yes, I think so. Whenever she can,' Mrs Howard replied. 'She's coming this weekend so I can pop over and visit my sister.'

Alice-Miranda decided to search the rest of the house and then quickly say hello to Bony and Chops before breakfast. The ponies had been delivered back to school on the previous Saturday, having spent the term break at Highton Hall. Max, the Highton-Smith-Kennington-Joneses' stable-hand, had put the pair on a strict regime of diet and exercise. Alice-Miranda had hoped that Bony's manners might have improved, although, given the number of times he'd bitten Chops's tail when she and Millie had been riding on Sunday afternoon, she didn't think it was likely.

Alice-Miranda backtracked to Sloane and Caprice's room but it was still empty.

'Did you find her?' Millie asked, warily poking her head into the corridor.

Alice-Miranda shook her head. 'I'll talk to her later. Do you want to come up to the stables with me?'

Millie nodded. 'I'd better say hello to Chops or he'll think I don't love him anymore.'

The two girls darted along the hallway and out the back door.

'Do you think Miss Reedy is turning into a bridezilla?' Millie asked, thinking back to the night before. The English teacher had stopped in and had a very long conversation with her fiancé about table decorations. She was extremely particular and, although it was obvious that Mr Plumpton didn't mind what she decided, the woman had gone on and on and on. The girls didn't hear the final decision, as the couple had ducked out into the corridor, but if the stomping noises were anything to go by, Miss Reedy hadn't been happy.

Alice-Miranda giggled. 'If you'd asked me yesterday morning, when Sloane and I were talking to her, I'd have said no, but who knows after last night. Weddings can do strange things to people.'

'Just you watch,' Millie said. 'She's a control freak at the best of times and this is her *wedding*. As if she's going to leave that up to anyone else to organise.'

'I suppose you can't really blame her for wanting everything to be perfect,' Alice-Miranda said as they entered the cool brick building. 'Good morning, Bonaparte,' she sang out, poking her head over the top of Bony's stall door. The black pony was standing in the far corner with his eyes closed. 'Would you like some breakfast?'

At the mention of food, the pony spun around as if he were on ice skates, charging at the stall door and almost knocking his owner for six.

Alice-Miranda jumped back. 'Hey, watch out! I haven't got it yet. And please stop biting old ladies, you naughty boy. Mrs Howard is very upset with you. She told me what you did yesterday, almost taking her fingers off when she was just trying to give you a treat.'

Bonaparte stamped his foot and whinnied loudly, shaking his head up and down.

Alice-Miranda walked to the feed room, where Millie had already mixed up two small buckets of oats and bran. The child pulled the lid off the molasses container and drizzled a small amount on top of each.

'Sounds like someone's hungry,' Millie said. She smiled and picked up Chops's breakfast.

Alice-Miranda followed her with Bony's. She put it on the ground and opened the stable door. Bonaparte pushed and shoved, trying to get his head into the container. 'Stop that!' Alice-Miranda commanded. 'Go and stand back there or I'll walk straight out of here and give your breakfast to Buttercup.'

Susannah's pony was in the stall next door and whinnied when she heard her name.

'You'd think he hadn't been fed for a week,' Millie said as she filled Chops's feed bin. Her pony stood quietly in the stall on the other side, watching her like a perfect gentleman.

Bonaparte turned around and walked to the back of the stable, sticking his nose in the corner.

Alice-Miranda chuckled. 'You are such a sook.'

Millie closed Chops's stall door and poked her head around to see what the little black beast was up to. 'He's sulking.'

'You can't stand being told off, can you, Bony?' Alice-Miranda said.

The pony promptly lifted his tail, trumpeted loudly and filled the air with the most noxious smell.

'Oh, pooh!' Millie sputtered. 'You stink!'

Alice-Miranda chortled and gave him a playful smack on the bottom. 'When are you ever going to learn to behave yourself?'

Bonaparte turned his head around and bared his teeth.

'Did you see that?' Alice-Miranda exclaimed. She finished pouring the contents of the bucket into the feed bin. 'You can come and get it now.'

Bonaparte turned his head and eyed her warily.

'Come on,' she said. 'Stop that nonsense. You know it doesn't work on me, mister.'

Bonaparte whinnied and wheeled around. He rubbed his chin on the top of Alice-Miranda's curls and then licked her cheek.

'Oh, just what I love first thing in the morning – horse slobber.' She kissed the tip of his nose and walked out of the stall, taking care to lock it behind her. She and Millie walked back to the feed room to return the buckets. Suddenly, they heard a loud thump.

'Whoever's kicking their stall had better stop that right now or Mr Charles will be very cross,' Alice-Miranda called out.

Millie handed Alice-Miranda her bucket and headed into the main part of the stable, her eyes darting from stall to stall. As far as she could tell, all of the horses were standing quietly. 'I don't think it was any of them,' she called back to Alice-Miranda, who finished tidying the feed room and walked out to join her friend.

There was another loud *whump*, followed by the rush of running water.

Millie glanced up. 'It sounds like it's coming from the flat.'

'It's probably one of the stable cats, chasing mice,' Alice-Miranda said.

'What? Then drowning them?' Millie giggled.

Alice-Miranda spotted the stable clock and gasped. 'Gosh, look at the time.'

'I'm in enough trouble this week without being late for breakfast,' Millie said as they charged outside into the sunshine.

The girls hurried down the roadway to the boarding house. As they reached the garden gate, Alice-Miranda was surprised to see Caprice behind them. She looked to be coming from the direction of the stables too. 'Hi there!' she called out to the girl.

Caprice jumped at the sound.

Millie groaned. 'I really don't want to talk to her.'

'Hi,' Caprice muttered, pushing past Alice-Miranda and Millie and making quickly for the back door.

'Where have you been?' Alice-Miranda asked.

'Just out for a walk if it's any of your business,' Caprice snapped.

'Did you go for a swim?' Millie said, noticing the front of the girl's school shirt was soaking wet.

'No, of course not.' Caprice glanced at her uniform and gulped. She hadn't realised it was quite so obvious. Bathing that pup had been much more of a challenge than she'd imagined.

'What really happened with the paint bombs, Caprice?' Alice-Miranda decided that now was as good a time as any to ask.

Millie's stomach lurched. 'Don't worry about it,' she said, tugging Alice-Miranda's arm.

'Ask *her*,' Caprice said, glaring at Millie.

The red-haired girl could feel her neck and face getting hotter and hotter. 'You know it wasn't me,' she retorted.

Caprice narrowed her eyes. 'Prove it.'

'I don't understand,' Alice-Miranda said.

'I can't help it if you're not very smart,' the girl spat at Millie. 'Maybe you should have worn gloves like I –'

Alice-Miranda's eyes widened.

'What – wear gloves like you did?' Millie said, eyeballing the girl. 'Who's the stupid one now?'

'I didn't say that,' Caprice snapped. 'Anyway, you can't prove a thing.' She turned around and reached out to push the door just as Mrs Howard pulled it open. The girl fell flat on her face.

'Oh, are you all right, dear?' the old woman fussed.

'I'm fine,' Caprice huffed. She scrambled to her feet and fled down the hall.

'I think that's about as close to a confession as we're going to get,' Millie muttered.

Alice-Miranda squeezed her friend's arm. 'Maybe her conscience will get the better of her.'

'Don't count on it,' Millie said as the two girls hurried past Mrs Howard and ran to get their books.

Chapter 9

Silas Wiley re-read the letter on his desk and checked the calendar for the fifth time. How anyone had made such a glaring error was almost beyond comprehension. Now he had Alistair Foxley, the Chairman of Chudleigh's Dog Show, the most prestigious event in the nation's canine calendar, due in his office in half an hour.

Silas pressed the intercom button on his telephone. 'Mrs Mereweather, could you come in here, please?'

A titter of laughter rang out from the other end. 'Be there in a minute, sir. Would you like me to bring you some tea?'

Silas's stomach grumbled. 'No, thank you,' the man sighed. 'I need to discuss something with you urgently.'

Thirty seconds later there was a sharp knock followed by Mrs Mereweather poking her head around the door. The middle-aged woman was Silas Wiley's latest secretary, a jolly creature with the unfortunate propensity for ill-timed fits of giggles. 'What can I do for you, sir?' she asked, walking into the newly furnished office. She passed the forest-green leather sofas and the enormous antique mahogany desk, which Silas had bought with council money from a local auction house.

'Are you absolutely certain that the quilting club has booked the showground for the same dates we've got down for Chudleigh's?' he asked.

Nancy Mereweather frowned. She wondered if perhaps the man was losing his hearing. Or maybe he suffered the same affliction as her husband, Roy – a condition she liked to call 'domestic deafness', although in this case it was possibly a bout of selective comprehension. 'Yes, Mayor Wiley. Nothing has changed in the past hour.'

'And you've spoken to Mrs Sudbury about the possibility of moving her event?' Silas looked at the dismal list of alternative options he'd scribbled on the page.

'I'm afraid it's the one hundredth anniversary of the Downsfordvale Quilters' Association and they are hosting quilting groups from all over the country as part of their exhibition. They've already issued invitations and Mrs Sudbury was adamant that they are not willing or able to reschedule the event,' Mrs Mereweather replied, giggling.

Silas Wiley looked up at the woman. 'I don't consider this to be a laughing matter.'

'Oh, neither do I,' Nancy chortled. She composed herself and thought for a moment. Suddenly, the woman's blue eyes popped open. 'What about the showground at Winchesterfield?'

Silas shuddered. 'Good heavens, no!'

'But why not? There's the lovely hall, which has only recently been renovated, and there are lots of outbuildings. If that's still not enough space, you could always have the overflow events in the school halls at Fayle or Winchesterfield-Downsfordvale Academy for Proper Young Ladies,' the woman said, visibly excited by the idea.

'But that would mean putting Myrtle Parker in charge,' Silas replied, aghast at the thought.

'What's wrong with Myrtle? She's a wonderful President of the Show Society. I've recently joined the committee myself. I can guarantee that Mrs Parker would make Chudleigh's a show to remember.'

Silas Wiley swallowed hard. He'd forgotten that Mrs Mereweather lived in Winchesterfield and was now one of Myrtle Parker's cronies. The last thing he needed was to get on the bad side of that woman or she'd be fronting up to council meetings even more often than she already did.

'Well, sir, I suggest you come up with another brilliant idea quick smart as Major Foxley is due in fifteen minutes,' Nancy said, turning on her heel and walking out the door.

Silas Wiley cradled his head in his hands. He had to think of something. Perhaps he could ask the local high school to host the event. He buzzed the intercom. 'What about Downsfordvale College?'

'Too small,' the woman replied.

'Bramstead Hall?'

'The house has just changed hands and the new owners are gutting the place. It won't be ready for at least a year.'

Silas glanced at the clock on his desk. Ten minutes. What was he going to tell the man? 'All right,' he sighed, 'get me Myrtle Parker on the phone.'

Mrs Mereweather laughed loudly. She had already dialled Myrtle's number. 'Very good, sir. Putting you through now.'

Silas Wiley listened as the telephone rang. He was bracing himself, fully aware of the monster he was about to unleash.

Myrtle Parker put down the telephone. 'Reginald!' she shrieked loudly. 'Reginald, you're not going to believe this!'

She wondered where on earth that husband of hers had got to. Myrtle charged down the hallway, checking each room to no avail. She decided he must have gone outside, and grabbed a cardigan on her way through the kitchen.

'Reginald!' Myrtle yelled.

'I'm in here, dear,' the man called from the shed at the bottom of the garden.

'Ah, there you are! I've got news,' the woman shouted, hurtling along the path. She stopped at the shed door to catch her breath and was surprised to find Barry Dankworth enjoying a cup of tea. 'Oh, you're here,' she said.

Barry smiled at her and stood up. 'Hello Mrs Parker. I hope you don't mind – I popped round to borrow a drill. Mine's on the fritz and Roberta has a few shelves she wants me to put up.'

'Of course she does,' Myrtle mumbled.

'What's this exciting news then?' Reginald asked.

'I've just had a telephone call from Mayor Wiley,' Myrtle began. She paused for a moment, anticipating some sort of indication that Barry Dankworth was impressed with her connections, but the man stayed annoyingly silent.

Reginald looked at his wife. 'And?'

Myrtle was hopping from one foot to the other, barely able to contain herself. 'He asked if the Show Society would like to host Chudleigh's Dog Show,' she replied.

Her husband raised his eyebrows. 'That is quite an honour. Shall we go along to this year's event? Barry was just telling me it's on in a couple of weeks' time.'

'No, no, no,' Myrtle said impatiently. 'I'll be hosting *this* year's event at the end of the month.'

Barry Dankworth's face crinkled into a deep frown. 'I thought it was being held in Downsfordvale.'

'It was but the council has double-booked the venue and now Mayor Wiley's come to me begging.' Myrtle exhaled loudly.

'What did you say?' Reginald asked. He didn't like to second-guess his wife as he usually turned out to be wrong.

'What do you think I said?' Myrtle replied, rolling her eyes. 'I said yes, of course! I could hardly say no when Her Majesty will be there to present Best in Show, could I? She knows what a good organiser I am. We'll have to set to work right away. There's no turning back now. The committee will be here tonight to get things rolling. This is going to be the best Chudleigh's ever!'

'It's a massive undertaking,' Barry warned. 'Where are you going to accommodate everyone?'

Myrtle blanched. 'Whatever do you mean?'

'Well, people come from all over the country and they need to stay somewhere,' he said.

Myrtle hadn't even thought about that. 'Where do they usually stay?' she asked.

'Lots of people bring their caravans and tents, but there are usually hotels and guesthouses close by that they can book into,' the man explained.

'Won't most of them be staying in Downsford-vale?' Myrtle surmised, given that it was the original location for the event. 'I imagine they'll have their lodgings sorted already.'

'Yes, but knowing the dog show people, they won't want to stay that far from the venue,' he said. 'And there's not really much around here. Perhaps you can see if there are any locals willing to billet the entrants.'

'Billet?' Myrtle's face scrunched up. 'As in have people stay in private houses with their dogs?'

Barry nodded. 'I'm sure they'd be most appreciative. We've got a couple of spare rooms but Roberta will be run off her feet with all the preparations, so I don't think I'll suggest it until you're absolutely desperate. I'm happy to lend a hand, though.'

'Good heavens. I didn't realise I was going to have to play the role of travel agent as well as show convenor,' Myrtle blustered. 'No time to dally, then. I've got a million things to do. Reginald, you'll have to come and help me right away. Mr Dankworth, you'd best be going.' Myrtle gave a nod, then turned on her heel and stalked up the garden path to the back door.

Barry placed his cup back onto the bench and Reg tipped the last of the tea into the small sink. 'Sorry about that,' he said.

'Don't be,' Barry replied. 'I really must get home.'

The two men walked out into the garden. 'I suspect life is about to get a bit busy,' Reginald sighed, patting his new friend on the back.

Barry nodded. 'I think you're right about that.'

Chapter 10

Ophelia Grimm set down the telephone and massaged her left ear. Myrtle Parker was an excitable woman at the best of times, but the mayor's invitation for Winchesterfield to host Chudleigh's Dog Show seemed to have almost sent her over the edge. Myrtle had asked Ophelia to commit the school to assist in whatever capacity was needed. She could hardly say no, given the woman said Fayle had agreed to do all that was necessary to make sure this was the best Chudleigh's ever. Ophelia scribbled the date on a piece of paper. As far as she could see there was nothing on that weekend, although a vague thought was scratching at the back of her mind.

Ophelia pressed the button on the intercom. 'Louella, could you come in for a second?'

Seconds later Louella Derby poked her head around the door. 'Is everything all right? Mrs Parker seemed terribly wound up.'

'Could you add some dates into the calendar? The school is going to be helping with Chudleigh's Dog Show in a couple of weeks' time,' the head-mistress said, motioning for her to sit down. 'It's the twenty-ninth and thirtieth of the month.'

Louella Derby's face went pale. 'That's the weekend Mr Plumpton and Miss Reedy are getting married.'

Ophelia bit her lip and gently smacked her forehead. 'Oh heavens, I completely forgot. It was supposed to be the week after when Josiah first discussed it with me but then he brought it forward because of the honeymoon expedition.' She sighed heavily and shook her head. 'We're just going to have to manage the two. The wedding's on the Sunday, isn't it?'

Mrs Derby nodded.

'Well, Mrs Parker said it will all be over by three o'clock, and the wedding's not until half past four,' Ophelia said with a grimace. 'So it shouldn't be a problem.' She didn't know if she was trying to convince herself or her secretary, but she was sure neither of them believed it.

'Of course not,' Louella said, avoiding eye contact.

'I'll have to make an announcement straight after lessons. They already know about it at Fayle and that ship has more leaks than the *Titanic*.' Ophelia Grimm glanced at the clock on her desk. 'I want to catch the children before they go off to their afternoon activities. If I don't tell them now they're bound to hear about it from someone else and I'd rather quell the excitement until we know exactly what's expected.'

'What about Mr Plumpton and Miss Reedy?' Louella asked. 'Aren't you going to speak with them first?'

'I'll try to grab them on the way, but I'm afraid they're just going to have to work around it. I've promised Myrtle already. Could you imagine the fallout if I say that I've changed my mind? We'd be on the village blacklist forever.' The headmistress stood up and straightened her grey skirt. She pulled on her blazer and quickly applied some pink lipstick. 'Could you ask all of the students and staff to meet me in the dining room immediately after their last lessons?'

Louella Derby nodded. 'Of course, Miss Grimm.'

And with that, the headmistress rushed out the door.

The loudspeaker in the quadrangle crackled to life. 'Good afternoon, girls and staff. Miss Grimm has asked that everyone please meet in the dining room for a special announcement at afternoon tea. Thank you.'

Alice-Miranda closed her locker door and walked outside. 'Millie, wait for me!' she called, scurrying over to her friend, who had just come out of French class.

'What do you think this is about?' Millie asked.

Sloane sidled up to the pair. 'Maybe Caprice owned up and you're about to be pardoned in front of the whole school.'

'I doubt it,' Millie said, rolling her eyes. 'Not after what happened this morning. She practically admitted it and then lied again.'

'Do you want to go for a ride this afternoon?' Alice-Miranda asked. 'Mr Trout cancelled choir practice and I really want to give Miss Hephzibah and Miss Henrietta their chocolates from Switzerland.'

'Good idea,' Millie said. 'I don't think they'll last much longer sitting on the shelf in our bedroom – they'll probably go off.'

'Or you'd eat them, more likely,' Sloane teased.

'Do you want to come with us?' Alice-Miranda asked. 'We could walk if you'd rather not ride.'

'No, it's fine,' Sloane replied. 'I have to finish that book, and you know me and horses are still not exactly the best of friends.'

The girls hurried into the dining room, where a long queue of students had already formed at the servery. The smell of grilled cheese filled the air and it wasn't long before everyone was seated and enjoying their afternoon tea.

Millie looked around as she munched on her cheese toastie. 'So where is Caprice?'

'See, I might be right,' Sloane said. 'Any minute Miss Grimm's going to march her in here and she'll make a full confession.'

Millie shook her head. 'No way.'

Seconds later, Ophelia Grimm entered the dining room alone and glanced around.

'Told you,' Millie said.

But Alice-Miranda was curious as to where Caprice could be. It seemed as if everyone else was present – even Mrs Howard and Mr Charles were in the room. Mr Trout was there too, so Caprice couldn't have been at another rehearsal.

The headmistress walked to the podium and switched on the microphone. She'd looked everywhere for Miss Reedy and Mr Plumpton but hadn't been able to locate either of them. The news couldn't wait any longer; they'd just have to find out about the dog show at the same time as everyone else. 'Good afternoon, girls and staff,' she began. 'I have some rather exciting news and I wanted to tell you all straight away. We're going to have to form working groups immediately as time is of the essence.'

There was a hush of whispers around the room while girls speculated about what this big announcement might be.

'Who likes dogs?' Miss Grimm asked, and hands shot up all over the place. 'Good, because in a couple of weeks' time Winchesterfield is going to be hosting the largest and most prestigious dog show in the country,' the woman declared.

Chatter erupted around the room.

'Cool,' Sloane said. 'I wonder if there'll be some really weird ones, like those hairless Chinese.'

'I think they're called Chinese crested,' Alice-Miranda said with a smile.

Millie's eyes widened. 'What about those huge Bernese mountain dogs, like the one we saw in Switzerland? They're gorgeous.'

'Hopefully there's none like Princess Gertie,' Sloane said, wrinkling her nose.

'Can we enter our own dogs if our parents will bring them?' a young girl called Ella asked.

'Everyone, please calm down,' Miss Grimm ordered. 'And no, Ella, this is a professional event. It's a bit like,' the woman hesitated, thinking about how she was going to put it.

'Miss Universe for dogs,' Sloane called out. 'Except that some of them are boys.'

The girls laughed.

Millie put up her hand. 'Are we hosting Chudleigh's Dog Show, Miss Grimm?'

'Not hosting – just helping – but, yes, that's the event, Millie,' the woman said with a nod.

'Wow, Chudleigh's is big,' Millie said. 'I've been with my mother. She was one of the official vets a couple of years ago.'

'You might be able to give us some pointers then. All I know at this stage is that Mrs Parker, as President of the Winchesterfield Show Society, is in charge and she is enlisting as much help from everyone in the village as possible. It's likely that we will be having some events here at school and we'll also be sending teams of girls to assist with all manner of other things,' the headmistress explained.

'Bags not being on pooper-scooper duty,' Millie said.

Sloane pulled a face. 'Ew, that's disgusting.'

'Seriously, that's a job,' Millie said. 'There were all these guys in white hazmat suits with long gloves walking around everywhere making sure there was no –'

'Thank you, Millie. We get the picture,' Miss Grimm said. 'I suspect we might be acting as guides and ushers and serving afternoon tea.' Though, there were a few girls she wouldn't have minded putting on pooper scooping.

Ophelia spied Livinia Reedy and Josiah Plumpton entering the room, looking sheepish. The pair quickly took the empty seats at Alice-Miranda's table.

'Excuse me, girls, what's the big news?' Mr Plumpton whispered.

'The village is hosting Chudleigh's Dog Show in a couple of weeks,' Millie fizzed.

Livinia Reedy's eyebrows knotted. 'It had better not be the weekend of the wedding.'

'Surely not,' Mr Plumpton said, flashing his fiancée a reassuring smile. 'We couldn't be that unlucky.'

The headmistress cleared her throat. 'I'm off to a meeting with Mrs Parker this evening, so I'll have more news to share tomorrow. Enjoy your afternoon, everyone.' Ophelia stepped down from the podium and strutted towards Alice-Miranda's table. 'Excuse me, Miss Reedy, Mr Plumpton, might I have a word outside?' she asked, smiling tightly.

Livinia Reedy's stomach twisted. 'I don't believe this,' she hissed under her breath. Josiah Plumpton reached across and squeezed Livinia's hand. 'I will not have our wedding hijacked by a pack of mangy mutts,' she whispered in her fiancé's ear as they followed Miss Grimm into the courtyard.

Chapter 11

Roberta Dankworth finished brushing Citrine's ears and leaned over to plant a kiss on her wet nose. 'You are so beautiful,' she cooed at the creature. 'You make Mummy very proud.'

The hound nuzzled her owner and looked for all the world as if she were smiling, until a series of high-pitched barks interrupted the tender moment.

Roberta turned and looked at the poodle, who was strapped into a tiny high chair attached to another grooming table behind her. The hair on top of the dog's head was expertly parted and rolled up into six curlers. 'You make Mummy proud too, Farrah, but I'm not happy about those dark circles under your eyes.' Roberta opened a drawer underneath the bench Citrine was perched on. She fished around and found what she was looking for, then unscrewed the lid. 'All the top models swear by this,' she said as she dabbed some haemorrhoid cream under Farrah's eyes. 'Now, sit here and rest while Mummy finishes up your sister.'

Roberta had been practising putting false eyelashes on Citrine all day, which the hound hadn't appreciated in the slightest. This time she was determined to make them stick. Roberta pulled another packet from the drawer.

Citrine flinched and turned her head away. The grooming bench, which Roberta had designed herself, boasted a giant tub at one end, complete with a hydraulic lift, which left no chance of injury to either animal or human at bath time. At the other end was a low bench for the beasts to stand on while they were being dried. Several wide drawers contained supercharged hair dryers, curling irons and crimpers as well as a vast array of beauty products. To finish the room, a mirror spanned the length of an entire wall, allowing the animals to admire themselves while they were being primped and preened. A smaller bench stood along another wall. It had been built especially for Farrah as Roberta didn't want her to feel left out. The whole space looked rather like an upmarket beauty salon.

Roberta took out a small pair of clippers and began to cut Citrine's toenails with the utmost precision. Although the woman currently had six Afghans in her kennel, Citrine was her favourite, particularly having taken out Best in Show at last year's Chudleigh's. It was the first time one of her dogs had received the honour. Her hounds had won their division many times, of course, but Best in Show was the grand champion, the competition where all of the divisional winners went head to head.

There had been whispers that she had only won because of Becca Finchley's absence from the show that year. It was true Roberta had always felt miffed that the woman's husband was a judge. Even though Sandon Finchley hadn't overseen his wife's categories, it just hadn't seemed fair, really. But how people could suggest such cruel things, Roberta couldn't understand. She'd won Best in Show because Citrine was magnificent and Roberta was the most dedicated breeder in the country and now she had her heart set on backing up with a second crown. On top of everything else that had happened to the Finchleys last year, while Becca was in hospital her dogs had been caught up in one of the largest kennel thefts in the country, so the poor woman hadn't had a single dog to show even if she'd wanted to.

Roberta picked up a toothbrush and some paste. 'You love having your teeth brushed, don't you?' she said as she pressed the button and the hound opened her mouth. The device hummed away for a pre-programmed three minutes after which Citrine lapped some water from a ceramic dish the woman placed in front of her. Citrine was the daughter of Roberta's first champion, Emerald, who now sat pride of place in a silver urn on the mantle above the fireplace in the master bedroom. The past year had been a roller-coaster in the Dankworth household. From the highs of Citrine winning Best in Show to the sudden death of Roberta's beloved Emerald, the year couldn't have been any starker in contrast.

Emerald's death had shattered Roberta, who had insisted on a full funeral and wake. It had been a dark time in the Dankworth household, quite literally with Roberta and the dogs wearing only black for months. Barry had begun to worry that his wife was never going to smile again and called in a grief counsellor to help her to process her emotions. It turned out they were all depressed – Roberta *and* the dogs. Things had taken an upward turn, though, when Roberta received the phone call from the producers of *Dog Days*, saying they were planning to feature her and her hounds in a special series. From that moment on, life had been full steam ahead again. It was fortunate that they had already purchased their new home, though the plans for the doghouse went from practical to palatial overnight. Barry had almost fainted when he got the bill for the fit-out, but there had been no point in arguing. If that was what his wife wanted, he knew he'd do himself no favours to deny her.

'Are you here, Roberta?' Barry called as he pushed open the front door to the Poochie Palace. The place was laid out with a sitting room at the front, where the dogs could socialise and watch their television. There were also hundreds of photographs of Roberta and her children, mostly with them dressed in matching outfits. Adjacent to the room was a kitchen, complete with food-preparation area, two enormous refrigerators stocked with fillet steak, salmon and free-range chicken, a sink and a dishwasher. Beyond that were six individual rooms containing oversized beds, pillows and fluffy duvets. Roberta had a bedroom for herself too, in case she needed to stay overnight. At the rear of the building was the grooming salon and a walk-in wardrobe for all the dogs' accessories, outfits and toys. Outside, a covered veranda, which overlooked a sprawling exercise yard and a lap pool, housed day beds for each dog.

Barry walked through the central hallway to the rear of the building. 'She's looking good,' he said, stroking Citrine's back. Farrah sat up and began to yap at the man. Barry turned and put his finger to his lips to shush the little creature.

'Good? Is that all you can say?' Roberta pouted.

'She's beautiful, Roberta – stunning, in fact,' Barry tried again, overcompensating horribly. 'I think she's a shoo-in for Best in Show.'

Roberta rolled her eyes at him. 'Stop going on, Barry. Where have you been, anyway?'

'I've got some *very* interesting news. Chudleigh's is going to be held here in Winchesterfield.'

'No, it's not,' Roberta said firmly. She finished buffing Citrine's nails and retrieved a bottle of clear polish from the drawer. 'It's in Downsfordvale.'

'Well, it was *supposed* to be, but it's been moved this morning,' Barry said. He enjoyed knowing something that his wife didn't for a change.

'Who told you that?' Roberta asked, refusing to look up from her task. She was very careful not to get any polish on Citrine's fur.

'I popped in to borrow a drill from Reg Parker and Myrtle came out all abuzz about having just been contacted by the mayor,' the man explained. 'I told her that, if she needed, I could help out and you might be able to offer some advice too.'

Roberta's head snapped up. 'Why would you do that?'

'I just thought . . .'

Roberta looked back at the dog's claw and realised that she'd accidentally painted the tip of Citrine's paw. 'Look what you've made me do. You don't *think*, Barry. That's the problem. I don't have time to help that bossy woman. I have preparations to make and we have to practise. You know what it's like – I'll be out here sixteen hours a day. You don't get to be Chudleigh's Best in Show without putting in the work.'

The man grimaced. 'Sorry, it's just that there's no one in the village who has more experience with dog shows than you.'

'Of course there's not, but I don't have time. Sounds like the whole thing is going to be a disaster, anyway. You can't organise Chudleigh's at the last minute. Have they thought about where they're going to accommodate everyone and how they're going to cater for it?'

Barry tried hard not to smirk. Now that he'd told his wife what was going on, he knew that she wouldn't be able to help herself.

Chapter 12

Caprice Radford carefully snibbed the lock behind her as she entered the flat. She shivered as she hurried across the sparsely furnished sitting room and past the kitchenette. The place was silent apart from the creaks and groans of the timbers and the odd neighing and nickering of a pony down below. Out of the corner of her eye, she noticed an old electric coil heater and thought of using it to warm the place up a little. She walked into the bathroom and pulled aside the shower curtain. 'You'll need to wake up, little man,' she said.

The creature was curled into a tight ball, trembling like a half-set blancmange.

'What's the matter?' Caprice picked him up and realised that his fur was still soaked from the bath she'd given him that morning. He was freezing. She'd towelled him off as best she could but, without the aid of a hair dryer, it was impossible to get him completely dry. She set him back down and raced into the bedroom, where she had found the towels the night before. She snatched another two from the cupboard and fled back to the pup. Gathering him up in her arms, she wrapped the towels around his shivering body.

The creature whimpered and burrowed into the folds.

'Are you hungry?' Caprice asked. She reached into her pocket and pulled out a bread roll she'd saved from lunch.

The pup sniffed the food, then turned its head away. Its high-pitched squeaks were growing louder and louder.

'Shush, be quiet or someone will hear you,' Caprice pleaded. No matter how much she cuddled him, his shuddering wouldn't stop. 'It's all right,' she cooed. 'I'll put the heater on.'

Caprice placed the pup onto the threadbare couch and unwound the frayed cord on the electric heater under the window. She glanced around for somewhere to plug it in and discovered a socket just behind the old television set. Within minutes the coils began to glow.

The girl sat back on the floor beside the pup, enjoying the warmth. 'That's better now, isn't it?'

The pup looked up at her with his big brown eyes. A few minutes later, his nose twitched and she felt around for the bread roll. Before long he'd gobbled it down and was crying for more.

'Hello Mr Charles!' Alice-Miranda waved to the gardener, who was up a ladder trimming a hedge opposite the stables.

'Afternoon, girls,' he called back.

'That's exciting news about the dog show,' Alice-Miranda said.

The man grinned. 'I don't know if I'm excited or terrified, lass. I just hope that all those pooches get along.'

'It was fun when I went with my mum,' Millie said, 'although I do remember one very bolshy sausage dog that kept on trying to eat the tails of the big dogs. Eventually, this Great Dane turned around and opened his mouth and the sausage dog's whole head disappeared.'

Charlie cringed. 'Oh, I don't like the sound of this.'

Alice-Miranda's eyes widened. 'My goodness, what happened then?'

'The dachshund's owner screamed and people came running from everywhere. I remember the handler of the Great Dane just telling him calmly to spit it out. There was a horrible hoicking noise and out popped the sausage dog, covered in slime. It was gross but it could have been much worse, I guess,' Millie said.

'It certainly could have,' Charlie agreed.

Following Miss Grimm's thrilling announcement, the two girls had rushed to get changed into their jodhpurs and boots and Alice-Miranda had located the beautiful box of Fanger's Chocolate that she'd bought for Miss Fayle and Mrs Sykes.

'Is Elsa around?' Alice-Miranda asked.

'No, she's busy with her studies today. I'll feed the ponies when I'm finished here, unless you girls would like to give me a hand. Millie, I could let Miss Grimm know that you've been awfully helpful and perhaps she'll give you Sunday afternoon off,' he said with a wink.

The girl smiled. 'Sounds like a plan to me. We're on our way to see Miss Hephzibah and Miss Henrietta for half an hour, so we'll take care of everything when we get back.'

'Rightio.' The man waved goodbye and continued with his pruning.

Millie charged into the stables with its smell of dust and manure, lucerne and molasses. 'Hey, fatso,' she called to Chops, who was dozing with his head over his stall door. She walked into the tack room and took the pony's bridle from its hook on the wall.

Bonaparte spotted his mistress and whinnied loudly.

'Sorry, Bony, no treats for you,' Alice-Miranda said. She laughed as the pony shook his head up and down as if to disagree. The girl located Bonaparte's bridle and grabbed her saddle too, taking them both over to the pony's stall.

There was a loud thump from upstairs.

Millie looked up at the timber ceiling and frowned. 'Seriously, are those mice having a party?'

The girl hitched Chops's reins to his saddle and left him standing in his stall while she scurried to the staircase at the end of the building. Alice-Miranda was attempting to tighten Bonaparte's girth strap but the pony was doing his best impersonation of a bloated beer belly and she could barely get it to the first notch.

'Breathe in, please,' she begged, but Bony clearly didn't feel like going anywhere this afternoon.

Millie reached the upstairs landing and turned the handle. 'That's weird – the door's locked,' she said.

'Maybe Mr Charles decided it would be better not to leave it open,' Alice-Miranda called back.

Millie shrugged and thumped down the stairs.

Inside the flat, Caprice held her breath. When she was convinced she could hear whoever it was walking away, she exhaled and carried on with her search for food. She opened the last cupboard door and came face to face with the twitching nose of a tiny brown fieldmouse.

Caprice squealed, then clamped her hand over her mouth. The mouse took one look at her and scampered away.

In the sitting room the pup had managed to free himself from the towels and padded out to the kitchenette. His wet nose touched Caprice's leg and she leapt into the air.

'What are you doing in here?' she berated the creature. 'You're supposed to be keeping warm by the heater.'

The puppy looked up at her and began to whimper.

'I've already told you I don't have anything more for you to eat. There's nothing in here apart from disgusting mice. Hey, what's that smell?'

Caprice sniffed the air. She spun around to see white smoke rising from the pile of towels in front of the heater. A small flame flickered to life. Caprice froze and the puppy ran away into the bedroom.

'Come back!' Caprice yelled, chasing after it as the flames licked the bottom of the curtains.

Chapter 13

Bonaparte's nostrils flared and he kicked up at his belly.

'What's the matter with you, mister?' Alice-Miranda said. She gave him a pat and tried again to tighten the strap. In the box next to him, Chops whinnied loudly.

Millie opened her pony's stall door and grabbed his reins. Chops's eyes darted all over the place and he stomped on the ground. 'Stop that,' she said.

'I hope Bony hasn't given himself another stomach-ache,' Alice-Miranda said. 'There's a lot of sweet clover in the field at the moment and you know what a greedy-guts he is.' Her pony was susceptible to bouts of colic, usually brought on by a visit to a vegetable patch and his particular predilection for cabbages, though he had been known to get sick on lush grass too.

Buttercup was in the stall on the other side of Chops, pawing at the ground.

'They're all a bit nuts this afternoon,' Millie said. There were three more horses in the stables whinny-ing and thumping about.

Alice-Miranda raised her nose into the air. 'Can you smell smoke?'

'Maybe Charlie has a bonfire in the garden somewhere,' Millie said.

Alice-Miranda inhaled deeply. 'No, it smells different to that.'

Out of nowhere, a bloodcurdling scream echoed overhead. 'Fire!' a girl shouted. 'Help!'

'There's someone in the flat!' Millie exclaimed. She immediately flew into action, pushing Chops back into his stall and slamming the door.

Alice-Miranda left Bonaparte and fled upstairs with Millie right behind her. She tried the handle but it wouldn't budge.

'Help me!' the girl shrieked on the other side, pounding the door.

Alice-Miranda's eyes widened. 'It's Caprice,' she gasped. She was about to race downstairs in search of a spare key when the door burst open and Caprice flew out, coughing and sputtering. A pall of thick smoke billowed onto the landing.

Spotting a fire extinguisher outside the office, Millie shoved Caprice out of the way and dashed down to get it.

Alice-Miranda looked at Caprice, whose face was blackened with ash and streaked with tears. 'Go let the horses out and get Mr Charles,' she said, before covering her mouth and nose and running into the flat.

Caprice stumbled down the steps as Millie wrenched the extinguisher out of its bracket and charged back upstairs.

'Alice-Miranda, where are you?' Millie shouted, choking on the toxic grey smoke.

'In here!' Alice-Miranda ran into the sitting room to find the curtains ablaze. She fled through the smoke to the kitchenette, where an old plastic tub was sitting in the sink. She quickly filled it with water and raced back to throw it on the flames.

Millie appeared beside her with the fire extinguisher. 'How do you do this again?' she said. Panic was beginning to take hold as she fiddled with the top of the metal handle.

'Release the pin,' Alice-Miranda yelled, running back to the kitchen for more water.

Millie felt for the pin and pulled hard. 'Got it!' she cried out.

Alice-Miranda dumped another bucket over the flames, then threw the container to the ground. 'You take the hose and I'll press,' she shouted above the crackling and hissing. Her eyes were bleary with tears and they felt as if they were being stung by a swarm of angry bees.

Millie pointed the nozzle at the fire while Alice-Miranda grabbed the handle with both hands. A blast of water shot towards the blazing drapes. Millie sprayed the flames until the jet slowed to a trickle.

Charlie Weatherly burst into the room carrying another extinguisher. He had the pin out and was dousing the last of the flames in seconds. Without a word, Millie let go of their hose and ran to refill the plastic tub. By the time she returned the fire was out.

Charlie dropped the extinguisher with a thud and coughed violently. In the distance a siren screamed louder and louder until it stopped just outside the building. Minutes later, a fireman trundling a thick hose raced up the stairs and into the flat. Several more firemen charged into the room, shouting instructions at one another.

'Is everyone okay?' an older chap called. He looked at the girls and their smudged faces. Alice-Miranda's white shirt was covered in soot and Millie's hair resembled a bird's nest.

The girls turned and hugged each other fiercely, relief flooding through their veins.

'Wow, that was intense,' Millie said before launching into a series of wheezy coughs.

Alice-Miranda nodded. 'I'm just glad the fire's out,' she rasped. As the smoke began to clear, she spotted something lying in the bedroom doorway. 'What's that?' Alice-Miranda said, wading through the haze to investigate.

Millie squinted, struggling to see.

'It's a puppy!' Alice-Miranda exclaimed. She quickly scooped it up and checked that it was still breathing.

Millie clasped her hands together and bit down on her thumbnail. She hoped it was all right.

'We need to get you all out of here,' the fire captain instructed. He gestured to one of his colleagues, who ushered the children and Charlie downstairs.

As the four survivors emerged into the late afternoon sunshine, drinking in the fresh air, Miss Grimm hurtled towards them. 'Oh, thank heavens!' she exclaimed, throwing her arms around the girls and hugging them tightly. 'Are you all right?'

Alice-Miranda nodded. 'Thanks to Millie,' she croaked. 'She got the extinguisher.'

A crowd of onlookers had gathered outside the stables and there were still more girls and staff rushing up to see what was going on, having heard the sirens and seen the fire truck careering up the drive.

Ophelia Grimm stepped back and noticed the fourth member of the party. 'What have you got there?' she asked.

'A puppy. I found him in the flat,' Alice-Miranda said, as she cradled the fluffy creature against her chest.

The headmistress frowned. 'How on earth did he get up there?'

'We don't know,' Alice-Miranda replied.

The fire captain walked out of the building towards them. 'Hello Miss Grimm,' he greeted the headmistress. 'You owe a great debt of gratitude to Charlie and the girls here. If it had been just a minute or two longer, that whole place would have gone up. It's rare to have a stable fire that doesn't end badly.'

Miss Grimm paled. 'Do you know how it started?' she asked.

'There was an electric heater upstairs and it looks as if some towels were dropped right in front of it,' the man informed her. 'Is someone living up there?'

The woman reeled. 'No!' she said. 'I wonder if we have a squatter.'

Millie shook her head. 'It was Caprice. She was in the flat when it started.'

There was an audible gasp from everyone within earshot.

'What was she doing up there?' Miss Grimm demanded.

Millie shrugged. She opened her mouth to say something but was overtaken by another coughing fit.

'Where's Caprice now?' The headmistress looked around at the crowd, but the girl was nowhere to be seen.

'I told her to let the ponies out,' Alice-Miranda said. She could see Bony and Chops and the others running about at the top of the driveway. Miss Wall was trying to herd them through the open gate into the field.

Mrs Howard arrived huffing and blowing. 'Is everyone safe?' she puffed, completely out of breath. A look of relief washed over her face when she saw Alice-Miranda and Millie with Charlie. 'Where's Caprice? She was screaming about a fire, so I called the brigade, but then she disappeared before I had time to find out what was going on.'

The fire captain stepped forward. 'I think you should get the doctor to check this lot over and probably take that little fellow to the vet too,' he said to Miss Grimm. 'You'll want to make sure they aren't suffering from smoke inhalation.'

Another siren wailed in the distance. 'That will be the ambulance now,' the housemistress said. 'I called them and the police, just to be on the safe side.'

'Well done, Mrs Howard. I'm glad someone had their wits about them,' Ophelia Grimm said gratefully. She looked over at her secretary, who had just raced up the drive and was being caught up on the drama by Miss Reedy.

The girls and teachers were clamouring to see what had happened, asking Alice-Miranda and Millie if they were all right, and admiring the unexpected newcomer.

'Oh my gosh, he's so cute,' Sloane gushed.

'Mrs Derby, can you call Dr Davidson and tell him we've found a stray pup?' Miss Grimm asked.

Sofia Ridout sighed, watching the animal rest his head in the crook of Alice-Miranda's elbow. 'I wish we could keep him.'

'A school dog!' Sloane exclaimed. 'We could all help to look after him in the boarding house.'

'That's a lovely idea, girls, but I suspect someone will be missing him very much,' Miss Grimm said. She was quite taken with the little bundle of caramel fur herself. She reached over to stroke his head and the tiny pup gave her a lick.

'I have enough to look after without adding a four-legged child to the mix,' Mrs Howard tutted.

There was a groan of disappointment from the girls as Alice-Miranda passed the puppy to Mrs Derby.

'There's Caprice!' one of the girls shouted. Everyone turned to see where she was pointing. The girl was partially hidden behind a hedge, as if she was looking at what was going on while trying not to be seen.

'Right, Mrs Howard, can I leave you with the girls?' the headmistress asked. 'Miss Reedy, please come with me.'

113

'Do you *really* need me?' Miss Reedy huffed. 'There are quite a few things I simply must organise by this afternoon.' Learning that her wedding weekend had quite literally gone to the dogs had not put her in a very good mood, to say the least. She still needed to make several phone calls to suppliers before they closed for the day.

Miss Grimm was surprised by the woman's tone. 'We've just had a very serious incident, Livinia, and I think Caprice might be in shock.'

Livinia Reedy checked herself. 'My apologies, Miss Grimm, of course,' she mumbled, and followed the headmistress over to the hedge.

'I'm so glad everyone's safe,' Alice-Miranda said. She linked arms with Millie and rested her head on the girl's shoulder. 'Bye, little puppy.'

Mrs Derby smiled at the girls. 'Don't worry, Dr Davidson will take good care of him.'

Mrs Howard put her arm around Millie. 'Come along, then. Let's have the paramedics take a look at you two.'

'Cool,' Millie said. 'Can we sit in the back of the ambulance?'

Chapter 14

'Whatever is the girl doing?' Miss Reedy said as she and the headmistress trotted down the driveway. They could see Caprice peering out from behind the hedge as clear as day.

'Your guess is as good as mine, but she'd better have a very good reason for being in that flat.' Ophelia frowned. 'Caprice, come out here at once!'

The girl shrank down and froze.

'Now!' the headmistress boomed. She was in no mood to be toyed with.

'Yes, Miss Grimm,' Caprice replied, her voice wavering, as she emerged from behind the bush. Her face was smudged with black and her uniform was filthy.

'Are you hurt?' Miss Grimm asked.

Caprice remained tight-lipped and cast her eyes to the ground.

'Perhaps we should go to your study and we can talk there,' Livinia suggested quietly. 'And if we need to, we can ask the paramedics to come down and make sure that she's all right.'

'That's a very good idea,' Ophelia said, nodding. The shadows were long and the sun was low in the sky. There was a slight chill in the air too. The head-mistress placed her hand on the girl's shoulder and steered her down the road. They walked directly to the back of Winchesterfield Manor and through Mrs Derby's office to the headmistress's study.

'I'll get us some tea,' Miss Reedy said. 'And a hot chocolate for you, Caprice.'

'Thank you,' Miss Grimm replied. 'I think we could all do with a drink.' She motioned for Caprice to sit on one of the dark green leather chesterfield lounges. Ophelia waited for Miss Reedy to return with the refreshments before pressing on. She wanted to have a witness to their discussions.

'Here we are,' Livinia said, setting the mugs onto the coffee table.

'Now, Caprice,' Miss Grimm began gently, 'I hear that you let the horses out and alerted Mrs Howard to the fire. Well done for that, but I do need to know what you were doing in the flat in the first place.'

The girl gulped and glanced around the room.

'The truth is all I'm interested in, Caprice. Millie and Alice-Miranda both saw you. They said you were pounding on the door to get out.' Ophelia looked at the child. 'I can't tell you how relieved I am that you're all right.'

Caprice blinked her big blue eyes. Tears welled and then spilled onto the tops of her cheeks. Miss Reedy jumped to grab a tissue and handed it to the girl.

'I . . . I went for a walk to the stables after school and I heard a noise upstairs, so I had a look,' Caprice began, then paused.

'Go on,' Miss Grimm urged. She wondered why Caprice went to the stables in the first place. She didn't have a pony at school and hadn't seemed even vaguely interested in horseriding since she'd arrived, despite having told the headmistress about her champion dressage horse in her interview.

'Daddy said that he might buy me another pony, one I could bring to school because my Lipizzaner is far too valuable to have here,' the girl explained, as if reading Ophelia's mind, 'so I went to see if there was a spare stall.'

'What did you find upstairs?'

Caprice stared at her hands and began to pull apart the tissue she was holding. She swallowed hard. 'There was someone up there.'

'A member of staff?' Miss Grimm pressed.

'I don't think so,' she replied, her voice barely more than a whisper.

'Oh, goodness,' Livinia Reedy gasped. 'Did they hurt you?'

Caprice shook her head.

'Well, what were they doing?' Ophelia Grimm asked, leaning towards the girl.

'I don't know,' Caprice said. Then the words began to tumble out, as if someone had pulled an orange from the bottom of a shop display and now the whole lot was falling fast. 'I heard a noise in the bedroom. I pushed the door open and saw someone go out through the window, then I turned to run downstairs and tell Charlie but I must have tripped over and hit my head. When I woke up there was smoke everywhere and I had to get out because I couldn't breathe. I thought I was going to die.'

'Oh, Caprice, you poor thing.' Livinia Reedy went to comfort the child. She placed her arm around the girl's shoulders and Caprice buried her head against the woman's chest.

A row of lines formed across the headmistress's forehead. 'Did you see what the person looked like?'

Livinia Reedy sat back and allowed the girl to speak. Caprice sniffed and wiped away her tears. 'No, I couldn't even tell if it was a man or a woman.'

Ophelia Grimm stood up and walked to her desk. She picked up the telephone and buzzed her secretary. 'Mrs Derby, could you get hold of your husband and Charlie and ask them to come to my office immediately?' There was a long pause as Mrs Derby explained what had happened with the puppy. 'That is good news. Thank you.' The headmistress hung up and turned around. 'Constable Derby and Charlie will be here in a few minutes,' she said, sitting back down.

Caprice chewed on a nail. 'But I don't even know what the person looks like and I'm not hurt.'

The headmistress frowned. 'No, you don't appear to be but you must have hit your head if you blacked out. We'll need to have the paramedics take a look at you and we must investigate the incident properly. We can't have a stranger roaming about the campus. Did you see the puppy in the flat?'

Caprice shook her head sharply. 'What puppy?' she asked, wide-eyed.

'Alice-Miranda and Millie found a puppy lying on the floor after they'd put the fire out,' Ophelia explained. 'It's a wonder the creature didn't die from smoke inhalation.'

'Is he all right?' Caprice asked.

'Yes, Mrs Derby says he seems fine. It appears we'll be looking after him until we find the owner or until Dr Davidson returns from his holiday – whichever comes first. Perhaps he belongs to the stranger you saw.'

'Well, I'd say they're dreadfully irresponsible,' Miss Reedy sighed. 'People like that shouldn't be allowed to own pets.'

Caprice sat silently, staring at the door.

'Livinia, could you ask the teachers and any support staff who are not currently on duty to meet in the teachers' lounge in fifteen minutes?' asked the headmistress.

There was a sharp knock on the door and Louella Derby poked her head around. 'Hello Miss Grimm. Constable Derby and Charlie are here,' she announced.

'Please send them in,' Ophelia said.

As the woman opened the door, a ball of caramel curls raced ahead of them.

'Come back here, you naughty little thing,' Louella called, but the creature was on a mission. He ran into the room, dodging the furniture and Miss Grimm's legs, and stopped in front of Caprice. The girl flinched and tried to shoo him away but the pup would not be deterred. He jumped up onto the couch, then leapt up and licked the girl's cheek.

'Eww!' Caprice squealed. But she couldn't resist his charms and was soon cradling him against her chest.

'He's sure taken a shine to you,' Mrs Derby said, reaching out to take the puppy. The girl reluctantly handed him over.

Miss Grimm welcomed the men. 'Good evening, Constable Derby. Hello Charlie. Please take a seat. You need to hear what Caprice has just told us about what happened in the flat.'

Caprice sat up straight and flicked her copper-coloured locks over her shoulder.

'How are you feeling, Charlie?' Ophelia asked.

'Fit as a fiddle, Miss Grimm, and thankfully Alice-Miranda and Millie are too. Talk about brave. I don't know how many children would have had the wherewithal to locate the fire extinguisher and know how to use it. Seems like those lessons we gave them a while ago paid off,' Charlie Weatherly said with a grin.

The woman nodded. 'They certainly did.'

Constable Derby took out a notebook and pen from his top pocket. He looked at the girl, who was fidgeting with the cushion on the seat beside her. 'All right, Caprice, let's start from the beginning, shall we?'

Chapter 15

Millie and Alice-Miranda were given a thorough check-up by the paramedics. A friendly young woman called Kate had listened to their chests, monitored their heart rates and examined their airways for signs of smoke damage. Both girls were given a clean bill of health and instructions to have a shower and wash the smoke smell out of their hair and skin.

'Have you got shampoo?' Millie called out.

Alice-Miranda passed her a bottle around the partition. 'Here you go. We'll have to wash the ponies and air out all the blankets tomorrow too. I hope Bony doesn't make himself sick in that field tonight. He always eats more when he's upset.'

Alice-Miranda hopped out of the shower cubicle in her underwear with a towel wrapped around her head. She pulled on a pair of jeans and a blouse and gathered their smoky clothes into a pile.

'Pooh, they stink!' Sloane said, walking into the bathroom.

Alice-Miranda chuckled and waved a sock towards her. 'I thought you were going up for dinner,' she said.

'We're not allowed to leave until everyone is ready,' Sloane said, wrinkling her nose and batting the sock away. 'Mrs Howard's been acting weird about us going anywhere on our own.'

Millie turned off the water. 'Caprice has probably told a big fat lie about there being a prowler or something. But I'm sure there was no one in that flat except her and the puppy.'

'Maybe they escaped out a window,' Sloane said with a shrug.

'And maybe Caprice should be in the running for an Academy Award.' Millie stepped out of the shower with a towel wrapped around her and picked up a wide-toothed comb.

'Do you think Caprice started the fire?' Sloane asked.

'Who knows?' Millie said.

'She might be a bit unpredictable and have a short temper at times but, really, Millie, setting fire to the stables on purpose? She could have killed someone, including herself,' Alice-Miranda said.

Sloane leaned in close to one of the mirrors, examining the blemish on her forehead. 'Well, if we find out that pyromania is one of her new vices, I'm requesting another room mate.'

Mrs Howard appeared in the doorway. 'Girls, I hate to rush you, but we need to head over to the dining room. Get dressed and I'll be back in a minute with some hair dryers. You can't go out in the night air with wet hair.'

'What happened to Caprice?' Millie asked, running the comb through her matted curls.

'I don't know for sure but Miss Grimm would like to talk to everyone at dinner and she's given me strict instructions not to leave the house until we can all go together. Miss Reedy and Mr Plumpton are on their way down to accompany us,' the housemistress explained before scurrying away.

Sloane looked at the girls.

'There's no way I'm buying any of Caprice's stories,' Millie said, shaking her head.

Alice-Miranda looked at Millie. 'Let's just give her the benefit of the doubt – at least for the moment.'

The atmosphere in the dining room was electric as everyone waited for the arrival of the headmistress. The girls had traipsed in a long line from the boarding house, with Miss Reedy and Mr Plumpton leading the charge and Mrs Howard bringing up the rear. Millie had complained that being marched around together felt like they were back in infants school.

Miss Grimm strode in not long after they were all seated, with Caprice in tow. The woman headed straight for the podium and switched on the microphone. 'Good evening, girls and staff. I'm sure that you are all aware of the events that unfolded in the stables this afternoon. We have had a very lucky escape thanks to the quick thinking of three of our students and Mr Weatherly. Alice-Miranda and Millie, would you please stand up?'

The girls rose to their feet, and the students stamped the floor and clapped loudly. Millie's face flushed the same colour as her hair and Alice-Miranda gave a wave to acknowledge the applause.

'Thank you, girls,' Miss Grimm said, waiting for the students to calm down. 'Now, we've been investigating the cause of the incident and it would appear that there may have been someone using the flat without our permission.'

'You mean like a prowler?' Sloane called out.

Ophelia sighed. That was just the word she had been trying to avoid. 'I mean that it is possible there has been someone on the school campus without our knowledge.'

'This morning we thought it was just one of the stable cats but they were thumping about a lot,' Alice-Miranda whispered with a frown.

The girls looked at one another.

'Caprice might be telling the truth for once in her life,' Sloane said quietly.

Millie rolled her eyes. 'Remember it's Caprice we're talking about. I bet she found that puppy and was hiding him for herself and now she's gone and told the police that there's a prowler just so she doesn't get into trouble.'

'Surely she wouldn't lie about something so serious,' Alice-Miranda said.

'She probably set the place on fire,' Millie said, 'and now she's trying to cover it up.'

The headmistress cleared her throat. 'Constable Derby and his men will be searching for further evidence. Until then, I don't want anyone wandering around on their own – to class, to after-school lessons, to the stables. Travel in groups of three, not two, and if you see anything suspicious at all I expect you to seek help from the nearest adult. Now, enjoy your dinner, girls, and please don't worry. I have every confidence that Constable Derby will get to the bottom of this soon.'

'That's stupid,' Sloane grouched. 'It's hard enough to get one girl to come with me to look after the worm farm, let alone two.'

Ophelia Grimm stepped away from the microphone and walked down to join Mr Grump, who had just returned from a day in the city.

'It's a load of rubbish,' Millie grumbled.

'But if she'd found the puppy and taken the time to hide him and look after him, why did she leave him there?' Sloane said. 'He could have died.'

'Maybe he ran away and she couldn't find him,' Alice-Miranda said. 'Lying to the police will get her into a lot more trouble than if it was just an accident.'

'And I wouldn't want to be Caprice when Constable Derby finds out what really happened,' Millie said, standing up. 'She might get expelled or, even better, go to juvenile detention.' The girl's green eyes lit up at the thought.

'Millie, you don't mean that,' Alice-Miranda chided. Though, she had to admit there was something awry about the whole affair. The girl's mind raced. She had to find out the truth before Caprice dug herself in any deeper.

Chapter 16

Vera Bird lifted the discarded newspaper and fished around for the telephone. She dialled the number and waited for the operator to connect.

'Hello, I'd like one of those kitchen wizards with all the attachments and that exercise thingamajig – the one you just have to stand on and it vibrates the pounds away. Oh, and while I'm at it, I'd like that set of saucepans with the bonus steamer,' she said, and reeled off the digits of her credit card. 'Yes, that's it for now. When will they arrive? Goody! Yes, it's a post-office box.'

Vera hung up the phone and pushed herself out of the armchair, her spectacles swinging wildly on the chain around her neck. Tall pillars of boxes arranged according to their contents, which included everything from dolly tea sets to microwave ovens, televisions, a treadmill and just about any other household item you could imagine, lined the room. There was barely enough space for a walkway but there was an order to it all. The fact that she couldn't recall the last time she'd set foot in the dining room, let alone glimpsed the table, was beside the point.

The woman walked through the maze and into the kitchen, where bundles of cutlery and piles of plates towered on every surface. There were at least sixteen boxes of brand-new saucepans in the corner, and on the stovetop, a single battered pot held the remnants of last night's soup.

A stack of recipe books teetered ominously on the bench while cake tins of all shapes and sizes spilled from another box on the floor. Although the house was overflowing, and Vera could barely move, it was remarkably clean. She spent countless hours wiping down the surfaces and used her cordless swivel-headed vacuum to keep the walkways clear.

Her bedroom was similarly crammed with goods, and the bathroom was almost impossible to enter these days, filled with everything from flat-pack bookshelves to cast-iron coat racks, boxes and boxes of face creams, soaps, toothpaste and enough toilet rolls to supply the entire village of Winchesterfield for at least a year or two.

Vera picked up an envelope that was sitting inside the gleaming new toaster on the bench and slid her long nail under the flap, easing it open. She slipped on her spectacles and squinted at the amount on the bottom of the page.

'That can't be right,' she said to herself. 'I don't remember spending that much last month.' She ran her finger down the list and mentally ticked off the things she'd picked up from the post office. 'Hmph. Well, perhaps I did.' At least she didn't have to worry about money these days. Her investments were doing very well.

Vera walked to the corner of the room and squeezed her tiny frame between a stack of *Kennel and Kibble* magazines and a barbecue, retrieving a chipped cookie jar in the shape of Mickey Mouse. She unscrewed the lid and pulled out a bundle of notes. Vera peeled off the amount she needed and returned the rest to its rightful place.

Tomorrow she would drive to the village and pay the credit card bill, then she'd pick up the new hair curlers and finally be able to try that deluxe gold-leaf curling serum she'd bought a couple of weeks back. Or had it been a couple of years? Vera had always been a collector. It was an addiction of sorts. It used to be about winning but that was long gone. Now it was shopping.

As she turned to leave, something on top of the kitchen cupboard caught her eye. She located the little stepladder that was often carted through the house with her and wheeled it over. She climbed up and reached forward onto the tips of her toes. Her fingers latched onto the ribbon and pulled, dropping the box to the floor. She gingerly climbed back down again, waving away the plume of dust, and took the box into the sitting room, where she untied the ribbon and lifted the lid.

'Oh my heavens,' she said as she pulled out photograph after photograph. 'Look at you. My beautiful, beautiful boys.' A sharp pain clawed at her chest. She sat down in the armchair and leaned forward. It was then that she saw his face, beaming at the world. 'Why? Why did you have to take it all away?' she whispered.

Chapter 17

The sitting room at Grimthorpe House was unusually crowded for a weeknight. Some girls had brought their homework with them while others were playing cards or reading. Mrs Howard walked out of the kitchenette with a cup of tea in her hand. Although the girls had made a great show of their bravado, it was clear that the possibility of an unknown person on the school grounds had rattled them and, truth be told, Mrs Howard would feel a lot better too once the culprit was caught. She sat down beside Mimi

Theopolis, who was writing a book review at the dining table.

A stocky brunette girl called Anna looked up from the couch. 'Excuse me, Mrs Howard, would you like me to check that all the windows and doors are locked?'

'Thank you, dear, but Charlie's already been down and done that. There's no need for you to worry,' the old woman reassured the child.

'Oh, I wasn't worried,' the girl said, smiling awkwardly.

'You shouldn't be,' Millie quipped, 'because I doubt there is a prowler *at all*.'

Mrs Howard frowned. 'I think we'll leave Constable Derby to decide on that. In the meantime we will look after each other, won't we, Millie?'

The girl bit her lip and nodded begrudgingly. Without absolute proof, there was no point saying anything else. She'd just be in Howie's bad books.

'Do you want a hot chocolate?' Alice-Miranda asked her friend.

Millie nodded and the pair walked across to the kitchenette.

Mrs Howard glanced around the room and counted the children in her head. Everyone was there except for Caprice, which seemed odd given that she was the one who had encountered the intruder. Perhaps Millie's accusations were true but, goodness, if that were the case, the girl was going to be in terrible trouble for bothering the police about nothing. Thankfully, despite having bumped her head and fainted, Caprice had received a clean bill of health from the paramedics. All the same, the housemistress made a note to check on her if she didn't appear shortly.

'Do you think we'll get to play with the dogs when the show is on?' Anna asked.

'I don't know, but maybe one of the jobs might include walking them,' Mrs Howard said. 'That would be fun, don't you think?'

The girl nodded. 'We have a dog called Brutus but he's nothing like a brute at all. I love taking him for walks.'

The girls began to speculate about what responsibilities they might have at the show. Mrs Howard was glad that the event was taking their minds off other things when suddenly the telephone rang, sparking a wave of squeals. The housemistress almost jumped out of her seat too. 'Could someone answer that, please?' she said, taking a moment to recover.

Alice-Miranda dived around the corner to the little office and picked up the handset. 'Good evening, Grimthorpe House, this is Alice-Miranda speaking,' the child said, walking back to the kitchenette. There was a short pause. 'Oh, hello Mrs Parker, how are you? And Mr Parker? I was hoping to pop by on the weekend, if I may?'

'Who is it?' Mrs Howard called from the other room.

'Nosey Parker,' Millie called back.

Alice-Miranda barely got her hand over the mouthpiece in time. She widened her eyes at Millie, who giggled and shrugged.

'Would you like to speak with Mrs Howard?' Alice-Miranda asked.

The housemistress was walking towards the child and shaking her hands like windscreen wipers on high speed.

'She's right here,' Alice-Miranda said.

The old woman's shoulders slumped and she reluctantly took the telephone.

'I don't think Howie wanted to talk to her,' Millie said, heaping several spoonfuls of cocoa into two mugs.

Alice-Miranda grinned. 'You know Mrs Parker. She'd only call back later.'

'Hello Myrtle,' Mrs Howard breathed.

The girls in the sitting room giggled as they heard Mrs Parker's shrill voice blasting through the receiver.

'Excuse me, Myrtle,' Mrs Howard blustered, raising her voice. 'We've had a near catastrophe here this afternoon and, no, I did not get your message about the emergency meeting, so you can jolly well calm down.' Mrs Howard stormed into her office and closed the door behind her.

Millie picked up the two steaming mugs and passed one to her friend. 'What do you think all that was about?'

'Mrs Howard must have missed something important,' Alice-Miranda replied. She and Millie wove a path through the girls who were sitting on the floor, making their way to two empty beanbags in the corner of the room.

Sloane was there, resting on her elbows and reading a book. She looked up as the girls approached. 'It's nice having everyone here together for a change,' she said, wriggling over to make room for their legs.

Millie nodded. 'It feels like the weekend.'

'I suppose we have Caprice to thank for that,' Sloane said.

'She's not getting any thanks from me,' Millie grumbled. 'I thought Miss Grimm might have let me off gardening duties after what happened, but she didn't say anything at dinner.'

'She probably wasn't even thinking about that tonight,' Alice-Miranda said. 'Where is Caprice, anyway?'

Sloane put aside her book. 'In bed. She said she was exhausted but I'm pretty sure she was crying when I left to come down here. I asked her what was wrong and she just snapped at me like always.'

'Maybe I should go to see her,' Alice-Miranda said. 'Even if there wasn't a prowler, maybe she feels guilty about the fire and the puppy.'

'Let her! That puppy could have died and, now that I think about it, we could have too,' Millie said, taking a sip of her drink.

Alice-Miranda thought for a moment and then stood up. 'I'll be back soon.'

Chapter 18

Alice-Miranda knocked gently on the door and waited a few moments before pushing it open. 'Caprice, are you all right?' Alice-Miranda whispered. 'I thought you might like to talk to someone about what happened this afternoon.'

The girl was lying on her bed and rolled over to face the wall. 'Go away,' she ordered, her voice muffled beneath the covers.

Alice-Miranda closed the door behind her and sat down on the edge of Sloane's bed. She looked around the immaculate space, which these days resembled a page from a catalogue. If nothing else, Sloane had certainly learned a lot about house-keeping from her room mate. 'But I'm worried about you, and the other girls are too,' she said.

'Sure they are,' Caprice huffed.

Alice-Miranda decided to try a different tack. 'I'm so glad the puppy is okay. It would have been horrible if anything had happened to him.'

A small sob came from the other side of the room.

Alice-Miranda walked over and placed her hand on Caprice's shoulder. She could feel the girl's body shuddering. 'Was there really someone up there?' Alice-Miranda asked. There was a long silence. 'Please talk to me.'

Caprice's body tensed. 'I don't want to! Just leave me alone.'

'You have to tell the truth, Caprice,' Alice-Miranda said. 'If you lie to the police you can get into serious trouble.'

The girl suddenly threw off the covers and sat up. 'And wouldn't that just suit all of you? Millie is probably rubbing her hands together at the thought.'

'That's not true,' Alice-Miranda said firmly. 'But you know everyone would like you more if you didn't pick on her.'

Caprice looked away. 'I don't pick on her.'

'Well, why did you set her up to take the blame for the paint bombs?' Alice-Miranda said.

'You don't know that.'

Alice-Miranda raised an eyebrow. 'I haven't said anything to Miss Grimm, but there seemed to be a lot of curly caramel hairs on your wet uniform this morning. I'm sure you didn't start the fire on purpose, Caprice, but you really should own up.'

Caprice's jaw flapped open like a stunned carp. For once in her life she didn't know what to say.

'All the girls are terrified there's a prowler on the school grounds and we won't have any freedom while Miss Grimm thinks someone is lurking about,' Alice-Miranda said. 'It will make our preparations for the dog show awfully tricky.'

Caprice drew up her knees and hugged them to her chest. 'It was an accident,' the girl said softly. 'The puppy must have gone too close to the heater and the towels snagged on the coils. I was just trying to warm him up.'

Alice-Miranda's eyes widened. She never imagined Caprice would actually confess. 'But why did you leave him there?' she asked.

'He ran away and hid and I couldn't find him and then the smoke was getting thicker and I thought I was going to die.' Tears began to stream down the girl's face.

Alice-Miranda put her arm around Caprice's shoulders. 'You have to tell Miss Grimm the truth.'

'But she's going to be so angry,' Caprice blubbered. 'And what if she calls my parents?'

'Miss Grimm will be mad for a while but, believe me, she'll be happy that we don't have to be on the alert for an intruder,' Alice-Miranda assured her. 'Where did you get the puppy?'

Caprice blinked her big blue eyes and snatched a tissue from the bedside table. She wiped away the tears. 'I found him in the garden when I was on the way back from my singing lesson,' she explained. 'I knew Miss Grimm would have called the dog catcher, so I thought about where I could hide him and the stable flat seemed the best place.'

'Someone would have found him sooner or later,' Alice-Miranda said, smiling at the girl. 'He would have got bigger and noisier and I don't know how you were planning to feed him.'

Caprice shrugged. 'I don't know either. It was a stupid idea.' She swallowed hard and looked Alice-Miranda in the eye. 'Are you going to tell Mrs Howard?'

The girl shook her head.

'Why not?'

'Because you're going to tell her yourself.'

'I don't know if I can,' Caprice said, her eyes awash with new tears.

Alice-Miranda patted the girl's hand. 'You'll feel better once you get it off your chest.'

Caprice sniffed. 'Will you come with me?' she asked.

Alice-Miranda smiled and nodded. She was pleased the girl wasn't concocting yet another lie to cover her tracks.

Caprice swivelled her feet to the ground and stood up. She pulled on her dressing-gown and found her slippers at the end of the bed.

'Where are you going?' Alice-Miranda asked, surprised by the girl's burst of energy.

'To see Miss Grimm,' Caprice replied. 'I'm not going to be able to sleep if I leave it until tomorrow, and if I don't sleep I might get sick, which would be a total disaster. I always get throat problems when I'm stressed, plus I have a rehearsal with Mr Trout and Mr Lipp that I can't afford to miss.'

Caprice opened the door and turned to find Alice-Miranda still sitting on the bed. 'Come on, slow coach, some of us have other things to do, you know.'

'Sorry,' Alice-Miranda said, grinning as she got up and followed Caprice out of the room.

Chapter 19

Cornelius Trout watched from the organ balcony upstairs, awaiting his cue from Miss Reedy, who always gave him a nod when the staff were gathered at the assembly-hall door. It was his prompt to commence the processional and the first song of the day. When the microphone crackled to life, he swivelled his head and was shocked to find the head-mistress and her entourage already on stage.

Having spent the best part of an hour with Caprice and Alice-Miranda the night before, Ophelia

Grimm was determined that this was going to be the end of the drama and, frankly, she just wanted to get the whole thing over and done with. 'Girls,' she began, 'I am pleased to report that the issue of the trespasser has been resolved and you have absolutely nothing to worry about.' She cast a glare in Caprice's direction. 'The fire was an unfortunate accident and, as I said yesterday, we must be thankful that no one was hurt. I'd ask that we now lay this incident to rest and I will have no further speculation about blame. We all make mistakes, and something that warms my heart is when people are mature enough to own up to them. Rest assured that there will be consequences for the girl responsible.'

Wild whispers filled the air until a stern tap from the headmistress's foot silenced them as swiftly as they had begun.

'Now,' Miss Grimm continued, 'I have some exciting news about the dog show and what is in store for us over the coming weeks. I hadn't quite realised the enormity of the event but I'm looking forward to everyone pitching in to help.'

Livinia Reedy's eye twitched. Despite the headmistress's assurances that the dog show would be over before the wedding began, she was nervous. These things were unpredictable and she would have much preferred to have the day to herself. At least Ophelia had agreed to her request that Chudleigh's not be allowed to use the dining room or the chapel and that she and Josiah would not, under any circumstances, be on duty that day.

Ophelia Grimm was feeling somewhat overwhelmed herself, having been presented with the list of demands from Mrs Parker the previous evening. She had been livid upon discovering that Professor Winterbottom hadn't committed the boys to assist with the show until after being told Ophelia had already agreed to do so. When confronted about this, Myrtle replied that it surely didn't matter who'd offered to help first and that it was heartwarming to know both schools were so willing to be part of what was to be a monumental occasion. 'Monumental' seemed appropriate, but 'monstrous' was the word that kept flashing through Ophelia's mind.

Sloane raised her hand in the air.

The headmistress looked over and nodded. 'Yes, Sloane?'

'What happened to the puppy?' the girl asked.

'Mrs Derby is looking after him until Dr Davidson returns from his holidays,' Ophelia replied.

'And we'll be assigning some girls to put up posters of him around the village.' Onstage, sitting beside the Head Prefect, Livinia Reedy pursed her lips. The last thing they needed was a puppy to take care of as well as everything else that was going on.

'What if no one claims him?' Millie asked.

'I imagine we'll cross that bridge when we come to it,' the woman replied.

'Could we keep him, Miss Grimm?' Mia said. 'It would be lovely to have a school dog and we could all help to look after him.'

There was a murmur of agreement through the hall.

'Let's not get ahead of ourselves, girls. We must do our best to find the puppy's owner. If no one comes forward after a reasonable amount of time, then I will think about it,' the woman said.

'Yes!' the girls hissed while fists pumped around the room.

Alice-Miranda nudged Millie. 'Miss Grimm thought he was adorable.'

'Caprice will probably still think he belongs to her because she found him,' Millie grumbled.

'I can't imagine it,' Alice-Miranda replied. She had watched the girl's torturous exchange with the headmistress the night before, followed by Constable Derby giving Caprice a stern talking-to about wasting police resources. 'I suspect she might lay low for a little while.'

Caprice was sitting further along the row, her back straight like a soldier, looking as if there were a thousand things and nothing going through her head.

'I wonder if Miss Grimm is going to let me off gardening duty,' Millie whispered.

Alice-Miranda shrugged. 'I'm not sure. Caprice didn't own up to having planted the paint bombs.'

'I suppose that would have been too much to hope for,' Millie said. 'What's her punishment?'

The headmistress's voice boomed into the microphone. 'What matters is that the puppy is being properly cared for. Now, girls, I'm going to put volunteer sheets up on the noticeboard outside the dining room at morning tea time. There are lots of different things you can help with, so please make sure that you add your name to at least three different activities and we'll announce after school which of those you'll be assisting with.'

'Tell me later,' Millie mouthed.

Alice-Miranda wasn't sure if she should divulge the girl's punishment, seeing as though it required

Millie and Caprice to work together over the weekend. It sounded like Caprice was going to be busy every weekend for the rest of the term. Miss Grimm's first reaction had been to ban her from competing in the National Eisteddfod, which Caprice had begged her to reconsider. In the end, the pair had come to an agreement involving considerable garden duties and mucking out the stables under Charlie's strict supervision. There was no weekend television and no outings either, so she was pretty much under lock and key. When Miss Grimm told the girl that her parents would have to be informed, Alice-Miranda thought the exchange would descend into chaos, but surprisingly Caprice didn't object too loudly.

'I hope Miss Grimm's got a pooper-scooper group. I'll be putting Caprice's name at the top of that list,' Millie said, grinning slyly.

Alice-Miranda smiled. 'No, you won't.'

Millie rolled her eyes. 'But you know I want to.'

Chapter 20

The second half of the week passed quickly without any more nasty dramas. There was great excitement about the dog show as well as extra rehearsals for the Winchester-Fayle Singers for their performance at Miss Reedy and Mr Plumpton's wedding. The children had been surprised to learn that Chudleigh's was to be held on the same weekend as the wedding and wondered why Miss Grimm had agreed to it, but it was too late to change anything. Preparations for both events were in full swing. There were workmen measuring up for marquees and Charlie Weatherly had hired additional manpower to help mark out the parking areas and to clip and snip the gardens to their absolute best. Miss Reedy seemed to be forever dashing from one place to the next with a thick folder in her arms, which Millie nicknamed the Wedding Bible. When it went missing after lunch on Wednesday, you'd have thought she'd lost the crown jewels. Fortunately, it was found among a pile of dirty laundry, although how it got there was anyone's guess.

Alice-Miranda, Millie and Sloane had put their names down to work as ushers at Chudleigh's as well as volunteering to work on food stalls and the cleaning crew. When the various teams were decided, the girls had all wound up on different activities. Sloane was assigned to cleaning, Millie was on food duty and Alice-Miranda was to be an usher. They hadn't seen Jacinta all week and wondered what she and the girls from Caledonia Manor had been allocated.

During all of this, Caprice kept her head down in classes and quietly went about her after-school activities, avoiding everyone as best she could. Alice-Miranda was pleased to see the girl taking her punishment on the chin, though Caprice still hadn't owned up to the paint bombs, which meant Millie was still on gardening duty all day Saturday and Sunday. Mr Charles had already told the girl he was negotiating with the headmistress to give her an early mark on Sunday afternoon.

On Friday night the girls from Caledonia Manor joined the rest of the school for a special dinner. Millie took the opportunity to regale Jacinta with the news of the week, albeit quietly, as she didn't want Miss Grimm or any of the other teachers to hear her. Alice-Miranda had asked Caprice if she wanted to sit with them, but the girl had taken herself off to sit with Mr Trout and some of the younger students.

'So where's the puppy now?' Jacinta asked.

'Mrs Derby has been looking after him during the day in her office, but she and Constable Derby have gone away for the weekend, so Miss Grimm's got him,' Millie said.

'Really? Is he here?' The girl looked at the head table, where Miss Grimm was sitting with Miss Reedy and Mr Plumpton.

'I don't think so,' Millie replied.

'There he is!' Sloane pointed at the door as Mr Grump walked in, carrying the bundle of curls in his arms. The pup was wearing a bright red collar with a matching lead. 'So much for not getting too attached to the little guy.'

The headmistress's husband walked past the girls, who all cooed at the puppy.

'Isn't he sweet, Mr Grump?' Alice-Miranda sighed. She broke off a small piece of naan bread and offered it to the pup, who gobbled it down.

'Yes, except that he just chewed my slippers,' the man said, ruffling the puppy's ears. The creature growled playfully and nipped at his fingers.

'He's very small,' Alice-Miranda said.

'Yes,' Mr Grump replied. 'Dr Davidson was concerned about his age when he checked him over before jetting off on holiday. Apparently, this one's too young to be away from his mother and there were signs of malnutrition. Good news is, I think he's gained quite a bit of weight over the past few days,' Mr Grump said. 'His soft paw pads were cut to shreds too – he's obviously walked some distance to get here.'

'That's awful, and his poor mother,' Alice-Miranda said with a frown.

'Yes, we suspect he might have escaped from somewhere,' the man said.

'Maybe he was dumped,' Millie suggested. 'People do that, you know. Mummy sees it quite often in her surgery.'

Jacinta shook her head. 'What sort of person could leave that gorgeous pup by the side of the road? People like that don't deserve to have pets.'

'Mrs Derby took the most adorable picture of him for the posters we're putting up in the village tomorrow,' Alice-Miranda said.

'Yes, I know a couple of people who are going to find it very hard to say goodbye to him when the time comes,' Mr Grump nodded in the direction of his wife.

'*You* and Miss Grimm,' Millie said cheekily.

'No, *Mrs Derby* and Miss Grimm,' the man replied. 'Oh, and I will just a smidge, unless he keeps eating my shoes.'

The man said goodbye and walked over to join his wife, who'd brought the puppy's basket with her from the office. Silence descended over the table as the girls got to grips with the delicious curry Mrs Smith had made.

'What's everyone doing for the dog show?' Jacinta asked, snapping a pappadum in half.

The girls talked over the top of one another, explaining what they'd been assigned.

'What about you?' Alice-Miranda asked.

'I'm ushering, so we'll be together,' Jacinta replied. 'Mummy told me Nosey Parker's up to ninety about the whole thing. And we've got new neighbours at the end of the road who breed dogs. Mummy's having a welcome barbecue for them tomorrow night and you're all invited.'

Millie's face dropped. 'I doubt I'll be allowed to go.'

'We can ask,' Alice-Miranda said. 'And if you can't, I'll stay here with you.'

Millie grinned at her friend. 'Thanks but you don't have to.'

'Isn't Ursula looking after us this weekend because Howie's going to see her sister?' Sloane said.

'Oh yeah,' Millie said, perking up. 'Ursula's a big fan of Monopoly, so if I'm not allowed to go out, we can revisit the Grimthorpe House Monopoly Championships.'

'Do you want to come and help us put up the posters around the village in the morning?' Alice-Miranda asked Jacinta.

'I would but I have training,' the girl replied. 'I've got the National Gymnastics Championships coming up and at the moment I don't think I'll even qualify.'

'Of course you will,' Sloane said. 'You're amazing.'

Jacinta shook her head and frowned. 'I used to be, before I broke my toe in Paris. Since then I just can't seem to get it together. My coach also says it might be because I'm having a growth spurt. I don't know . . . sometimes I think that maybe I'm growing out of gymnastics, although I don't want to give it up completely.'

'Maybe you should try acrobatics for a change,' Sloane said. 'I saw this incredible video of some acrobats who could pretty much turn themselves inside out. My muscles hurt just from watching them.'

Jacinta nodded. 'That sounds interesting. I mean, gymnastics is great but there are loads of other things I'd like to do too.'

'Like meeting up with your boyfriend,' Millie teased.

Jacinta rolled her eyes and poked out her tongue.

'Speaking of Lucas, have you seen him this week?' Alice-Miranda asked.

Jacinta shook her head. 'No, but he and Sep are coming to the barbecue tomorrow night.'

'Good. I want to show him some pictures Aunt Charlotte sent me of the twins,' Alice-Miranda said.

'He's the most adorable big brother. Mummy told me that he's started reading books to them on the phone every night and, even though they're just babies, their eyes get really big and they make all sorts of funny excited noises when he appears on the screen.'

Millie snorted and almost sent a chilli up her nose. 'That's what happens to Jacinta when she sees him too,' she joked, and all the girls burst out laughing.

'Very funny,' Jacinta said, trying to look cross. After a few seconds she broke into a huge grin. 'He really is going to be the best father ever,' she sighed.

Chapter 21

The lad glanced into the cage and counted again. He pointed at the creatures and racked his brain. 'Hey, Damon, what happened to the other puppy?' he yelled.

'I don't know,' the younger lad snapped. 'How many are there supposed to be?'

'Seven, and now there are six,' Declan said, the heat rising to his neck. He paced the length of the shed, ignoring the howls and cries. 'You must have let one out, you moron.'

'Why's it always my fault? I didn't even know there was one missing,' Damon replied. They'd had an escapee once before but had realised almost straight away and had found the creature under a thicket on the edge of the woods. If Declan was right this time around, it meant that the pup would have been missing for at least a couple of days.

'What are we gonna say?' Declan muttered. He kicked a cage door, causing the pups inside to cower.

His brother shrugged. 'The truth.'

'Were you abducted by aliens or something? Do you know what that pup's worth?'

'Well, we can't do anything about it now.' His brother sniffed and wiped his nose on his sleeve. 'We'll say it died.'

'What if the boss wants proof?'

'We buried it already,' the scrawny lad replied.

Declan turned around and grinned a yellow smile. 'Sometimes you're not as dumb as you look.'

'Where are they going to this time?' Damon asked.

'How would I know? We don't ask questions. We just do as we're told,' Declan replied.

He retrieved a fruit box from the end of the shed and strolled back to the cage. As he opened the door, the mother looked up at him. She knew what was coming next. The lad reached in and pulled the pups out one by one and plonked them into the empty box. Each one whimpered and whined, their tiny bodies quivering. The mother turned her head to the back of the cage as if she couldn't bear to say goodbye.

'The old girl doesn't look too good,' Declan said. 'Better not tell the boss or that'll be the end of her. You'd better hurry up and finish feeding this lot. Have you done the others?'

'Not yet,' the lad replied.

'Well, get on with it. We've gotta take these to the drop-off.'

Sloane Sykes grabbed her jacket and poked her head into the room next door. Millie was sitting on her bed doing up her shoelaces and Alice-Miranda was rummaging around in her backpack. 'Ready to go?' the girl asked.

Alice-Miranda looked up and smiled. 'I was just checking we've got everything.'

'Has Caprice left already?' Millie asked.

Sloane nodded. 'A few minutes ago. You know,

she's actually been really nice to me since the fire,' Sloane said. 'Maybe it was like an epiphany or whatever you call that thing when you realise something huge about yourself.'

'I'll believe it when I see it,' Millie said.

'Everyone can change, Millie,' Alice-Miranda said.

Millie looked over at Sloane.

'What are you staring at me for?' Sloane said, feigning offence. 'I was never as bad as . . . Okay, I was. If I can change, anyone can.'

Millie stood up and put an arm around Sloane's shoulders. 'Yeah, I really didn't imagine we'd ever be friends and look at us now.'

'I can assure you the feeling was mutual.' Sloane grinned at Millie, who screwed up her nose.

'I wish I could come with you two, but I'd better get going or I'll be in trouble again. I can't wait to see Caprice's face when Charlie tells her she's going to be up to her elbows in manure for most of the day,' Millie said, grinning.

'We'd better get going too,' Sloane said. 'I don't want to miss lunch. Mrs Smith's making pizza.'

The girls left through the sitting room, bidding farewell to Ursula, and went their separate ways.

Sloane and Alice-Miranda took a short cut across the field, following a lane that led to the edge of Winchesterfield. They spent the next hour trekking up and down the streets and lanes on the east side of the village. They were going to visit some of the shops before tackling the west side, where the Fayle School was located, and then finish up at Rosebud Lane, which was only a short walk from the school.

Fluffy white clouds drifted across the blue sky as Sloane taped another poster to a timber lamppost. The golden leaves at her feet foretold the colder months to come but for now the village sparkled in the sun.

'You do realise that we're going to have to take all of these down again once someone claims the puppy,' Alice-Miranda said.

Sloane looked at her in alarm. She had been enjoying the task right up until that moment. 'Really?'

'Absolutely,' Alice-Miranda replied. 'Don't you remember when we did the play with the boys at Fayle and we put posters up around the town? Mrs Parker nearly had a fit that they were still there the morning after the performance.'

Sloane pulled a face and shook her head. 'Actually, no. I was already halfway back to Spain by then.'

Alice-Miranda smiled at her. 'Oops, I forgot about that. Never mind. Things worked out in the end, didn't they?'

'Yes, thanks to you,' Sloane said, grinning. She pointed to the general store across the road. 'Do you want to get a drink?'

'Sure, I'll ask Mr Munz if we can put a poster in the window,' Alice-Miranda said.

As the girls walked through the door with the tinkly bell, an ancient white van with more dents than a golf ball squeaked to a halt across the road. Two young men, one tall and solidly built, the other much shorter and slighter, got out. The taller lad walked into the hardware shop while the shorter lad stood in the sunshine, leaning against the driver's door.

Declan emerged from the hardware shop with a large bag of dog food slung over his shoulder. He opened the van door and dumped it inside. 'Get in,' he ordered.

'But I want something to drink,' Damon said.

'Why didn't you go when I was in the shop?' The older lad rolled his eyes and sighed. He pulled a couple of notes from his wallet and shoved them into Damon's hand. 'Get me a bag of crisps and a cola while you're at it, and hurry up – they're starting to get antsy in the back.'

Damon jogged across the street to the general store. He was about to go in when he noticed the poster in the window and stepped back to read it. 'Oh heck,' he breathed.

Alice-Miranda glanced at the young man by the shop window. She and Sloane had decided to have their drinks before tackling the rest of the village and were sitting on the bench by the door. The lad's shorts and singlet looked as if they hadn't seen the inside of a washing machine in a while and he seemed to be studying the flyer intently. Alice-Miranda jumped up and hurried over to him.

'Hello,' she said. 'Do you know who owns him?'

The lad flinched, startled by the small girl. 'Why would I know that?' he said, taking a step back.

'You just seemed to be looking closely, that's all, and we'd love to find his owner. He's a gorgeous little pup and he's probably too young to be away from his mother.'

'No, he's not,' Damon said, curling his top lip.

'Really?' Alice-Miranda frowned, wondering how he could be so sure. 'Well, if you do know who owns him, please tell them that he's being well cared for at our school and they can come and pick him up at any time. Hopefully someone will be missing him. We've delivered plenty of flyers around the village and put posters up on the lampposts too.'

'Oi, what are you doing?' another young man yelled from across the road. He was leaning out of the van window and Alice-Miranda noticed a large tattoo of a star on his upper arm. 'We gotta go!'

'I'm coming,' the skinny chap shouted. He stalked across the road and jumped into the passenger seat without looking back.

'Where's my stuff?' Declan growled.

The younger lad swallowed hard and nodded towards the two girls sitting on the bench. 'We've got trouble. They have the pup.'

Declan stared at the girls. 'How d'you know that?' he said.

'There's a poster in the shop window,' Damon explained. 'She says that whoever owns him can go to the school and pick him up.'

'Did she say what school it was?'

'No, but it must be that big posh boarding school on the edge of the village because the school in town is closed on the weekends, isn't it?'

Declan glanced at his watch. 'There's no time to go there now.'

'Well, if we can't get him now, we can't get him at all or the boss'll know we lied about him dying,' Damon said as his brother turned the key in the ignition. 'Oh, crumbs!'

'What now?' Declan sighed. He eased the sputtering van out from the kerb.

'The girl said they've put up posters all around the village and they letterbox-dropped everyone. What if the boss sees?'

'We're goners, that's what.' Beads of perspiration began to trickle down the older lad's temple. 'Fine. Let's make the drop, then come back and take them all down as quick as we can,' he said.

Damon's face lit up. 'Why don't we come back and collect the pup?'

'What are you talking about?' Declan barked. 'We just said we can't!'

'We could sell him ourselves,' Damon suggested, his face splitting into a grin.

'If the boss found out, I can only imagine what would happen to us,' Declan said.

'We could leave it at the school until we have a buyer and then we can just pick it up and deliver direct,' the younger brother said. He clenched his fists like a prize fighter. 'And if it works, who knows where that might lead?'

'Don't get ahead of yourself, moron,' Declan spat.

'But it could work, couldn't it?'

The older lad crunched the gears. 'I don't know.'

'Well, I think I'm a genius.' Damon picked at a pimple on his cheek as his brother finally found second and the van sped out of town.

Declan shook his head. 'You would.'

Chapter 22

The doorbell buzzed sharply and Myrtle Parker scurried down the hallway to get it. She had asked her committee members to be there at nine o'clock sharp so she could organise the tea and biscuits before their guest of honour arrived. Most of them had obeyed her instructions, but she was still waiting on Mrs Howard, who had been less than enthusiastic about attending. She swung open the door to find a tall man wearing a very stylish navy suit standing on the porch. He leaned on a polished timber walking stick, its brass handle the head of a handsome-looking hound.

'Good morning, Major Foxley, and welcome to Winchesterfield,' Myrtle sparkled. She held out her hand and stared at the man, simply taken aback.

He smiled, revealing a perfect set of white teeth, and shook her hand. 'Thank you for having me, Mrs Parker,' he said, wondering if the woman's grip was always so firm.

Myrtle sighed. With his tanned complexion and full head of silver hair, the man could have stepped straight out of an old Hollywood film. 'Please, do come in,' she said, patting her bouffant curls and straightening her floral skirt. 'Most of the committee members are here already – well, those who could make it this morning. Unfortunately, several have been detained by work engagements. I told them this was far more important but, for whatever reason, some people are reluctant to put their community commitments first. But you have no worries about that with me.'

The woman ushered him in, then briefly stepped outside to see if there was any sign of Mrs Howard, but she could hardly look past the glistening black Range Rover parked in the driveway. Major Foxley simply exuded elegance, from his immaculate clothing to his impressive vehicle. Myrtle closed the door and turned to the major. She'd noticed he had quite a pronounced limp and stared at the stick in his hand.

He saw her looking at it too. 'Nothing to worry about, Mrs Parker – just an old war injury. That's what you get when you save an entire battalion.'

A dreamy look clouded Myrtle's face as she found herself imagining the man in his battle fatigues, throwing men the size of lumberjacks over his shoulder and spiriting them to safety.

'Are you all right, Mrs Parker?' Major Foxley asked.

'Yes, of course,' Myrtle said, crashing back to reality. 'We're just through here in the sitting room,' she said, and held out her arm for the man to go ahead of her. 'Ladies,' Myrtle fizzed, 'I'd like you to meet Major Alistair Foxley, Chairman of Chudleigh's Dog Show.'

There was an audible gasp as the women stood up to greet the man. Major Foxley walked around the room with Myrtle as she introduced each member of the committee to him.

'This is Mrs Singh. She and her husband own the local curry house,' Myrtle said.

'How divine. I love a good curry,' he purred. Mrs Singh offered her hand, which the man shook gently. But when he tried to take it away, her grip tightened.

'Indira,' Myrtle snapped.

The woman released Major Foxley and giggled like a schoolgirl. Myrtle continued around the room, introducing Doreen Smith from the girls' school, Marta Munz, Evelyn Pepper from Chesterfield Downs, Nancy Mereweather and Deidre Winterbottom, wife of the headmaster of the Fayle School. All of the women seemed to have fallen under some sort of charm spell, and Myrtle made sure to mention several times that, in addition to being Chairman of Chudleigh's, he was also a decorated war hero.

Alistair Foxley leaned down to give the pristine West Highland terrier at Mrs Winterbottom's feet a pat. 'What an adorable little chap,' he said.

'His name is Parsley,' Myrtle chimed. 'He's gorgeous, isn't he? A pedigree, I believe. Isn't that right, Deidre?'

The woman nodded obediently. On past occasions when Parsley had accompanied her, Myrtle Parker had made him sit in the kitchen on a mat. Some days he'd even been relegated to the utility room. He usually wasn't allowed within cooee of Myrtle's precious sitting room, but today Parsley had received his own special invitation. Professor Winterbottom had been quite miffed not to be able to take him to the morning's rugby matches, but Deidre insisted that Myrtle had been very specific that Parsley attend the meeting, and everyone knew that it wasn't worth upsetting her.

'Do you have a dog yourself, Mrs Parker?' the man asked as she showed him to the armchair in the middle of the room.

'Sadly not,' she said, handing him a fine china cup and saucer. 'My Reginald has been unwell for the past few years, so there was just no time for one. I couldn't bear the thought of not devoting all my energy to a pet – it just wouldn't be fair.'

Deidre Winterbottom sputtered. It was common knowledge that Myrtle wasn't at all partial to animals, particularly dogs, but this offer to host Chudleigh's had seen quite the most remarkable about face in the woman. Deidre glanced over at Nancy Mereweather, who gave her a sly wink. The two women found themselves having to contain a rising fit of giggles.

Myrtle turned and gave them both a stern glare. 'Whatever's the problem, Deidre?'

'Nothing. I was just thinking about something funny that Wallace said to me this morning,' the woman replied. She recovered her composure and didn't dare look at anyone for the next few minutes – especially not Mrs Mereweather.

'Right. Major Foxley, I think we should get on with the business at hand.' Myrtle produced a clipboard and proceeded to distribute the agenda for the meeting. 'Item one: Her Majesty's attendance,' Myrtle began.

'Oh dear,' Nancy Mereweather said with a giggle. 'I think there's been a mix-up. Her Majesty is to be the guest of honour at the Quilters' Exhibition, not Chudleigh's. I believe Major Foxley will be presenting Best in Show.' She smiled at the man and chortled.

Myrtle Parker looked up sharply from the agenda. Her face seemed set to explode. Around the room, the women held their collective breaths. 'Oh, never mind,' Myrtle said, her face softening as she gazed at Major Foxley. 'Her Majesty comes to our events all the time. It will be a breath of fresh air to have a man of Major Foxley's standing among us.'

The committee members eyed each other warily, exhaling in unison just as the doorbell rang.

'I'll get that,' Doreen Smith said, jumping up from her seat. She didn't think Mrs Howard deserved to be on the receiving end of Myrtle's wrath for being late. Several minutes later Mrs Howard followed Mrs Smith into the room and quietly took her place in the corner.

'Nice of you to join us, Mrs Howard,' Myrtle remarked before introducing the woman to their special guest.

'My apologies, Major Foxley,' Mrs Howard said. 'One of my girls was terribly homesick this morning and I couldn't leave the poor poppet until we'd had a soothing cocoa and some cuddles. Given I won't be there this evening and her parents are uncontactable, I thought it only fair.'

'Oh, Mrs Howard, you're a gem. I wish my boarding mistresses had been as kind and compassionate as yourself. I spent many a year crying myself to sleep,' the man replied.

'I'll give you a hug now if you like, Mr Foxley,' Marta Munz said cheekily. The other women tittered until Myrtle Parker cast death stares at all of them.

'You're a cheeky one, Mrs Munz. I can see I'm going to enjoy working with you lot.' Alistair laughed. He cleared his throat and the ladies all settled down.

Myrtle was about to resume the meeting when Major Foxley beat her to it.

'Well, thank you all for agreeing to host Chudleigh's. It is a huge undertaking but one that I am assured by Mayor Wiley that you can not only cope with but will excel at.' He tapped a shiny gold pen on the notebook he'd just pulled out of his suit pocket and looked expectantly at the group, who stared at the man with the doe-eyed looks of lovestruck teenage girls.

Chapter 23

The telephone rang as Becca Finchley finished making her son's bed as best she could. She fumbled with the wheels of her chair and tried to push herself backwards, only to have one of them jammed by a stray sock.

'Would you get that, please, Daniel?' she shouted. 'Daniel! Please answer the phone,' she called again, but it rang and rang until it was interrupted by the tinkling of the front doorbell.

It must have been about the fourth time she'd missed the phone this week and no one was leaving messages. She made a mental note to check if she'd set the thing up properly. The woman gave a sharp shove, releasing the stuck wheel and manoeuvring her way out of the room. She pushed down the hallway to the front door and turned the lock.

'Have I got you at a bad time, dear?' the old woman asked. She was holding a large round tin in one hand and a carton of eggs in the other.

'Oh, no, Mrs Bird, I was just making the beds,' Becca replied.

'What are you doing that for? Your son is old enough to help with the household chores,' Mrs Bird tutted.

'Please come in.' Becca pushed back, trying to spin the chair around but the hallway was narrow and she found it a challenge, to say the least.

'Let me help you.' The old woman dumped the goods she was carrying into Becca's lap and grabbed the handles. 'Speaking of Daniel, where is he? I would have thought he could have answered the door for you.'

'I'm not sure,' Becca said, hoping he didn't suddenly appear. She never liked having to explain herself to anyone, including their kindly old neighbour.

They reached the kitchen and Becca was surprised to see that the washing up had been done.

'I'll put the kettle on,' Mrs Bird insisted. 'And I've made you some biscuits. I know what it's like living with boys.'

Becca Finchley thought Mrs Bird's name rather suited her. A small woman with a nondescript face, she looked like one of those television mothers from an advertisement for washing powder – pleasant but not especially memorable. She had been particularly kind, though, since the accident. Funnily enough, they'd not had much to do with her beforehand. She'd wave as she drove her ancient white sedan past the house and the Finchleys presumed she lived somewhere at the end of the road, but they'd never been invited up and she never mentioned a family. The Finchleys had only moved to Winchesterfield a year and a half ago, and renovating their own house and the outbuildings to accommodate Becca's kennels had been their priority. Daniel had settled in well at the village school and they'd only just started getting to know people when their life was turned upside down.

'Milk and sugar, dear?' Mrs Bird asked, jolting Becca from her thoughts.

'Just milk, thank you,' she replied. The sound of tapping claws tripped down the timber hallway and into the kitchen. Becca put down her hand for the dog to nuzzle. 'Hello my gorgeous girl.'

'She's looking good,' Mrs Bird commented.

'I've entered her in Chudleigh's,' Becca said.

'Really?' the old woman said in surprise. 'How are you going to manage it?'

Becca smiled and cradled her teacup in her hands. 'I'll be fine. You know I'm driving again now, and Daniel will help me.'

'Are you sure you want to? I mean, it's going to bring back a lot of memories,' the old woman said.

'I need to do something,' Becca replied. 'Maybe next year I'll start breeding again.'

Mrs Bird sat down at the kitchen table. 'Still no news from the police?'

'Nothing. Constable Derby said it was as if they vanished into thin air. Whoever took them was well organised. The police can't be sure if it was opportunistic or if the thieves heard about the accident and pounced, but, realistically, my babies could be halfway across the world by now,' Becca said, blinking back tears.

Vera Bird shook her head. 'Eight dogs going missing overnight is no mean feat.'

'It's lucky Siggy was at the vet's having her annual boosters or I'd have lost them all.' Becca bit her lip and wiped under her eyes.

Vera reached across and patted the younger woman's arm. 'Have faith, dear. Someone's looking after them,' she said with a smile.

'I can't believe anything different,' Becca sniffed. She pulled a tissue from her trouser pocket and blew her nose. She looked over at Siggy, who was tilting her head to the side and shaking her ear. 'What's the matter with you?' Becca said, glad of the distraction.

'Looks like an ear infection,' Vera said. 'Or mites. Have you checked lately?'

Becca shook her head. 'It's the first time I've seen her doing it.'

Vera Bird scooped the dog onto her lap and put on the reading glasses that hung around her neck. She lifted Siggy's ear and prodded around for a few seconds. 'Do you have a torch?'

Becca nodded. 'I'll get it.' She wheeled herself over to one of the kitchen drawers and pulled out a small flashlight, which she passed to Mrs Bird.

'Aha! I think little Siggy here's got a tick,' the old woman announced. She squinted and ran her finger along the inside of the dog's ear. 'Yes, it's a big brute.' Siggy yelped and Vera put her back down on the ground.

'Oh my goodness, I wonder when that happened,' Becca said, astonished that she'd missed it. 'She's barely been outside. Daniel took her for a walk a couple of days ago but I've been so focused on getting her ready for the show, I didn't want her being out much at all.'

'Do you have some tweezers, dear?' Vera asked, standing up. 'I'll get them.'

'In the bathroom,' the woman replied gratefully.

Vera walked down the hallway and off to the left, returning several minutes later with tweezers, antiseptic, rubbing alcohol and cotton buds. She placed Siggy on a chair, then wedged the torch under her chin and picked up the tweezers. Within seconds she had deftly extracted the wriggling mass, pincers intact, and disinfected the area inside Siggy's ear. The little dog rubbed her face against Vera's hand.

'You look as if you've done that a thousand times, Mrs Bird. Do you have dogs too?' Becca was suddenly reminded of the fact that she knew very little about her neighbour.

'Oh, I might have done it once or twice. I . . . my sister used to show dogs a long time ago,' the woman said, cuddling the thankful pooch in her arms.

The back door slammed and Daniel ran red-faced and puffing into the kitchen. He lunged straight for the sink and poured himself a large glass of water, then gulped it down.

'Daniel,' his mother said. 'Say hello to Mrs Bird.'

The old woman looked over and smiled at the boy.

'Hi,' Daniel said, still catching his breath. 'What's with the hospital?'

'Mrs Bird removed a big tick from Siggy's ear,' Becca said, pointing at the jar that contained the critter.

Daniel peered at it and shuddered. 'Gross. I hate ticks.'

'Yes, well, Siggy was none too happy about it, either,' Mrs Bird said, stroking the dog's long ears. 'So, dear, who's going to parade Siggy for you at Chudleigh's?'

Becca looked up at Vera blankly. 'I'll . . . I was planning to, but –' Becca glanced down at the wheelchair – 'I can't, can I? It didn't even cross my mind. Gosh, what was I thinking? We'll have to withdraw.'

Daniel turned around from the sink. He couldn't believe he hadn't thought about that either.

'Perhaps Daniel can do it,' Mrs Bird suggested.

Becca shook her head. 'He's too young. They won't allow it.'

Mrs Bird put the terrier onto the floor and clicked her fingers. 'Off to bed, Siggy,' the woman instructed. Siggy looked at her, then scurried across the floor to her bed in the utility room. 'She's such a good girl,' Vera said. 'Surely you have a friend who can help out.'

Daniel looked at his mother, and the pair of them looked at Vera. 'What about you, Mrs Bird?' Becca said.

'Oh, don't be ridiculous,' the old woman blustered. 'I wouldn't know the first thing –'

'I could help you. We could watch videos of past dog shows, and Siggy adores you. She's more obedient with you than she is with me,' Becca pleaded.

Mrs Bird shook her head adamantly. 'No, I couldn't possibly.'

'Please, Mrs Bird. You know it would make Mum so happy,' Daniel said.

Vera thought for a moment. There was a part of her that wanted to shout yes from the rooftops, but what if . . .? 'I'll think about it,' the woman said finally. She walked to the sink and washed her hands.

'Oh, Mrs Bird, that's wonderful,' Becca said, smiling widely. 'We could start practising tomorrow, if you've got time.'

The old woman frowned. 'I haven't said yes, dear.'

The telephone on the side table rang, and Becca looked at her guest apologetically.

'Go on, I'll let myself out,' Vera said.

'Daniel, can you see Mrs Bird to the door?' Becca asked as she wheeled herself to answer the telephone. 'Thank you for the eggs and the biscuits, and the tick.'

Vera Bird picked up her handbag and followed Daniel down the hallway and out onto the porch. He was about to close the door when he stopped. 'Mrs Bird?' he said.

'Yes, Daniel?' She turned and looked at the boy.

'Can you please help Mum with the show? I know how much she'd appreciate it.'

The old woman sighed. 'She's a good person, your mother, and she certainly didn't do anything to deserve all this,' Vera said. 'All right. You tell her that I'll be back in the morning and we can start.'

Daniel Finchley's face split into a smile. 'Thank you, Mrs Bird,' he said, feeling the pinpricks of tears at the back of his eyes. 'I'll let Mum know.'

Vera Bird smiled and turned to walk down the garden path. Thirty years had surely been long enough. No one would recognise her these days anyway, and if she couldn't help her neighbour in need, what sort of a person had she become?

Chapter 24

'Isn't that Howie's car?' Alice-Miranda said, pointing to the small green sedan across the road. 'I thought she was going to visit her sister for the weekend.'

'There must be another meeting at Mrs Parker's.' Sloane stuffed a flyer into Ambrosia Headlington-Bear's letterbox. Given the number of cars in the lane, there was certainly something going on. Just as the girl finished saying so, the Parkers' front door opened and several women spilled out onto the porch.

'Thank you, ladies,' Mrs Parker trilled. 'Don't forget our next meeting is on Tuesday evening. I want you to have put *all* of the things we discussed in place by then. I will speak with Miss Grimm and Professor Winterbottom this afternoon to give them the details and lock down that plan for the accommodation.'

'Hello Mrs Parker,' Alice-Miranda called out.

'Oh hello dear,' the woman replied, then promptly turned her attention back to her guests.

Alice-Miranda greeted the other committee members as they trickled down to their cars and squeezed in a quick conversation with Evelyn Pepper. She and the woman had grown close when Bonaparte and Rockstar, Aunty Gee's prized race-horse, had become the best of friends and Rockstar had won the Queen's Cup.

'You'll have to come and see us soon. Rockstar would love a visit,' Evelyn said. 'He hasn't seen Bonaparte in ages.'

'Bony would love that too. Perhaps we'll come tomorrow afternoon,' the child said.

'I'll bake some scones just in case.' Evelyn Pepper smiled and hopped into her battered Land Rover. The woman gave a wave as she drove away.

Alice-Miranda skipped up the driveway. She wanted to ask Mrs Parker if there was anything more she and the girls could do to help with the dog show. The woman was talking to a man in a smart suit. He had a thick head of silver hair and was one of those people her mother would have called immaculate, from his shiny shoes to the polished buttons on his double-breasted jacket.

'Alice-Miranda,' Myrtle warbled, 'may I introduce you to Major Alistair Foxley? He's the Chairman of Chudleigh's Dog Show.'

'Hello Major Foxley, I'm Alice-Miranda Highton-Smith-Kennington-Jones, and I'm very pleased to meet you,' the girl said, shaking hands with the man.

Alistair smiled. 'Lovely to meet you too.'

Sloane had jogged to the end of the cul-de-sac to deliver the second-last flyer and was about to stuff the final one into Mrs Parker's letterbox when the woman caught sight of her.

'What on earth are you putting in there, Sloane Sykes?' she bellowed. 'If you have mail, don't you think it would be easier just to hand it to me?'

Sloane looked at the page in her hand and dawdled up the driveway. 'Sorry, Mrs Parker, I thought you were busy,' she said sheepishly.

'Major Foxley, this is Sloane Sykes,' Alice-Miranda said.

'What have you got there?' he asked, glimpsing the photograph of the pup.

'Yes, and did I see you girls putting something on that post?' Mrs Parker squinted down the street.

Alice-Miranda quickly explained the situation with the lost pup.

Major Foxley looked closely at the photograph. 'He's a gorgeous little thing. A cavoodle, I'd say.'

'What's that?' Sloane asked.

'It's a crossbreed, between a cavalier King Charles spaniel and a toy poodle,' the man replied. 'These designer dogs are very popular, and they each bring a small fortune too. Where did he come from?'

'We don't know,' Alice-Miranda said. 'One of the girls found him at school. He's really small and probably shouldn't be away from his mother yet and Dr Davidson said that he'd covered some ground to get to us. The soft little pads on his feet were terribly cut up.'

Alistair Foxley frowned. 'Well, I do hope you find the owner. Someone will be missing him very much, I'm sure.'

'I trust you girls haven't polluted the whole village with your posters. As soon as someone claims the pup, I expect them to be taken down. We can't have the place looking unkempt, not with Chudleigh's coming up,' Myrtle Parker blustered.

'We'd already thought of that, Mrs Parker,' Alice-Miranda assured the woman. 'If no one comes forward, Dr Davidson offered to take him, but I think Miss Grimm might let us keep him for our school pet.'

'He's so tiny, especially compared to the dogs the new people at the end of the road breed,' Sloane said.

'And what do they have?' Major Foxley asked.

'Afghan hounds,' Sloane replied. 'It says it on the sign: *Nobel Kennels, Breeders of Exquisite Afghan Hounds.*'

The man raised his eyebrows. 'That's Roberta and Barry Dankworth. I hadn't realised they'd moved to Winchesterfield. Goodness me, Mrs Dankworth's Citrine is the current Chudleigh's Best in Show. I've never known a woman more dedicated to her dogs. You should see her come show day. She has the most comprehensive array of 1970s outfits and hairdos, which match her dogs splendidly,' he said, visibly excited by this news.

'We're going to meet Mr and Mrs Dankworth tonight at a barbecue across the road,' Alice-Miranda said. 'You're coming too, aren't you, Mrs Parker?'

Myrtle pursed her lips. She was quite sure that her husband and Ambrosia had cooked up the scheme when Reginald had been helping the woman in the garden. It was not how she cared to spend her Saturday evening at all. 'Yes, apparently we are,' the woman sniped, 'although I can't imagine we'll be there for long as I have so many things to do.'

Alice-Miranda wondered what the Dankworths had done to upset Mrs Parker already.

'I must pop by and see them before I go,' Major Foxley said, all aflutter. 'And you know, Mrs Parker, if the Dankworths have any time up their sleeves, I'd be asking them onto the committee *tout de suite*. There are very few people with more experience of the dog show circuit than them. Roberta was born into it and Barry has embraced it wholeheartedly.'

Reginald Parker had been walking down the hallway when he heard Major Foxley talking about the Dankworths. He did his best to smother the smile that was tickling his lips.

Alice-Miranda turned and spotted him as he reached the front door. 'Hello Mr Parker. How are you today?' she asked.

'Top of the world, my dear,' he replied. 'And what about yourself?'

She smiled. 'Very well, thank you.'

'Mrs Parker, why don't you and I say hello to the Dankworths? We can see whether they can offer any assistance in the coming weeks,' Major Foxley suggested.

Myrtle was ready and armed with an excuse. 'I'm sure they have enough on their plate unpacking and getting the house in order,' she said. 'I wouldn't want to trouble them.'

'Nonsense, Myrtle,' her husband weighed in. 'I'm sure Barry would be thrilled to help.' The man knew he was treading on thin ice but, given that they were going to be neighbours, he'd much rather that the Dankworths were friends than enemies. Myrtle would just have to get over her initial misgivings.

'Splendid!' Alistair Foxley looked over at Reg and grinned. He wasn't going to give Mrs Parker any time to back out.

'I think you'll be impressed with the Dankworths's doghouse,' Reg added. 'I've never seen anything like it and, apparently, that television show *Dog Days* is going to feature it soon.'

Alistair Foxley rubbed his hands together with delight. 'Ooh, I had always heard that Roberta had an extravagant facility at their previous home, but I never had the pleasure of visiting, so this will be a treat.'

'I'll get my coat,' Myrtle Parker said, looking as if she had just sucked a lemon. The woman trundled off inside, shooting her husband quite the glare as she walked past. 'We will talk about this later, Reginald,' she hissed.

'Do you girls know the Finchley lad?' Alistair Foxley asked. 'I think the boy would be similar in age and I suspect he goes to school here in Winchesterfield. The family moved to the area about a year and a half ago.'

Sloane shook her head. 'We don't have any boys at our school. Maybe he goes to Fayle or the village school.'

'I remember Mrs Howard telling us about a terrible car accident a while ago and I thought she said the name of the family involved was Finchley,' Alice-Miranda said, her forehead puckering.

'Yes, it was a tragedy. Sandon Finchley was killed and his wife Becca is now in a wheelchair. Their son wasn't with them that day, thankfully. It just occurred to me that you might know them,' the man said.

Sloane shuddered. 'How awful.'

'Are they friends of yours, Major Foxley?' Alice-Miranda asked.

'Sandon Finchley's father, Emerson, was one of the longest-standing and most respected canine judges in the country and a former Chairman of Chudleigh's. He passed away quite some time ago, and I took over, but Sandon was following in his footsteps. Becca breeds cavalier King Charles spaniels and miniature poodles, though in another dreadful twist of fate, all but one of her dogs were stolen while she was in hospital,' the man explained. 'It's such a pity – up until last year, the woman had won Best in Show three consecutive times.'

'Where do they live?' Sloane asked.

Major Foxley shook his head. 'I'm afraid I don't know.'

'Myrtle mentioned a family that sounds like them, out past Chesterfield Downs, first house on the left. There's just Mrs Bird after that,' Reginald weighed in.

'We're honouring Sandon and his father at this year's show with the inaugural Finchley Award for Excellence. I was hoping that Becca would present it, and I did see yesterday that she's entered Siggy, her previous champion, in this year's show, although goodness knows how she's going to manage it. I've tried to phone her a few times this past week with no luck. And I won't have time to get out there this afternoon.'

'I could go and see her tomorrow,' Alice-Miranda offered. 'I was going to take my pony, Bonaparte, for a ride to Chesterfield Downs. It wouldn't take long to pop a bit further down the road. I can ask her to phone you or at least pass on the message and she can decide for herself.'

'Are you sure? It would be wonderful if you could,' Alistair Foxley replied. 'I have to be on the other side of the country tomorrow to do some pre-show judging.'

'Don't worry, Alice-Miranda loves making new friends,' Sloane said with a grin.

Myrtle Parker strode down the hallway with her beige handbag swinging from her left arm. 'Come along then, Major Foxley, let's make this a quick visit, shall we?'

'Well, it was lovely to meet you all and I imagine I'll be seeing you again soon,' Major Foxley said, giving them a wave. He offered Mrs Parker his arm and the two of them descended the steps.

'Bye, Major Foxley! See you tonight, Mrs Parker,' Alice-Miranda called.

'We'd better get back to school,' Sloane said, her stomach grumbling. 'I can almost smell that pizza from here.'

Mr Parker rubbed his belly. 'Mmm, that sounds delicious.'

'You could come too,' Alice-Miranda offered. 'I'm sure that Miss Grimm wouldn't mind a visitor.'

The man smiled. 'I think my school days are long past, but thank you for the offer. I said I'd help Ambrosia get the barbecue sorted in a little while, so I'll see you all later this afternoon.'

Alice-Miranda leaned forward and hugged him around the middle.

'Now, what's this for?' The man grinned.

Alice-Miranda looked up at him. 'You're a miracle, Mr Parker, and I'm so glad that you're better.'

'Me too,' the man said. 'I don't think it would have been fair to keep Myrtle in that state of misery for another minute longer. And for all her huff and puff, that wife of mine has a heart of gold. It's just the tongue of acid that gets her into trouble sometimes.'

The girls giggled.

'I hope you find the owner of your puppy,' Reginald said, waving goodbye.

'We do too,' Alice-Miranda replied. 'Well, sort of. I think we'd all be very happy to keep him.'

'You never know your luck.' The man winked, then walked back inside, determined to have a cup of tea and a nap before his wife got back.

Chapter 25

As the girls headed across the quadrangle towards the dining room, the door to the headmistress's flat opened. A ball of caramel fur scampered out, dashing into the garden and nipping at the flowers. Ophelia Grimm and her husband followed the pup.

'Hello Miss Grimm, Mr Grump!' Alice-Miranda called. 'We've finished delivering the flyers and there are posters all over the village.'

Sloane ran to play with the puppy, who was now

charging at the flower heads and barking at his own shadow.

Miss Grimm smiled. 'Well done, girls. I wonder if anyone will come forward.'

'I saw a young man outside Mr Munz's shop and he seemed to take quite a bit of notice of the sign, but when I asked if he knew who might own the puppy, he said no,' Alice-Miranda told them. 'We also bumped into the Chairman of Chudleigh's. He's a very nice man called Major Foxley.'

Sloane picked up the puppy and cuddled him close as she walked back to join the group. 'We should give him a name,' she said, giggling as he licked her nose and cheeks.

Aldous Grump grinned at the girl. 'I've been saying that too.'

'Aldy, I've told you we can't name him because it will make it that much harder when his owner is found,' his wife scolded.

'If he does have to go, do you think we might be able to get a school dog, anyway?' Alice-Miranda asked.

Mr Grump was nodding his head at a great rate behind his wife, who was being much more coy.

'Well, perhaps we can think about it. It's just not a pet for term time, though. We'd have to work out who could look after the animal during the holidays as people often want to get away,' the woman said.

'Ophelia, there is always someone here,' her husband reasoned. 'Besides, you can play tough all you like, but I know you're hoping we get to keep him. You should have seen the pair of them curled up together on the lounge last night. It was adorable.'

She shot the man a reproachful look as Sloane gathered the creature into her arms. The pup wriggled around and pressed his wet nose against her cheek.

'It's true, Miss Grimm. He loves you,' Sloane said. 'Who'd have thought?'

'Excuse me, young lady,' the headmistress said, feigning offence.

'She's right, you know.' Mr Grump wrapped his arms around his wife and planted a kiss on her cheek.

The woman blushed a bright shade of red. 'Aldous, not in front of the children.'

'Yeah, we don't need any PDA around here,' Sloane said, looking green.

'PDA?' Miss Grimm frowned. 'What's that?'

Sloane and Mr Grump pulled faces at each other. 'Public displays of affection,' the pair said in unison. 'Snap!'

Ophelia laughed and shook her head, just as Miss Reedy and Mr Plumpton came out of the dining room on the other side of the courtyard. The woman was walking beside her fiancé, gesticulating wildly, and her face looked set to explode. The pair seemed completely oblivious to everyone else.

'Josiah, you promised me that you'd have your suit fitted this afternoon,' Miss Reedy fumed. 'We've only got a week until the wedding! What if you can't get your buttons done up on the day?'

'Livinia, darling, please calm down,' the man implored. 'I've made an appointment with the tailor for Monday afternoon. I wanted to help you today.'

'We have our staff meeting on Monday afternoon. Did you think of that? You didn't, did you?' she snapped. 'And we *still* have to choose the toppers for the cake. I asked you what you wanted last week and you *still* haven't told me. Why is this all up to me? It's not fair,' the woman said, her face beginning to crumple.

'Sweetheart, let me make you a cup of tea and we can talk about it then.' Mr Plumpton touched her shoulder.

'I don't want tea!' she yelled at him. 'I want a blinking decision!'

Livinia turned on her heel and stormed away, with her fiancé running double-time to catch up to her.

Mr Grump grimaced. 'Looks like there's trouble in paradise.'

'I think Miss Reedy must be a little bit stressed about the wedding,' Alice-Miranda said.

Ophelia Grimm sighed. 'Oh dear, and I haven't helped. I feel awful that I didn't realise the weekends were one and the same when I was roped into the dog show. I'll have a quiet word and see if there's anything I can do.'

'I'd stay right away at the moment, Ophelia,' her husband advised. 'A bolshy bride can be downright dangerous.'

Sloane giggled. 'Millie was right.'

'About what?' Mr Grump looked at the girl quizzically.

'She said that Miss Reedy was going to turn into a bridezilla,' Sloane said. 'And there the monster goes.'

Chapter 26

Millie sighed happily as she helped Jacinta set the long table under the wisteria-covered pergola in Ambrosia's back garden. She was pleased to have escaped the prospect of being stuck at the house with Caprice all night. 'How was training?' she asked.

Jacinta looked up from counting out the knives and forks. 'It was better. Maybe I'm not as bad as I thought.'

'Of course you're not,' Millie said. 'You can't give up now. We're all banking on you winning a gold medal at the Olympics.'

'As if,' Jacinta chuckled. She began to lay the cutlery for each place setting. 'Did you have to spend much time with Caprice today?'

'No, she was carting poop,' Millie said triumphantly, 'and tomorrow she's going to be doing it again when she fertilises the new vegetable patch.'

Jacinta grinned. 'She must be hating that.'

'Let's just say she hasn't been very talkative,' Millie replied. 'I'm glad that she's got a proper punishment for a change.'

Alice-Miranda was in the kitchen chopping cucumbers for the salad when the doorbell rang. 'I'll get it,' she called out, and wiped her hands on a tea towel before scurrying to the front door. She opened it to find Sep and Lucas on the porch. 'Hello, did you just walk over from school?'

'Yeah, sorry we're a bit late,' Lucas said as he and Sep followed Alice-Miranda to the back garden. 'The professor was going on about the dog show and we had to have a meeting about how we're going to help out.'

Ambrosia met them outside. With her blow-dried hair and immaculately made-up face, she could easily have graced the pages of *Gloss and Goss*. The house looked stunning, too, with its white-on-white accents and elegant furniture. In the pretty cottage garden, a border of purple salvias and verbena was still in bloom among the otherwise autumnal hues. A huge vase of pink peonies sat in the middle of the long white table.

'Oh, hello you two,' Ambrosia said, smiling at the pair. 'Thanks for coming.'

'Thanks for inviting us,' Lucas replied. He grinned at Jacinta, who was putting the finishing touches to the table settings. The girl looked up and melted. 'I'm really looking forward to a steak. Our cook only knows two recipes – mystery meat hotpot and sock pudding.'

Millie laughed. 'Sock pudding? It can't be that bad.'

'We'd happily trade old Sizzler for Mrs Smith any day,' Lucas said.

'Why do you call her Sizzler?' Jacinta asked. 'Is she hot or something?'

Lucas and Sep looked at each other and gagged. 'Hot?' Sep exclaimed. 'No, she's something – and that would be about one hundred.'

'We call her Sizzler because she burns every-thing,' Lucas explained. 'Even water.'

'Well, you can't have Mrs Smith,' Millie said. 'She's been really good ever since she and Mrs Oliver became besties and Dolly taught her how to cook. She even tried this ridiculously difficult chocolate gateau the other day for Ella's birthday and it was amazing.'

'Who wants to help me get the plates?' Jacinta asked.

'I will,' Lucas volunteered, and followed the girl inside.

'They're so cute,' Sloane giggled.

'They're just friends,' Sep said. 'They're way too young for anything serious.'

Millie smiled. 'I don't know. I predict we'll be going to their wedding in about ten years' time.'

The doorbell rang again. This time Ambrosia rushed off to answer it while Millie and Sep scraped the barbecue hotplate, and Alice-Miranda carried the salad and cheese platter outside.

Ambrosia led their guests of honour through the double doors at the back of the house. A blonde-haired woman in a pair of flared jeans with sky-high white heels and a white peasant-style blouse blanched at the sight of the six youngsters. 'Are they *all* yours?'

she asked. She was carrying a small poodle with a long fringe, which flicked out perfectly from her pointy snout. The dog was wearing a white trench coat.

'Yes, all mine,' Ambrosia said, winking at the children. 'Sextuplets.'

Jacinta rolled her eyes. 'Mummy, that's not even funny. You couldn't deal with me until recently, let alone six of us.'

'So they're not yours,' the woman said, visibly relieved.

'No, this is my daughter, Jacinta, and these are her friends,' Ambrosia said, and proceeded to introduce the group. 'Everyone, this is Mr and Mrs Dankworth.'

'Please, we're Barry and Roberta, and this is my baby, Farrah Fawcett,' the woman said.

'She's very, sweet,' Alice-Miranda said. She reached out to pat the poodle, but the creature growled and barked at her sharply.

'Farrah, stop that,' Roberta scolded. 'I'm sorry. She takes a while to warm up to people, but once she knows you she'll be your friend for life. Barry, why don't you set up her highchair?'

The man nodded and produced an odd little seat from his bag. It resembled something a child might sit on at the back of a bicycle and came complete with a harness. He attached it to the table with a series of clamps, then strapped in the dog.

'Is her name really Farrah Fawcett?' Sep said.

Roberta looked at him in surprise. She assumed the famous starlet would have predated the boy's knowledge. 'Do you know who that is?' she asked.

Sep nodded. 'She's one of my dad's favourite television stars from a long time ago. She was in that show called *Charlie's Angels* and she had really flicky hair and was very pretty.'

'Yes, you're absolutely right,' the woman replied, fluffing her own tresses. 'And do you think she looks like anyone you know?'

The boy shrugged. 'Your dog?'

'I've got a picture of her on my phone,' Roberta said, passing it to the lad. 'Now, seriously, who do you think she looks like?' The woman struck a model pose and awaited his reply.

Lucas leaned across to look. 'Now, *she's* hot!'

Millie walked over and had a peek, then gave Sep a sharp nudge. He looked up and caught a glimpse of Mrs Dankworth preening herself and tossing her hair about. She pouted her lips and rolled her shoulders. 'I think,' he said tentatively, 'that maybe she looks a lot like you, Roberta?'

Barry let out the breath he'd been holding. His wife was already wound up tighter than a yoyo string without some poor unsuspecting lad offending her.

'Do you really think so?' Roberta said, smiling from ear to ear. 'People tell me that all the time.' She covered Farrah's ears. 'In fact, I think my Citrine is probably more of a Farrah lookalike but the kennel club wouldn't let me call her that.'

Millie and Sep exchanged grins. 'You can thank me later,' Millie whispered. 'I think she'd have thrown you on the hotplate if you didn't work it out.'

'Can I get anyone a drink?' Ambrosia asked, getting up.

'Oh, yes please,' Roberta said.

Barry offered to help and followed their host into the kitchen.

'So you breed Afghan hounds, Mrs Dankworth?' Alice-Miranda said.

'Please, call me Roberta. It sounds like you're talking to Barry's mother and, believe me, I don't ever want to be confused with that old dragon,' the woman said. She flicked her hair and admired her long fingernails. 'Yes, my Citrine is the current Chudleigh's Best in Show.'

'Major Foxley told me,' the child said. 'You must work very hard with them.'

'Morning, noon and night, they are my number-one priority,' the woman confirmed.

Barry Dankworth emerged from the kitchen with a tray of glasses. He passed his wife a tall iced tea and walked around, offering the children a variety of coloured refreshments.

'I'd love to meet them,' Alice-Miranda said. 'I imagine they are incredibly beautiful.'

'Stunning,' Roberta said, nodding. 'I could take the six of you to have a look at the babies after supper if you like.'

'I'd love that,' Alice-Miranda said, and the rest of the children agreed.

Roberta cut a small triangle of cheddar and held it out for Farrah. The little dog licked it and took a nibble before Roberta popped it into her own mouth.

Millie screwed up her nose and looked at Sep, who made a silent gagging motion. 'Do you want us to put the sausages on, Ambrosia?' Millie asked.

Alarmed, Roberta turned to their host. 'Are we just having sausages tonight?'

'Oh no, there are some lovely fillet steaks as well,' Ambrosia said.

'That's a relief. Farrah only eats the best quality meat,' Roberta replied.

Just as she finished saying so, there was a rustling sound and Mr Parker appeared at the side gate.

'I don't know why we can't use the front door like every other civilised person on the planet,' Myrtle blustered from behind him.

'Good evening, all,' Mr Parker called cheerfully, holding the gate open for his wife. Myrtle cast him an evil glare as she tottered past, clutching a giant cake box.

'Welcome,' Ambrosia said, planting a kiss on Myrtle's cheek.

'Sorry we're a bit late,' Reginald apologised. 'But Myrtle —'

'I had to finish the lemon meringue pie,' the old woman griped. 'I hope it's edible. With everything on my plate at the moment, I just don't know what it will be like.'

'I'm sure it will be lovely,' Ambrosia said, flashing Reg a grin.

Myrtle stalked into the house and proceeded to move everything in the refrigerator to find a spot for it.

'Barry didn't tell me we were supposed to bring anything,' Roberta said through pursed lips.

'We've got plenty of food,' Ambrosia reassured her. 'Mrs Parker didn't have to bring anything, either.'

'Really? Well, you should have told me that before I started making the pie at four o'clock after a full day of meetings,' the woman called out.

'I did tell you, Myrtle, but you insisted, remember?' her husband reminded her.

'Who arrives at a barbecue for this many people without making a contribution?' Myrtle said, walking out onto the patio. 'That would be the height of rudeness.'

'Let's get you some drinks, shall we? I think we might put the rest of the meat on. How are those sausages looking, Millie?' Ambrosia asked.

'They're sizzling!' the girl replied. 'A bit like the atmosphere,' she whispered to Sep, who stifled a laugh.

Alice-Miranda turned back to Mrs Dankworth. 'Major Foxley is a lovely fellow,' she said.

'Oh, yes, he's a darling,' Roberta said, 'and he was overwhelmed by my facilities this afternoon, wasn't he, Barry?'

'Yes, dear,' the man said, nodding eagerly.

Roberta glanced at Farrah, who was wriggling about in her seat. 'Barry, she needs to go for a walk.'

Her husband immediately sprang into action. He unstrapped the dog and placed her on the ground, where she pranced like a pony across the paving stones to the grass. Once there, the poodle stood on tiptoes, trying to pick her way through the blades. She found a spot and froze, glancing back at the table.

Sloane giggled. 'She's so cute.'

'Please don't watch her,' Roberta said. 'She has a shy bladder.'

'A what?' Lucas snorted.

'It's no laughing matter, young man. Farrah finds it very hard to do her business when she knows someone is watching,' Roberta explained.

The boy looked confused. 'Seriously? But she's a dog. Dogs go everywhere.'

'Well, my dog doesn't,' the woman said firmly.

'What sort of dogs does Major Foxley have?' Alice-Miranda asked, trying to steer the conversation into more pleasant waters.

Roberta frowned, or at least she tried to. 'I don't know. Isn't that odd? He's been around forever but I've never thought to ask what sort of dogs he has. He doesn't actually show at all himself – it's against the rules. When Emerson Finchley died, he became the Chairman of Chudleigh's. I think they knew each other from the army but they didn't seem to like one another much from what I recall.'

'I wonder if Major Foxley's limp is the result of a war injury,' Alice-Miranda said.

'Oh yes, apparently he was a highly decorated hero,' Roberta replied. 'He's getting on a bit but he's still terribly handsome.'

'I'm going to meet Mrs Finchley tomorrow,' Alice-Miranda said.

Roberta's eyes widened. 'Do you mean Becca Finchley? Why? Does she live around here?'

Alice-Miranda nodded. 'Yes, just near Chester-field Downs. Major Foxley is inviting her to present the new award they've created in memory of her husband and father-in-law,' she explained.

'Oh, how lovely, that's such an appropriate honour. Those men worked so hard for many years in our industry.' Roberta smiled and lifted her glass to her lips.

Barry Dankworth rejoined the group at the table and strapped Farrah back into her chair.

'And Mrs Finchley's entering the show again,' Alice-Miranda added.

Roberta Dankworth made a choking noise and spat iced tea all over Ambrosia's white tablecloth, narrowly missing the top of Farrah's bouffant head. 'She's what?!'

'Are you all right, Mrs Dankworth?' Alice-Miranda rushed around and began to thump her sharply between the shoulderblades. She was worried the woman might have inhaled an ice cube.

Roberta coughed and sputtered until finally she took another sip and began to calm down.

'But I'd heard that her dogs had been stolen,' Barry said quietly.

Alice-Miranda nodded. 'Major Foxley said that she had one left – her grand champion. I think he called her Siggy.'

Roberta glared at her husband.

A feeble smile spread across his face. 'You know you've got this year in the bag, Roberta,' he whispered.

'I'd better,' she snapped.

Alice-Miranda walked back to the other side of the table and picked up her drink. She felt bad that she'd overheard their conversation. Apparently the competition at Chudleigh's was even fiercer than she'd imagined.

Chapter 27

Alice-Miranda clicked her tongue and Bonaparte began to trot. 'What a beautiful afternoon,' she said to Millie, who was jogging along beside her on Chops. The girls had just turned off the main road and were heading towards Chesterfield Downs.

'I'm glad Charlie let me off this afternoon. I mean, it wasn't exactly hard work puttering around in the boat while poor Charlie was pulling out the reeds, but I'd much rather be doing this,' Millie said.

Alice-Miranda smiled at her friend. 'I'm glad you could come too.'

'That barbecue last night was pretty funny,' Millie said, grinning at the memory. 'Did you see the look on Mrs Dankworth's face when you said Mrs Finchley was entering the show this year?'

'Mrs Dankworth is very passionate about her hounds, that's for sure,' Alice-Miranda said.

'Crazy, did you say? Who has a pool *just* for their dogs?' Millie shook her head. 'And that portable highchair for Farrah – I've never seen anything more ridiculous in my life. She makes Herr Fanger's dedication to Princess Gertie look positively neglectful.'

Alice-Miranda laughed. 'You have to admit the dogs are gorgeous.'

'That's true,' Millie conceded, 'but what's the point in having a dog if you can't play with it? Give me an ordinary old bitza any day of the week.'

Roberta Dankworth had taken the children on a tour of her kennels after dinner. But before they went anywhere, they were made to leave their shoes at the door and wash their hands with antibacterial gel. When Sep joked that she was probably going to make them wear surgical masks too, Roberta had spun around and told them that she only insisted on masks when one of her girls was having puppies.

Histrionics aside, Roberta's dogs were every bit as beautiful as she'd told them. The woman had allowed them to pet a youngster called Sapphire, who was still quite a way off her first show, but they weren't to go anywhere near the others. The children had all giggled at the sight of the dog wearing a large set of headphones, through which, Roberta explained, she liked to listen to country music. Apparently she'd experimented with a range of genres but country was the only style that the animal enjoyed. She certainly wasn't your average family pet.

'It should be quite a spectacle if everyone at the show is as fanatical as Roberta,' Alice-Miranda said, earning a nod from Millie.

They trotted up the hill and past the driveway at Chesterfield Downs. The dirt lane meandered through endless green fields and row upon row of smart white fencing. Several horses dotted the land-scape on the Chesterfield Downs side while on the other, flocks of woolly sheep bleated an afternoon greeting. After another mile or so, the white fencing gave way to regular wire and the girls could see a cottage in the distance on their left. The property was surrounded on either side by open paddocks, and thick woodland rose up at the rear.

'That must be the Finchleys,' Alice-Miranda said. 'Mr Parker said that it was the first house past Aunty Gee's on the left-hand side.'

As the girls neared the property, they could see a white station wagon parked in the driveway. Bonaparte and Chops slowed to a walk and the girls pulled up outside the gate. The house was close to the road with a walled garden at the front and several stone outbuildings behind. There was evidence of a once-loved plot but the flowerbeds were overgrown and the patchy lawn needed mowing.

Alice-Miranda slipped out of the saddle and pulled the reins over Bony's head. 'Can you hold him while I go and see Mrs Finchley? I won't be long.'

'Sure.' Millie slid to the ground and grabbed the two sets of reins. She led the pair of them to the other side of the laneway, where the greedy brutes thrust their heads into a thick patch of clover, tearing at the clumps.

Alice-Miranda opened the garden gate and walked up the weed-speckled path. She climbed the porch steps and rang the doorbell. It was some time before the door opened.

'Hello, may I help you?' asked a thin, dark-haired woman in a wheelchair.

Alice-Miranda stepped forward and shook her hand. 'Hello Mrs Finchley. My name is Alice-Miranda Highton-Smith-Kennington-Jones and I'm very pleased to meet you,' she said with a smile.

'It's lovely to meet you too,' Becca replied, her brow creasing in confusion, 'but you seem to already know who I am.'

'I go to school at Winchesterfield-Downsfordvale Academy for Proper Young Ladies and we're helping with Chudleigh's Dog Show in a couple of weeks' time. Yesterday I met the chairman of the show, Major Foxley, and he asked whether I knew you or your son,' Alice-Miranda began to explain.

'Oh, I see,' the woman said. Alistair Foxley hadn't even sent her a condolence card after her husband died, so she was surprised to hear that he was asking after Daniel. Her father-in-law had always been wary of the man, although, to be fair, Alistair had never been anything other than charming to Becca. She supposed she could have missed some of the mail after the accident – things had been in such a jumble for so long.

'Major Foxley has been trying to call you and said that he hasn't been able to get through,' the child said.

Becca frowned. 'Oh, my machine mustn't be working. I'm afraid that by the time I get to the phone it's quite often stopped ringing. I'm not as speedy in this thing as I'd like to be. Did he say what he wanted?'

'The committee would like to honour your husband and father-in-law at the show this year with the inaugural Finchley Award for Excellence,' Alice-Miranda said.

'Oh, really?' Becca felt a pang of grief in her chest. 'That's very kind of them and it's very kind of you to come all this way to tell me.'

'It was no bother at all. My friend Millie and I had planned to ride our ponies to visit Miss Pepper at Chesterfield Downs, anyway,' Alice-Miranda said, gesturing to where Chops and Bony were chomping away.

Suddenly, a pained yelp sounded from inside the house.

'Oh dear, what's happened?' Becca said, trying to wheel herself around.

'I can go,' Alice-Miranda volunteered.

'I think she's in the kitchen.' Becca pointed down the hallway as the poor creature's distress grew amid a series of loud thumps and bumps.

Alice-Miranda fled down the passageway and into the kitchen. What appeared to be a dog with a jar of peanut butter firmly attached to its face was rushing about, crashing into the table legs and cupboards. Alice-Miranda burst out laughing. 'You're all right,' she said in a soothing tone.

Becca wheeled into the room behind her. 'Oh good heavens, what have you done to yourself, Siggy?' she exclaimed, giggling. 'Alice-Miranda, you're going to have to grab her and hold on while I get that off.'

The child lunged at the dog and missed, then chased her around the table several times before finally scooping her into her arms. Siggy was scrabbling about, attempting to get free while Alice-Miranda was doing her best to avoid getting knocked in the head by the large jar.

'Siggy, how on earth did you get into that?' Becca could barely hold the jar for laughing. The woman pulled gently, causing the dog to whimper. 'I'm sorry, my girl, but this is really stuck.'

The container had created a suction effect and, combined with the gooey contents, was proving hard to remove.

'Why don't you hold her and I'll try?' Alice-Miranda suggested, putting the dog in Becca's lap. The woman held the spaniel as the child got a firm grip on the jar and began to ease it forward. There was a loud pop as the air rushed out and Siggy was free.

'Oh, thank goodness,' Becca said, cuddling the dog close. 'You silly girl! I must have left the lid off the peanut butter this morning and she'd somehow sniffed it out. That could have been a disaster.'

Siggy looked up at Alice-Miranda. She had the most beautiful big brown eyes the child had ever seen. Her tongue flicked at the fur around her mouth as she lapped up the spread that was smeared all over her face.

'You're a bit of a mess,' the girl said, chuckling to herself. She scurried to the sink and ran a dish-cloth under the tap. 'Is she your champion?' Alice-Miranda asked, walking over to the dog.

Becca nodded. 'Not that you'd know it looking at her now.'

Alice-Miranda grinned and began wiping Siggy's face. With the creature's caramel colouring, it was hard to tell where the peanut butter began and where it ended. 'Her eyes look just like the puppy that we found at school,' she remarked.

'Really?' Becca said.

'Except that Major Foxley said he's a crossbreed. Our little fellow is a cavoodle,' the child explained.

'I used to have cavaliers and toy poodles.' Becca's smile dissolved and she bit down on her lip.

'Major Foxley said they were stolen when you were in hospital,' Alice-Miranda said. 'That's terrible.'

'It seemed especially unfair, really. My heart was already broken what with my husband . . . Well, I'm sure you know what happened. Finding out about the dogs felt as if someone had shattered what was left of it into a million tiny pieces,' Becca said, staring into the distance. She was lost in her thoughts for a moment, then glanced over at Alice-Miranda and smiled. 'I'm sorry. I shouldn't be telling you my troubles.'

Alice-Miranda couldn't begin to imagine what the woman had suffered. She touched Becca's arm and smiled. 'You've been through an awful lot.'

The woman cleared her throat and, blinking back tears, patted the girl's hand in gratitude.

'I think you two have had enough grass for now,' Millie said.

She pulled on the reins and Chops lifted his head, but getting Bonaparte to play nicely was a much more difficult affair. She pulled and pulled but the pony was determined to get every last chomp. Millie tugged sharply just as he was lifting his head. The beast turned and glared at her with contempt.

'Serves you right for being so stubborn,' she said, giving the reins another yank so he knew who was boss.

Millie held both ponies and began to walk from the shadow of the willow trees to the other side of the road when, out of nowhere, a white van sped into view. It was hurtling so fast that for a second she didn't know what to do. Bonaparte whinnied and reared into the air, tearing the reins from Millie's grasp. He took off and galloped up the lane as Millie struggled to hold Chops. She grabbed him tightly and ran across into the Finchleys's driveway just as the vehicle rocketed past.

'Idiots!' Millie shouted. 'You could have killed us!'

Her heart was racing at such a speed that she thought it was going to burst through her chest. She pulled the reins over Chops's head and planted her left foot in the stirrup before hauling herself onto the pony's back. Her legs felt like jelly as she flicked the reins and dug her heels in.

'Come on!' Millie yelled, urging her boy forward. She swallowed dust as Chops raced to catch up with the van, all the while hoping and praying that Bonaparte had the sense to get out of the way.

Chapter 28

'Watch out!' Damon yelled. 'You almost hit that horse and I reckon we would have come off second best.'

'Well, we didn't,' Declan sneered.

'What if that girl reports you to the police?'

'Have you seen the number plates lately? She could be five feet away and still not be able to read them,' Declan said. He turned the van into a patch of thick undergrowth and screeched to a stop in front of a gate. 'Well, what are you waiting for?'

Damon grunted and hopped out. As he unlocked the gate and pushed it open, the van tore off up the track, which veered slightly to the right.

'Hey, dog breath!' he shouted. 'Have a nice walk.'

Damon slammed the gate shut. It wasn't as if it was the first time he'd walked the mile and a half to the sheds. For some reason his boofhead of a brother thought it was hilarious. It was old the first time he did it and now it was just downright ancient.

As the cloud of dust dissipated, Millie realised the van was long gone and Bonaparte was still nowhere to be seen. She slowed Chops to a trot and wondered if Alice-Miranda had realised they were missing yet.

'Where could he be?' Millie said aloud. She scanned the paddocks on either side of the road, looking for any open gates. Bonaparte wasn't renowned as a jumper, but she reasoned that he could have managed to leap over a fence if he was as terrified as Chops had been. She noticed the fencing had changed from wooden posts to barbed wire, and her stomach twinged.

Millie contemplated turning back and asking Miss Pepper and Mr Wigglesworth to help with the search. She tugged on Chops's reins. The poor pony was huffing and blowing. Millie's bottom was wet with sweat and she could only imagine how drenched Chops would be too, especially underneath the saddlecloth.

'Come on,' she urged, spinning him around. She was about to head back when she spotted a flash of black behind a tree far off in the field. 'Thank goodness,' she said, breathing a sigh of relief.

Millie looked along the fence for a gate and spied a fallen tree, which had taken out a section further along, creating a narrow opening. She clicked her tongue, and Chops whinnied and pawed at the ground before walking on. Millie squeezed her thighs and he began to canter.

'Bony!' she called. The black pony looked at her, his ears twitching back and forth. He whinnied and danced around in a circle. 'Stay there, please,' she begged.

But it seemed the little beast had other ideas. Bonaparte turned around and galloped deeper into the woods. Millie gritted her teeth and urged her boy to go further. He leapt over a low log and through the thickening woodland. She could still see Bonaparte up ahead and he seemed to be slowing down.

He trotted through the undergrowth until, finally, Millie spotted him by a stream. She pulled Chops to a halt and slid off the saddle, leading him quietly towards the other pony.

'Bony,' she whispered, trying not to startle him again.

The beast's sides were heaving and she could see that his reins were split and the saddle was askew. He lowered his head into the cool flowing water and slurped a long drink. Millie led Chops down to the stream too. He was just as parched and guzzled greedily.

Millie reached into her pocket and found a sugar cube. She let go of Chops and walked as stealthily as she could towards Bony. 'Hey, look what I've got,' she said, holding out her hand. The pony skittered sideways and turned to look at her. His ears twitched, then he leaned forward and nibbled the sugar from Millie's hand. The girl quickly grabbed the reins, giving him a gentle pat on the cheek and blowing softly into his flaring nostrils. 'You poor little man. You must have been terrified.'

Millie considered whether she might be better off riding Bony back and leading Chops. There was less of a chance of losing him that way and, even though he was skittish, she'd been on much worse.

'What do you think, fella? Shall we go and see Alice-Miranda?' Millie righted the saddle and tightened the girth. She tied the reins back together and lifted them up over Bony's head. She was just about to mount the pony when a sharp grating sound, like a metal shed door scraping on concrete, sent Bony reeling backwards. 'You're okay,' she cooed.

The wind caught another sound – of barking dogs. Millie wondered where it was coming from all the way out here. She peered through the foliage but couldn't see anything. Deciding to head back before Alice-Miranda mounted a search party, Millie gave Bony a pat, then put her foot into the stirrup and hauled herself up. She wheeled him around next to Chops and reached to grab her pony's reins.

'Come on, let's go,' she whispered, and dug her heel into Bony's flank.

The pony broke into a canter as they headed out of the woods and towards the Finchleys's place.

Alice-Miranda rinsed the dishcloth and handed it back to Becca, who gave the dog's face one last wipe.

'Now that's better,' the woman said.

The child rubbed Siggy's cheek. 'She's a gorgeous dog. No wonder she's a champion.'

'Yes, I suspect that might all be past tense now, but we'll give it a good shot, won't we, Sig? My neighbour will be the one in the ring with her,' Becca explained. 'I can't do it and Mrs Bird has agreed – and I can't tell you how amazing she is with Siggy. The woman hasn't ever shown before but you'd think she'd been on the circuit for years.'

'I can't wait to see them,' Alice-Miranda said, 'but I'd better be going or Millie will think I'm lost.'

Becca smiled at the girl. 'It was lovely to meet you, Alice-Miranda, and I'll call Major Foxley this evening.'

'I can let myself out. See you at the show,' Alice-Miranda said, and gave Siggy one last pat. 'And you'd better stay out of the peanut butter jar, young lady.'

Alice-Miranda opened the front door and was surprised to find Millie and the ponies were gone. She walked around to the side of the house and spotted a boy jogging across the field. He leapt over the stile and into the garden. From the photographs she'd seen inside, she gathered that he was Becca Finchley's son. 'Hello,' she called, giving him a wave.

The boy looked over at her in surprise and slowed to a walk.

'My name is Alice-Miranda Highton-Smith-Kennington-Jones,' she said with a smile. 'I was just visiting your mother.'

'Oh,' he panted. 'I'm Daniel.'

'It's very nice to meet you, Daniel. Have you by any chance seen a red-haired girl with two ponies? One is black and the other bay. I left her out in the lane but they seem to have disappeared,' she said.

The boy shook his head. 'Sorry, I haven't seen anyone.'

Alice-Miranda looked up and down the road, hoping they might have wandered over to another clump of grass.

'You can get a better view from around the back,' Daniel said, motioning for the girl to follow. They circled to the rear of the house. To the left of the driveway, a large mound of dirt overgrown with grass rose up steeply at the side of a stone outbuilding. 'Dad was using it for the garden, before . . .' Daniel stopped himself and scaled the pile.

Alice-Miranda scrambled up after him. 'That's a great view,' she said as she peered across the fields and down the road. 'There they are!' she exclaimed, pointing to two ponies in the distance. She squinted, wondering why Millie was riding Bony instead of Chops. 'Millie!' the girl shouted, waving her arms in the air.

Millie saw her and waved back. Alice-Miranda and Daniel thumped down the mound, sending little avalanches of dirt tumbling to the ground as the red-haired girl steered the horses into the driveway. She wiped her brow and slipped from the saddle, landing with a thud, then passed Alice-Miranda the reins.

'I need a drink,' Millie said, racing to a garden tap by the fence and guzzling water like a camel in the desert.

'What happened?' Alice-Miranda asked, noticing the tide line of sweat on Chops's flank.

Millie turned off the tap and patted her face. 'Some lunatics in a white van spooked them. Bony took off, and Chops and I raced after him. I was about to give up when I saw him way off in a field and then he ran into the woods and we had to go after him all over again.'

'I know that van,' Daniel said. 'Two young guys would have been in it. I don't know who they are but they're always roaring up and down the road.'

'Someone needs to report them,' Millie said, still peeved. 'We could have been killed.'

'But you weren't, so we should be thankful for that,' Alice-Miranda replied quickly, noticing the look on Daniel's face. The girl blew gently into Bony's nostrils and patted his cheek. 'It's okay, boy. You're safe now.'

'He's bleeding,' Daniel said, noticing a red trickle on the pony's foreleg.

Millie squatted down to inspect the cut. 'It's not deep, thank goodness. It's a miracle he's still in one piece, really.'

'You poor boy,' Alice-Miranda cooed. She reached into her pocket and pulled out a sugar cube, which Bonaparte hoovered from her outstretched hand.

'Do your neighbours have dogs?' Millie asked.

Daniel looked at her blankly. 'What neighbours?'

'Over there somewhere,' Millie said, pointing in the direction from which they'd come. 'I don't know how far we went, but when I finally caught up to Bonaparte he'd stopped beside a stream and I could have sworn I heard dogs barking and a shed door opening.'

'That's old army land,' the boy said. 'It used to be a target range and a munitions dump. Didn't you see the signs?'

Millie shook her head. 'Great, so we could have been blown up too.'

'Someone told my dad there's a bunch of old bunkers built into the side of the hill,' Daniel said.

'Does the army still use it?' Millie asked, relieved that she didn't encounter any tanks or soldiers on training exercises.

'I don't know,' the boy replied. 'I just know that there are a lot of "Keep Out" signs, which is why I never run there.'

'Well, I'm pretty sure I heard dogs,' Millie insisted.

Daniel frowned. 'I don't know why they'd be up there, unless they belong to the army.'

But Alice-Miranda had a strange feeling. It seemed odd to her that there were a whole lot of barking dogs in the middle of nowhere. 'Did the police search that land for your mother's dogs?'

'I suppose so,' Daniel said. He looked at her as the same thought dawned on him.

'Please don't go there,' Alice-Miranda said. 'It sounds dangerous. I'll talk to Constable Derby.'

Daniel nodded. 'Okay, but let me know what he says.'

'I will,' the girl said. 'We should be going. Miss Pepper will have something we can put on that cut. It was good to meet you, Daniel.'

'Yeah, it was good to meet you too,' he replied.

'See you at Chudleigh's,' Alice-Miranda said as she pulled the reins over Bony's head and threw herself into the saddle.

'It was a bit scary, really,' Millie admitted as they trotted along the road. 'I just had no idea whether Bony would be in one piece or if I'd ever find him.'

Alice-Miranda leaned forward and patted the pony's head. 'That was brave, going after him.'

'More like stupid, especially now that I know about the munitions base,' Millie said, grinning. 'I clearly missed all those signs on the road.'

The girls continued along the lane, where the overhanging trees created patterns of dappled sunlight. They reached the entrance to Chester-field Downs and turned into the driveway, just as a sparkling black four-wheel drive with tinted windows roared past.

Alice-Miranda turned her head. 'That's odd,' she said. 'That looked just like Major Foxley's car.'

'Maybe he decided to see Mrs Finchley himself,' Millie said.

'Perhaps,' Alice-Miranda replied. 'It's just that he said he'd be on the other side of the country today. Of course, his plans could have changed.' The child shrugged and thought no more of it.

Chapter 29

Roberta Dankworth put down the telephone and squealed like a pen full of piglets. 'Barry!' she screeched. 'Barry! Where are you?'

Her husband was at the other end of the house, locked in the study and up to his neck in paperwork. At the sound of his wife's voice, he leapt from the chair, flung open the door and ran down the hallway to the kitchen, where Roberta was jumping up and down on the spot. 'What's the matter? What's happened?' he gasped.

'They're coming at the end of the week!' she said, blinking back tears.

'Who's coming?'

'*Dog Days*! They've decided they don't want to do a one-off special on the Poochie Palace, they want to devote *three* entire episodes to me and my babies.' Roberta smiled as a huge tear wobbled from her eye, splashing onto the top of her cheek.

'But what about Chudleigh's?' the man said. 'You need to stay focused, darling.'

'They're going to film that too,' Roberta replied.

'Are you sure you want a camera crew traipsing around after you in the lead-up to the show?' He looked at his wife, unsure whether she was crying tears of joy or devastation.

'Of course I do! Citrine's already firmed as favourite to take out Best in Show again. Can't you just see the look on everyone's faces when they find out the cameras are there for *me*?' Roberta pushed her hair behind her ear. 'You'll need to make up the bed in the spare room right away.'

Barry frowned. 'Why?'

'Well, the crew are going to stay in their campervan but we can hardly expect Darius Loveday to rough it now, can we?' Roberta pulled some lip gloss from her jacket pocket and began to apply a liberal slathering.

Barry's eyes widened. 'What's Darius Loveday got to do with this?'

'He's the new host,' Roberta said.

'But he does all those serious current-affairs shows,' Barry said. 'Has he been demoted?'

Roberta's mouth dropped open. 'Don't you think my babies are serious news?'

'I didn't mean it like that,' Barry said quickly. 'It's just that he's a well-respected journalist, that's all, and you could hardly put him and that ditzy Penny Bell in the same basket.'

'She was lovely and so pretty,' Roberta said, 'but they've obviously decided they need someone with a more impressive pedigree.'

'So Loveday's staying here? With us?' Barry asked.

'Yes, until Chudleigh's is finished.' Roberta fluttered her eyelashes as she caught sight of her reflection in the huge mirror overhanging the fireplace.

'Why can't he find his own accommodation?' Barry mumbled to himself. He had a bad feeling about all of this. It was one thing for *Dog Days* to do a one-off special on the Poochie Palace, but having the crew follow Roberta around for the next week didn't seem like the best idea. Describing the lead-up to the show as stressful didn't cover half of it, not to mention the fallout if Citrine didn't win.

'I don't know what you're upset about, Barry,' Roberta snapped. 'Your business is going to get loads of publicity too. Anyway, don't just stand there. This place has to be spotless from top to bottom.' She pointed at two boxes in the sitting room. 'All that mess there needs to be sorted out. I'll be in the Poochie Palace. Sapphire needs a full hair treatment and I'm going to give her some highlights. Her coat's been very lacklustre lately. And look at you, Farrah – my goodness, what is that you've got on yourself?'

'Roberta, take it easy. You're not showing Sapphire and I'm sure that no one will notice if Farrah's got a couple of dirty smudges,' Barry said.

'How can you say that, Barry?' Roberta gasped. She beckoned Farrah to her, and the little poodle leapt into her arms. 'Daddy didn't mean it, baby girl. He knows you hate it when you don't look your best.'

'I'll give Farrah a bath later,' Barry offered. 'Why don't we work together to get the rest of the house unpacked and then I can help you with the dogs?'

Roberta raised her pointer finger in the air to shush him. 'Don't interfere, Barry. You know this is a very tense time for me.'

The woman turned on her heel and flounced out the back door, leaving her husband in the kitchen rubbing his temples. Talk about *Dog Days*, he was having one himself.

Vera Bird held Siggy's lead in her left hand and together they pranced through the centre of Becca's dog kennel like a pair of consummate professionals.

'Mrs Bird, that was fabulous,' Becca said, clapping from the other end of the building. 'You look as if you've done this a thousand times before.'

'You're a natural,' Daniel agreed.

The old woman turned and smiled. 'I think it's got more to do with Siggy than me, dear. She's wonderfully obedient and not the least bit overexcitable, which can cause all sorts of problems in my experience . . . from watching my sister showing her dogs years ago.'

Becca and Mrs Bird had been practising for over an hour. Daniel was there too. He had been different the past couple of days. He'd told her about meeting Alice-Miranda and her friend and the dogs Millie thought she'd heard on the defence land. Becca had immediately telephoned Constable Derby the next morning and, true to her word, Alice-Miranda had spoken to him too, but the man assured Becca that they'd searched all over the neighbouring properties for her dogs and there was no evidence of them there or anywhere else close by. Although she and Daniel were both disappointed, working towards this year's Chudleigh's had lifted their spirits.

Inside the shed was a large central area designed as a practice show ring, with oversized kennels lining the walls on either side. There was a separate grooming room too. The set-up was far from plush but it served its purpose and had cost a considerable amount nonetheless.

'Now, Daniel,' Vera said, 'how about you pretend to be a judge? I'll get Siggy to stand and you can come and inspect her.'

Becca smiled. For someone who claimed to know very little about dog shows, Vera Bird was remarkably in tune with things. She wheeled herself to the side while Daniel made his way to the centre of the ring. He waited for Vera to run past, then watched her stop and put Siggy into position with her legs spaced apart and her head up. Daniel walked over and studied the dog's face and then ran his hands down her legs and along her back, examining the creature for bone structure. He went on to check her coat, ears, mouth and eyes too.

Daniel didn't say a word, just as the judges never did either. He looked at Mrs Bird and nodded, which was her signal to move on.

'Well, that was perfect,' Vera said.

Daniel grinned. 'Remember that Siggy has known me since she was born. Let's hope she performs as well with the judges.'

Vera Bird patted the dog and removed her lead.

'I can't imagine after all this time away that we'll get anywhere near the winner's podium,' Becca said, coming to join them, 'but goodness me, Siggy, you're looking fabulous.' The dog walked over to her and she gave her a pat.

'I think we should go in with our hopes held high,' Vera said. 'Wouldn't it be lovely to win? I'm sure that would make many people extremely happy.'

Becca pulled a face. 'Perhaps not everyone.'

'Is the show scene very competitive these days?' Vera asked.

Becca laughed. 'I take it you've never met a woman called Roberta Dankworth then.'

'She's horrible,' Daniel groaned. 'She's this big show-off who always dresses like her dogs.'

'She wouldn't be the first to do that, dear,' Vera said, chuckling. 'I remember a fellow called Lexington Smythe. He had a black standard poodle called Pelican and you could barely tell them apart in the show ring. They used to prance about and the entire audience would fall all over themselves laughing.'

'Oh, I remember him,' Becca said, her eyes lighting up.

Vera's face froze. 'Really?'

'Well, not personally but I remember my husband telling me about him from when he was a boy,' Becca said.

'Did your husband tell you lots of stories?' Vera asked quietly.

'Only the funny ones,' Becca said with a sad smile. She missed Sandon so desperately, her chest ached at the very mention of him. 'Now, I think we should have some supper. Would you like to stay and join us, Mrs Bird?'

'I should be getting home,' the woman said.

'Are you sure? I've got what I hope's a half-respectable stew on the stove and Daniel was going to warm up some rolls too,' Becca said.

'Thank you, dear, but I'd best be off,' Vera said. She had a car full of things she needed to unpack and there was a new vacuum that was coming on the market this evening.

'Where do you live, Mrs Bird?' Daniel asked. 'I know it's down the road somewhere but how far is it?'

'Quite a way,' the woman said, gathering her things.

Daniel frowned. 'I've never seen your house when I've been out running.'

'It's much too far,' the woman said. She picked up her handbag from the chair inside the door. 'I'll be up first thing tomorrow. I think we need some more practice on the obedience testing.'

'But I haven't entered her in that category,' Becca said.

Vera's shoulders sagged. 'What a pity. I wonder if we could get a late pass. Never mind, we can work that out tomorrow. Goodbye, Siggy, my darling girl.' Vera bent down and kissed the dog's snout, then dashed out the door.

'Do you think it's a bit strange that Mrs Bird hasn't invited us to her place?' Daniel asked.

Becca shrugged. 'Some people don't like having guests. All I know is, she's wonderful with Siggy and I'm excited about the show. Have you thought whether you'll help me present the Finchley Award?'

Becca had telephoned Alistair Foxley, who had been most apologetic about his lack of contact. He'd said that the Chudleigh's committee wanted to honour her husband and father-in-law and he hoped that she would agree.

Daniel nodded. 'I know that's what Dad would have wanted.'

Becca's eyes brimmed with tears. 'He'd be so proud of you,' she said, hugging him around the middle.

'I just wish he were here,' Daniel replied.

'Oh, sweetheart, you and me both,' Becca said, and kissed her son's cheek.

Chapter 30

Jacinta hopped off the school minibus that had brought the older girls over from Caledonia Manor for their choir practice.

'Hey,' Lucas called, jogging towards her. 'How was your day?'

The girl turned and smiled. 'Busy. I can't believe how much stuff we've been given to do for the dog show on top of all our lessons and homework, and I still have to train every afternoon too.'

Lucas nodded. 'It's crazy at Fayle as well.

Mrs Parker's been over every afternoon bossing the professor around. We've been building portable enclosures this week because Nosey says we need extra accommodation for the dogs. She's even talked him into handing over the dormitories,' Lucas said.

'Where are you going to sleep on the weekend?' Jacinta asked.

'We're putting up tents on the oval. At least Professor Winterbottom said that he'd make it count towards the next level of the Queen's Colours,' the boy replied with a grin.

Millie, Alice-Miranda and Sloane caught up to the pair, and Sep hurried up the driveway with George Figworth.

'So I gather your puppy's gone?' Sep asked.

Millie shook her head. 'No, he's still here. Miss Grimm let us keep him in the boarding house last night.'

'I bet Howie wasn't too thrilled about that,' the boy said, his eyes twinkling.

'She complained and moaned and said that she had too many things to do without having to look after a puppy as well, but when we were having our cocoa, he climbed up on her lap and just sat there looking at her with those adorable big eyes. We're keeping him for sure,' Millie added. 'Why did you think he was gone?'

'The posters have disappeared,' the boy said.

Millie looked at Alice-Miranda and Sloane. 'Did you take them down?'

Both girls shook their heads.

'I bet Mrs Parker did. She wasn't happy about them going up in the first place,' Sloane said.

'Sep and I did see a guy jump out of a white van and grab one when we were walking to Ambrosia's last weekend,' Lucas said.

'Yeah, we thought he might have been the owner,' Sep added. 'I forgot about that.'

Millie frowned. 'The ponies and I were nearly mown down by a white van when we were out visiting Mrs Finchley, but I suppose white vans aren't exactly rare.'

'This one was pretty beaten up,' Sep said.

Alice-Miranda bit her lip. 'Sloane and I saw a white van too, when we were putting the signs up in the village. A young fellow seemed really interested in the pup but then he said he had no idea who owned it. That van was really banged up as well. Seems strange that they'd take the posters but not come for the puppy.'

'Daniel said that van we saw near the Finchleys's belonged to two young guys and they were always tearing up and down the road,' Millie said. 'I didn't see where they went but I heard dogs going crazy in the woods. It was weird.'

'Constable Derby said they'd searched up there and found nothing.' Alice-Miranda shrugged. 'Maybe the dogs were miles away. Sound does travel.' Despite a niggling feeling, she trusted what the man said.

'I suppose so,' Millie agreed.

The children walked into the music room.

'Speaking of weird, has anyone got some sunglasses?' Sloane shaded her eyes as she caught sight of Mr Lipp. Renowned for his colourful outfits, today's offering was no disappointment. It consisted of a canary-yellow jacket and navy pants with a bright red bow tie.

Millie shook her head. 'That's hideous.'

'I think Mr Lipp is brave,' Alice-Miranda said. 'We should applaud a man who knows what he likes.'

Millie grimaced. 'Well, I know what I like and it's definitely *not* that.'

Harold Lipp clapped his hands and ordered the children into their positions. 'Ladies and gentlemen, we haven't got all night. In addition to the other songs we've been rehearsing, Mr Plumpton has made a special request for the wedding and I want it to be perfect. Caprice, have you learned your part?'

The girl nodded. 'Yes, sir,' she replied softly.

'She's been so strange since the fire,' Millie whispered to Jacinta, who was standing right behind her.

'If I didn't know better, I'd say she might actually be really sorry,' the girl whispered back.

Cornelius Trout's fingers danced across the piano keys.

Sloane burst out laughing. 'Is this a joke, sir?'

Harold Lipp shook his head. 'No, this is what Mr Plumpton requested, and who are we to question the man's taste in music?' he said pointedly.

The children glanced at one another and giggled.

'Who's singing the other main part?' Figgy asked.

'I thought you might like to have a go at it,' the teacher replied.

The boy sighed. 'I'll do it, but you know they're both boys in the movie.'

'Yes, I'm well aware of that,' Mr Lipp said, passing out musical scores along the front row. 'Now, is everyone ready?'

Chapter 31

Almost three hours had passed since Darius and his crew had arrived at Barry and Roberta's house. So far all they'd managed to do was drag an enormous amount of equipment into the sitting room, drink several cups of tea and poke about in the Poochie Palace and the garden.

'Does it always take this long to set up?' Roberta asked Darius. The man seemed to spend an awful lot of time checking the messages on his telephone between admiring his tanned reflection in the mirror.

'I'm afraid there's a lot less glamour in television than most people think,' he replied. 'It can take days to get the right shots.'

'Do you have a plan?' Barry asked.

Darius pulled a piece of paper from his back pocket and passed it to Barry. 'This is the rough running sheet.'

Barry studied it closely. 'So you're not going to be trailing Roberta for the whole time?'

'No, we'll just film short segments and then get out of your hair. I want to grab some location shots and follow the setting up for Chudleigh's as well,' Darius said. 'Oh, and I've heard that Becca Finchley is back in the game, so we're organising to interview her as well.'

Roberta blinked, her smile freezing on her face. 'But I thought this was all about me?'

Darius chuckled, revealing an even whiter set of teeth than Roberta's. 'Are you kidding, honey? This is television. It's all about *me*.'

Barry gulped.

'Why's Becca Finchley going to be on my series?' Roberta blurted. 'She only has one dog left and she's in a wheelchair. I don't know how she's even going to show it properly.'

'It's a great story,' Darius said. 'I think the woman's a miracle, especially considering what happened with her dogs. The public will be so thrilled to see her. Imagine if she took out Best in Show – our ratings would go through the roof!'

Barry pressed his palms against his forehead, wishing that overblown peacock would close his big mouth.

Chapter 32

Alice-Miranda walked into the classroom and looked around. For a moment she wondered if she was in the right place. Over the back of each chair hung long rose-pink sashes, and attached to the whiteboard were two giant pieces of cardboard, with fabric samples and pictures of flowers, food and other wedding decorations pasted all over them. They looked similar to the inspiration boards her mother used for planning events or deciding on new decor for the house.

'Hello?' the child called out.

There was a loud thud as Miss Reedy appeared from under her desk. The woman rubbed her head and glanced at the clock. 'What time is it?' she asked.

'I'm early,' Alice-Miranda replied. Poor Miss Reedy looked to be in such a muddle – things had really got out of hand. 'Um, Miss Reedy, I think there's a piece of pink marshmallow stuck to the side of your face.'

Livinia touched her cheek and prised off the offending sweet. She registered the state of the room and began to panic. 'Oh, heavens, I have to get this place cleared up,' she said.

Alice-Miranda looked around the desk, where the remnants of last night's roast dinner were congealed on a plate. There were fabric scraps strewn all over the floor along with bundles of clear cellophane bags stuffed full of pink and white lollies with the odd green one too. A long roll of pink ribbon, the same colour as the sashes, cascaded down the side of the desk.

The woman's eyes filled with tears and she began to sob loudly.

Alice-Miranda rushed to comfort her. 'Miss Reedy, what's the matter?' she asked, throwing her arms around the woman's waist.

'It's all too much,' Livinia sniffled. 'I'm calling the whole thing off.'

'Surely it's not that bad,' the child said.

'I should never have let Mr Plumpton talk me into getting married so soon. And now there's all the fuss about the silly dog show and I'm just so tired,' she wailed.

Other girls were beginning to arrive and had gathered near the door whispering.

Alice-Miranda stepped back and passed the woman a tissue from the box on her desk. 'I want you to sit down and tell me what else you need to do before the wedding.'

'I can't,' the woman sobbed. 'I have to teach you about dangling modifiers.'

Alice-Miranda spun around. 'Girls, does everyone know what that is?'

There were a few blank faces, then Sloane raised her hand. A frown perched on her forehead as she thought for a moment. 'A dangling modifier is a modifier that has nothing to modify.'

Livinia Reedy blew her nose loudly and stared at the girl.

'Is that wrong?' Sloane asked, biting her lip.

'No, that's perfect,' the woman whimpered.

'See, we do pay attention in class,' Alice-Miranda said. 'So, why don't you sit down and write that list? Sloane, can you make Miss Reedy a cup of tea? We'll get started right away. I think these ribbons need to be measured and cut and tied around the lolly bags, and I'm assuming you're making fabric bows for all of the chairs.'

The teacher gulped. 'But what if Miss Grimm –'

The school intercom system crackled to life. 'Miss Reedy, you are to do exactly as Alice-Miranda has told you and I will not hear another word,' a voice boomed. 'I'll be over to lend the children a hand in a minute.'

Miss Reedy's face crumpled and she began to cry all over again.

'Livinia, I can see you,' Miss Grimm said.

The children gasped. They had all thought the headmistress's secret spy system had been dismantled when she'd finally emerged from her study after all those years of hiding, but now it seemed that wasn't the case.

'Don't look so surprised, girls,' the headmistress said. 'I don't use it very often – this was an emergency.'

Alice-Miranda giggled and threw the roll of ribbon to Sloane.

Millie laid another triangle of bright red material on top of the pile. 'Forty-nine, fifty,' she counted, then pushed the bundle over to Mrs Howard, who was sitting at the dining-room table in front of her sewing machine. For the past couple of hours, the housemistress had been running up miles of red and navy bunting as quickly as the girls could cut the triangles. Miss Wall was supervising the patterns and cutting while Miss Tweedle was at a trestle table at the other end of the room, helping another team paste white fabric letters onto the triangles, spelling out the word 'Chudleigh's' over and over again. It was now Wednesday evening and Miss Grimm had decreed that all co-curricular activities were suspended until after the weekend. There were girls helping Mrs Smith in the kitchen while others had been assigned to sewing duties with Mrs Howard and another team was doing some twilight gardening with Charlie.

'I can't believe I let Mrs Parker talk me into making bunting for the dog show. We've got rolls and rolls of the stuff already but, no, she wanted more to string across the ceiling in the gymnasium, and *of course* it had to be branded,' Mrs Howard blustered as she pinned triangles onto the thin rope of fabric that was to hold them up. 'And I've still got to make another lot for the wedding. Miss Reedy's bought the prettiest floral fabric in pinks, blues and greens. It's going to look lovely in the dining room – that's if I can ever get this finished first.'

'I love her country wedding theme,' Alice-Miranda enthused. 'I'm so glad that Miss Grimm let us help her this morning. The poor woman was exhausted.'

'She's not the only one,' Mrs Howard sighed. The housemistress stopped what she was doing and glanced around the room. 'Has anyone seen the pup?' she asked. No one noticed the roll of red and blue bunting that was beginning to unravel from the end of the table.

'He was in his basket a minute ago,' Millie said. She walked over to the corner of the room, where the girls had set up a beanbag barrier to keep the puppy in. 'Uh-oh – he's gone.'

'Off you go and find him, please, and be on the lookout for puddles. That dog only has to see a water bowl,' Mrs Howard tutted.

The back door opened and the children were surprised to see the headmistress.

'Hello everyone,' Ophelia Grimm trilled. 'How's it going in here?'

'Hectic,' Miss Wall replied without looking up from her cutting station. Caprice was sitting beside the woman, working silently.

'It looks like you're all doing a great job. Mr Grump and I have just been sorting out how the seats are going to be installed around the edge of the gymnasium,' Ophelia said. Her gaze wandered around the room. 'Where's the puppy?' she asked.

Ophelia caught sight of the triangles at the end of the table flipping onto the ground. She ducked her head down to see the puppy stomping his paws and gathering a bundle of bunting on the floor. He looked up at her with his big brown eyes and barked playfully.

'Fudge, what are you up to?' the headmistress whispered, crawling over to him on all-fours. She pulled him to her chest and stood up.

Alice-Miranda and Millie looked at each other and grinned. 'Fudge?' said Millie.

The headmistress's cheeks were aflame, realising what she'd just said.

'Does that mean we're keeping him, Miss Grimm?' Alice-Miranda asked. Several other girls had left their jobs and hurried over to see what was happening.

'Pleaaaase,' the girls begged.

'You can't take him away now. We all love him so much,' Sloane said.

'It wouldn't be fair,' Millie added.

Mrs Howard nodded. 'And now that you've given him a name, well, that changes everything.'

'I didn't mean to. It was an accident, really,' Miss Grimm said. 'Mr Grump was having a piece of Mrs Smith's delicious caramel fudge and he hopped up to make a cup of tea. When he came back, this little fellow had managed to climb up on the lounge and was helping himself.'

'I love it,' Alice-Miranda said. 'Fudge is perfect.'

There was a chorus of agreement.

'I should have talked to Mrs Howard first, though, girls,' Ophelia apologised. 'I know that she's going to have to help look after him but we've all been so busy this past week.'

Ophelia Grimm deposited the pup into Mrs Howard's arms. 'You're going to have a lovely life here with us, aren't you, little man?' the old woman cooed. Fudge's tongue shot out and licked her cheek. 'Oh, you cheeky mite,' she said and gave him a squeeze.

Chapter 33

Myrtle Parker picked up her clipboard and eyed the list of jobs still to be done. The past week had been frenetic to say the least and now the competitors were arriving in their droves. Thank heavens the locals had got behind her and the Show Society Committee. There had been numerous offers of accommodation and Professor Winterbottom had agreed to hand over the dormitories at Fayle. Unfortunately, Ophelia Grimm had been unwilling to do the same, insisting that it was simply too disruptive for the girls, who also had a wedding to attend on Sunday afternoon. As she studied the plan for the layout of the hall, a man with a huge camera and another fellow holding a boom pole wandered into her peripheral vision. Myrtle's head snapped up, her pupils narrowing in on the intruders.

'Excuse me, what are you doing in here?' she called out, marching towards them. 'I *said* excuse me, who gave you permission to film in here?'

'Cut!' the cameraman yelled, visibly annoyed by the interruption. He turned to glare at her, revealing a third man with a microphone in his hand.

'Sorry, madam, but who are you?' the man with the microphone asked.

'Who am *I*?' Myrtle scoffed. She stared at him, thinking he looked vaguely familiar. 'I asked *you* first.'

'I'm Darius Loveday and we're filming for *Dog Days*,' the man said.

Myrtle blanched. 'Darius Loveday? *The* Darius Loveday, investigative reporter for *Prime Time Crime*?'

The man nodded.

'What are you doing working on a silly show about dogs?' she asked. Several of the Chudleigh's team shot the woman snarky looks. 'I mean, isn't that something of a step down for a journalist of your stature?'

Darius sighed and ignored her question. 'I don't believe we've met.'

'I'm Myrtle Parker, President of the Winchester-field Show Society,' the woman said importantly.

Darius smiled at her with his eyes and commenced his charm offensive. 'It's lovely to meet you, Mrs Parker. You've certainly got your hands full, taking on Chudleigh's at such short notice.'

Myrtle's lips twitched into a grin. There was a rugged handsomeness about the fellow. He looked like a very well-bred man of the land in his moleskin trousers and checked shirt. She assumed him to be in his mid-forties, although his tanned face could have belonged to someone at least ten years younger. 'What are you doing filming in here?' she asked, softening. 'I'd heard that *Dog Days* was all about my neighbour, Roberta Dankworth, and her hounds.'

'We've got permission from the Chudleigh's team to film the show as well,' Darius said. 'We thought we might get some shots of the setting up to use as a bit of a montage.'

Myrtle's lips tightened and she looked as if she'd swallowed something unpleasant. 'It would have been nice if someone had told me that.'

'My sincerest apologies, Mrs Parker, I thought they had,' Darius said smoothly. 'We'll get out of your way. You must have a lot to do.'

'Will I be on the show?' Myrtle asked.

'Well, I imagine so, if we continue filming,' the man said.

Myrtle smoothed her skirt and checked her curls. 'Would you like me to give you a tour?' she asked. She was warming to the idea of gatecrashing Roberta Dankworth's star turn.

Darius glanced at his crew, who were standing behind the woman and wildly shaking their heads.

'It's going to be much easier if I take you around, otherwise I just don't know if it's convenient, really,' Myrtle said with a pinched smile.

The cameraman and sound engineer's shoulders slumped.

'Thank you, Mrs Parker, that's very kind,' Darius said, plastering a grin on his face. 'We've only got about half an hour, though, as we have to pay a visit to Becca Finchley.'

'Is she part of your show too?' Myrtle asked. 'Poor dear, losing her husband like that and then her dogs too. It wasn't a very welcoming introduction to the village for her, was it? I've called on her a couple of times in the past few months but I can't be responsible for everyone's welfare, can I?'

In truth, Myrtle had dropped by once and left a casserole for the Finchleys at their front door but she'd never heard a word of thanks from the woman and so hadn't been again. If only Myrtle had known that the note she'd left wedged under the dish had flown away into the garden and Becca had no idea who the kind soul was who had left it for her.

'I heard that Mrs Finchley has one dog left that she's entering in the competition,' Myrtle said.

Darius nodded. 'Yes, and from what I hear she's a shoo-in for Best in Show.'

Myrtle's face split into a broad smile. 'Really? So you don't think Mrs Dankworth's hound will take out the top spot?'

'It'll be close I'm sure but, let's face it, people will be glad to see Mrs Finchley,' Darius said.

'So you think she'll get the sympathy vote from the judges?' Myrtle said.

Darius frowned. 'No, that's not what I meant.'

'Oh, that's all right,' Myrtle beamed. 'I'd love to see her win. It would be wonderful.'

Myrtle Parker returned home at the end of the day exhausted. Reginald was nowhere to be found in the house, so she tripped along the garden path to the shed. 'Reginald, I'm home,' she called.

Her husband stuck his head out the door. 'Hello dear,' he said. 'Would you like a cup of tea?'

'Oh, that would be lovely,' Myrtle replied.

'I've just made one for Barry and me,' he said.

Myrtle's face fell as she reached the shed and poked her head inside. 'You're here. Again.'

'Hello Mrs Parker,' Barry said with a grin. 'I just popped down to bring Reg's drill back.'

'Oh well, that does make for a nice change – a neighbour who actually returns things,' Myrtle said, noticing that the man hadn't come alone.

Farrah Fawcett was gambolling about, hoovering up the crumbs from the biscuits Reg and Barry were eating.

'How's everything going at the showground?' Reg asked. He'd offered to help but Myrtle had insisted that he'd only get in the way.

'Busy, busy, busy, and then would you believe I had Darius Loveday there for half the day too?' Myrtle began.

'Really?' Barry said. He'd been quite glad that the man and his crew had disappeared after breakfast as Roberta was getting more and more uptight about the show and really needed some time with Citrine on her own.

'Yes, he asked me to give him a tour, and afterwards I took him over to look at the schools so they could see how things were progressing there too, although I must say Miss Grimm and Professor Winterbottom were less than welcoming,' Myrtle fussed.

'You have to remember, Myrtle, Chudleigh's is not their primary concern – and they have been generous helping out,' her husband said.

'I know that, Reginald. But surely having the children miss a lesson or two wouldn't be such a big deal. Anyway, Darius and his crew left me to go and film Becca Finchley,' Myrtle explained.

'I wonder how she's going,' Barry said, taking a sip of his tea.

'Apparently she's doing very well,' Myrtle replied.

'Do you know who's going to be parading her dog?' Barry asked. He'd thought about that the other day when Alice-Miranda had mentioned she was entering the show.

'I'm not sure, but Darius thinks she's a shoo-in for Best in Show,' Myrtle said, enjoying the look of horror on the man's face.

'Did he really say that?' Barry asked.

Myrtle nodded. 'He said that everyone is going to be so happy to see her, there'd have to be something terribly awry with her dog not to win.'

Barry set his teacup down, his complexion suddenly pale.

'Are you all right, Barry?' Reg asked.

'I'd better be going – I said I'd help Roberta this afternoon,' the man said. He gave a wave and disappeared out the door.

'You shouldn't have said that, Myrtle,' Reg chided.

Myrtle looked at her husband blankly. 'What did I say?'

'You know full well that Roberta takes her showing very seriously and now poor Barry will be in an even bigger spin, worrying about how things will go for her,' Reg said.

'I was only telling him what Darius had told me,' Myrtle insisted.

Reg frowned at his wife. 'Gossiping.'

'That wasn't gossip, Reginald. I was just repeating what I'd been told. Now, did you manage to get dinner started while I was out working? I'm starving and I shouldn't have to make our tea on top of everything else there is to do.'

Chapter 34

Alice-Miranda and the girls arrived at the show-ground early on Saturday morning. They had been instructed to wear their school tracksuits, which the heads of both schools had agreed would be comfortable and identifiable. A huge sign hung over the entrance to the hall and there were miles of bunting strung up through the trees and traversing from building to building. A long line of stands had been erected on the perimeter with exhibitors showcasing their dog-related wares.

'Look, there's Mr Dankworth's Haute Hound Couture for Designer Dogs,' Alice-Miranda said, pointing at a supersized stand manned by a bevy of women dressed in outfits which matched those on sale.

'I hate to say it but Nosey Parker's done a great job pulling all this together,' Millie said.

'Hello girls,' Mrs Parker's voice warbled behind them. 'Are you ready to get your hands dirty?'

Millie jumped and spun around.

'Hello Mrs Parker,' Alice-Miranda said. 'We were just saying how fantastic the showground looks.'

'Of course it does, and I trust that your school gymnasium has come up trumps too,' the woman said, arching an eyebrow.

'It looks great,' the girl assured her. 'Is Mr Parker here?'

'He's on parking duty.' The woman waved to the flat grassy field, where cars towing a variety of dog trailers were arriving at a steady rate. 'Oh, there's Darius Loveday,' Mrs Parker sang, before scurrying away. 'Darius, could I have a word?' she called.

Everywhere the girls looked, dogs of all shapes and sizes were being primped and preened by their owners. Some were standing quietly while others danced about barking at the opposition. A giant poodle with a tail like a topiary ball caught Millie's attention.

'Imagine how long it takes to give that dog a haircut,' she said, ogling the perfectly formed spheres on its legs and the mass of fur on its torso and head.

'Or that one,' Jacinta said, spying a small black dog with hair like dreadlocks. 'How does it see anything?'

'That's a Hungarian puli,' Alice-Miranda said.

Sloane looked at her. 'How on earth do you know that?'

'I was reading up on dog breeds,' the child said. 'I thought it might come in handy, seeing as though I have to tell people where they need to be.'

The PA system blared, announcing the upcoming competitions. 'The preliminary judging of the hounds will take place in the hall starting at ten o'clock sharp,' a man's voice boomed.

'That's Mrs Dankworth's category,' Alice-Miranda said. 'We've got time to take a look before we start our shift.'

The girls walked into the hall, which was festooned in bunting and corporate signage. On the far end of the stage, tall plinths showcased beautiful silver cups and trophies. Two burly security guards stood on either side of them, watching over the treasures. On the rear wall at the back of the stage, twinkling lights spelled out 'Chudleigh's' across a black curtain. The wooden floor in the hall had been transformed into a lawn with astroturf, and tiered seating running the length of the building on either side was fast filling with spectators. The girls quickly found somewhere to sit and watched as the judging commenced.

'Good morning, ladies and gentlemen,' the commentator began, 'and welcome to the judging of the hounds. It gives me great pleasure to introduce our esteemed judge, hound expert extraordinaire, Mrs Malorie Sugsworth.'

The audience clapped loudly as an angular woman dressed in a dowdy brown suit walked into the middle of the hall. She wore her glasses perched on the tip of her pointy nose and carried a clipboard on which she was already scribbling copious notes.

'Now we'd like to welcome our first competitor, Ivan Scupper, and his beautiful basenji, Todd,' the commentator said.

A man in a green plaid suit ran along beside a small muscly dog with pointy ears and a tail as curly as a piglet's. He was tan with white markings and strutted along beside his handler. The man's wiry grey hair poked out in two tufts from either side of his deerstalker hat.

'I thought they'd all be Afghans,' Jacinta said.

'Apparently, the show divides the dogs according to categories,' Alice-Miranda said as the next dog and its owner appeared. This time it was a bassett hound with long droopy ears. Its stomach just about skimmed the ground as it paced along beside a woman who also seemed to have rather large lobes.

'Look, there's Mrs Dankworth!' Millie exclaimed as the woman was introduced.

Roberta wore a flared denim jumpsuit with cork wedges and a floppy hat, looking every inch the 1970s starlet. Her shoulder-length blonde hair was styled to perfection and Citrine's tumbling coat mirrored her owner's silky tresses.

Sep and Lucas slid onto the bench beside the girls. 'Whoa, Mrs Dankworth is really doing her best Farrah Fawcett out there,' Sep said with a grin. 'Dad would be impressed.'

Roberta pranced around the arena beside Citrine, who had all the poise of a dressage pony.

Another twenty hounds were introduced before it was time for the judge to assess each one individually. The dogs and their owners lined up in specially marked places along the hall. Some had a tall plinth beside them, on which to stand their beast. Malorie Sugsworth arrived at Citrine and ran her hands over the dog. She checked the Afghan hound's face and eyes and lifted her long ears, then looked into her mouth before holding her springy tail. She smiled at Roberta, who grinned widely and then patted Citrine.

Some members of the audience began to giggle.

'What's so funny?' Sloane said, looking around the ring. She spotted a beagle who was pulling determinedly on its lead and eagerly sniffing his neighbour's bottom. 'Oh, gross.'

The children laughed as the poor bloodhound, who was the object of the beagle's affections, stood there and put up with it.

The judging took a long time before Mrs Sugsworth was finally ready to announce the winners. The animals were lined up top to tail around the hall. All was going well until a haughty-looking dachshund took offence at the borzoi in front of him and attempted to take a bite of the unsuspecting dog's heel. There was a bit of a kerfuffle as the owners turned on one another.

'Well, we know who's *not* going to win,' Millie giggled.

Alice-Miranda spied Barry Dankworth standing near the entrance. He was tapping his foot nervously and seemed to have his fingers crossed. Mrs Sugsworth walked past the entrants at least twice more before she stopped in front of Roberta.

'And the winner of this year's Hound division at Chudleigh's,' the commentator boomed, 'is Roberta Dankworth and Nobel Citrine.'

Roberta beamed, striding out with Citrine to the winner's podium as the crowd clapped and cheered.

'Go, Roberta!' Millie called loudly.

The woman flicked her hair at the same time Citrine flicked hers. Truly, the pair was nothing short of magnificent.

Chapter 35

Once the judging was over, the children split up to attend to their volunteer duties. Millie was rostered on to help serve morning tea in the marquee near the stables while Alice-Miranda and Jacinta were to report to Mrs Mereweather at the information booth. Sloane and the boys were on cleaning duty with Mr Munz.

'Good morning, Mrs Mereweather,' Alice-Miranda greeted the woman, who chortled in reply.

'I hope you've brought your skates with you, girls,' Nancy said brightly, 'because we have been very busy directing all of these lovely patrons and their magnificent beasts to wherever they need to be.' She tittered as she located the girls' name tags.

Soon enough, a woman with a large chocolate-coloured neapolitan mastiff walked up to the booth.

'Hello there,' Mrs Mereweather giggled.

The woman looked at her and frowned. 'What are you laughing at?' she barked.

'Oh, nothing at all. I'm just thrilled to be here,' Mrs Mereweather replied.

'Are you laughing at my Stephanie?' the woman said, gesturing to her dog, who had more wrinkles than all the unironed shirts at Fayle put together.

Nancy could barely contain herself. 'No, of course not,' she said from behind her hand.

Alice-Miranda quickly stepped in to smooth things over. 'May we help you?' she asked.

The woman eyed her warily as Mrs Mereweather wiped the tears from her eyes. 'I'd like to locate the photographers, please,' she snipped.

'I can take you,' Jacinta volunteered.

Alice-Miranda watched the trio walk off and spotted Major Foxley standing to the left of the booth. He was dressed immaculately from the top of his coiffed silver hair to the tips of his shiny black brogues. The man turned her way and she gave him a wave. 'Hello Major Foxley!' she called.

'Oh, hello there, young lady. How are you enjoying the show so far?' he asked as he limped towards her.

'It's amazing. The dogs are so lovely,' Alice-Miranda replied.

'Yes, they certainly are,' the man said. 'I see Mrs Dankworth took out the Hound division this morning.'

The child nodded and smiled. 'She was magnificent, and so was Citrine.'

'It will be interesting to see who takes out Best in Show tomorrow. I think she's up against some stiff competition this year,' Major Foxley replied.

'Yes, it's wonderful Mrs Finchley is here,' Alice-Miranda said. 'Did you end up seeing her last weekend?'

Major Foxley shook his head. 'No, we spoke on the telephone.'

'Oh, that's funny,' Alice-Miranda said, frowning. 'I could have sworn I saw your car on the road when Millie and I were heading into the driveway at Chesterfield Downs.'

'Well, I can assure you it wasn't me,' the man snapped.

Alice-Miranda wondered what she'd said to turn Major Foxley's mood.

'Did you find the owner of your puppy?' he said quickly.

Alice-Miranda shook her head. 'No, but the good news is that we're keeping him. His name's Fudge and he's completely adorable even though his favourite pastime is to chew everyone's shoes.'

'What a *sweet* name,' the man said, smiling at his own joke.

A short queue was beginning to form and Alice-Miranda excused herself to deal with the next person in line. 'Hello, can I help you?' she asked a little girl who couldn't have been more than five years old.

'Can you tell me where the puppy farm is?' the girl asked.

Alice-Miranda frowned. 'What do you mean?'

Major Foxley, who was still standing close by, interjected. 'I'm afraid, young lady, that we have nothing of that sort here. Puppy farms are outlawed – they're *dire* things.'

The child's face began to crumple. 'Mummy said there'd be puppies I can play with, like when you have a baby animal farm at the show,' she explained in a wobbly voice.

'Of course,' Alice-Miranda said gently. 'There's a puppy petting station near the stables. Would you like me to take you?'

'Mummy's over there,' the child said, pointing to a woman wearing a red hat. She was eager to get away from the grumpy old man.

Alice-Miranda held the girl's hand and walked her to her mother, then directed the pair of them to the stables, where the most beautiful litter of golden retriever puppies was romping about. As she walked back across the showground, Alice-Miranda spotted Mayor Wiley. He was dressed in his complete council regalia, with the mayoral chain clanking around his neck, and looked to be shaking hands with anyone who came within shouting distance.

'Hello Mayor Wiley.' Alice-Miranda smiled at the man, who raised his sunglasses to see who was calling his name.

'Good morning, Alice-Miranda,' he said. 'Isn't this magnificent?'

The child nodded. 'Mrs Parker has done an amazing job.'

Silas Wiley's lip curled involuntarily as it always seemed to do at the mention of that woman's name. 'Yes, I suppose she has. Have you seen any dogs you like?'

'So many. There was the cutest cocker spaniel over there,' Alice-Miranda replied, pointing towards one of the pavilions. 'He was wearing slippers.'

'I've decided to get a dog myself,' the man said. 'But not one of these purebreds. They have far too many health problems apparently.'

'Ooh, what kind?' Alice-Miranda asked.

'Well, as it turns out, Major Foxley is getting me a cavoodle. That's a cross between a . . .' The man's brows furrowed as he tried to recall the names. 'Hmm, what was it now?'

'A cavalier King Charlies spaniel and a miniature poodle,' Alice-Miranda said.

'Yes, that's right. Cute as a button.' The man pulled a piece of paper from his pocket and unfolded it. 'Major Foxley showed me this just now.'

Alice-Miranda looked at the picture and gasped.

'I can't wait to get the little blighter. Life can get a bit lonely at times, you see.' Mayor Wiley noticed the girl had gone white as a sheet, and stopped. 'Is something the matter, Alice-Miranda?' he asked.

'No, of course not,' the child said, recovering quickly. 'Have a good day, Mayor Wiley. I have to run.'

She charged back towards the information booth, scouring the lawns for Major Foxley. She needed to talk to the man right away, but he was nowhere to be seen. She was so deep in thought that she'd walked straight past her booth. She turned around and almost fell into Becca Finchley's lap.

'Oh, Mrs Finchley! I'm so sorry – I didn't see you there,' the child apologised.

'Are you looking for someone?' Becca asked.

'Major Foxley,' the girl replied. She saw that Daniel was pushing his mother, and an older lady Alice-Miranda hadn't met before was leading Siggy and clutching a giant silver cup.

'Siggy won,' Daniel said, grinning from ear to ear.

Alice-Miranda clapped her hands together. 'Congratulations! That's wonderful news.'

'Thanks to Mrs Bird,' Becca said, smiling at the older woman.

'Hello Mrs Bird, I'm Alice-Miranda Highton-Smith-Kennington-Jones and I'm very pleased to meet you.'

The woman smiled. 'Lovely to meet you too, dear.'

'Mrs Finchley, do you know what sort of dogs Major Foxley breeds?' Alice-Miranda asked.

The woman frowned. 'I think he might have had poodles years ago.'

'It wasn't poodles,' Vera Bird said, shaking her head. 'I know that for sure.'

Becca looked at the woman, wondering how she could be so certain. 'Why do you ask?' she said to Alice-Miranda.

'Well, it's just that . . .' Alice-Miranda hesitated, not knowing exactly what to say.

'Becca, can we have a chat on camera?' Darius Loveday called, heading towards them. 'We've got everything set up now.'

Becca bit her lip. 'Sorry, Alice-Miranda. Can we talk later?'

The child nodded. 'Of course.'

Meanwhile, out the back of the Haute Hound stand, Barry Dankworth was trying to console his wife.

'Roberta, you know that Citrine is good enough to take out Best in Show,' he said, touching her gently on the arm.

'Don't do that, Barry,' the woman squawked. 'I can't believe *she* won. And who's that old bag showing Siggy? Where did she spring from with her pointy toes, prancing like a gazelle.'

Barry shook his head. 'Don't worry about Becca. You just have to do your best, darling. That's all anyone can ask.'

'My best!' Roberta screamed. 'I always do my best!'

'Why don't I take you and Citrine home and perhaps you can come back later and bring

Farrah for a walk?' Barry suggested, trying his best to placate her.

'You left her at home. I told you to bring her but, oh no, you said there was too much going on. Now Farrah's going to be upset too.' Roberta's face scrunched and huge tears wobbled in the bottoms of her eyes. 'And where's Darius? He's hardly filmed me at all the past couple of days.' Roberta sniffed.

Barry put his arm around the woman and she sobbed loudly.

'Hello there,' a familiar voice said to someone on the other side of the stand. 'Do you know where Roberta Dankworth is?'

'Um, she's out the back with Barry,' the young girl manning the stand replied.

A look of terror flashed across Roberta's face as mascara lines dribbled down her cheeks. 'I don't want to see him now!' she hissed to her husband. 'Get rid of him.'

Barry Dankworth nodded and slipped through the slit in the canvas. 'Hello Darius,' he said. 'How can I help you?'

'I just wanted to get a response from Roberta about Becca's triumphant comeback,' the presenter replied.

'Triumphant comeback, my eye,' Roberta muttered. 'I'll show him who's Best in Show!'

Chapter 36

Caprice Radford was not having a good day. In fact, she hadn't had a very good time since the fire a couple of weeks ago. Although she'd been allowed to continue with her singing rehearsals for the eisteddfod, and the other girls had stayed silent about what had happened, she just hadn't felt good about anything and that wasn't like her at all. Even the thought of another revenge plot on Plumpy didn't excite her and she was beginning to think she might do better to leave the man alone. Oddly, he'd been much nicer to her the past couple of weeks and had even asked her several times how the songs for the wedding were coming along. She thought he'd seemed nervous when they were talking about it, as if she might do something to ruin the day. But at this point she had no plans.

Caprice was glad that the puppy had been allowed to stay, but it wasn't the same as when he was going to be hers. It was a wonder the dog still went near her considering she almost killed him. For the first time in her life, Caprice had begun to question whether she was actually a good person.

Show day had finally arrived and, after a couple of weekends of her mucking out stables and carting horse manure, Charlie had decided she could have time off to take a look at the dogs who were competing at the school. But under no circumstances was the girl to go off campus. If she disappeared, Charlie said that he would have her on gardening duty for the rest of the year. So Caprice sat in the stands in the gymnasium and watched the Obedience division, which involved dogs being judged on how well they followed a series of instructions given by their owner. Most of the animals carried them out pretty well, although there was one Alaskan malamute who dropped and commando-rolled across the floor every time he was told to sit. He had the audience in stitches. It was the first time Caprice had smiled since the accident and it felt good to laugh again.

Afterwards, she decided to go for a walk and see what else was happening around the school grounds. The oval was being used for a car park and there were hundreds of people picnicking with their dogs. Every now and then a cacophony of barks shattered the peace as the dogs, not unlike people, Caprice thought to herself, got up each other's noses. She wandered back towards the dining room, hoping to find something for lunch, when she spotted Miss Reedy and Mr Plumpton. They were coming out of the chapel and neither looked like the picture of a happy bride and groom.

'I told you this whole weekend would be a disaster,' Miss Reedy blustered.

'I'm sure that the flowers will arrive soon,' the man said, mopping his shiny forehead with a hand-kerchief.

'They were supposed to be here first thing this morning so I could start on the arrangements,' Miss Reedy huffed. 'What am I going to do? Raid the gardens? Charlie will be thrilled about that!'

Caprice was about to change course when Mr Plumpton looked up and called out to the girl. 'Caprice, have you seen Charlie?' he asked.

She shook her head as the pair walked towards her. 'He's gone to get some extra water troughs to put around the grounds.'

'I see,' the man said. 'Would you mind giving Miss Reedy a hand while I go and chase up the flowers?'

Caprice shrugged. She was getting bored wandering around on her own, anyway. 'Okay.'

'Thank you,' Mr Plumpton said gratefully, then lowered his voice. 'I can't tell you how much this means to me. Miss Reedy is a little stressed.'

'What do you want me to do?' the girl asked.

'Could you help Miss Reedy tie the ribbons on the chapel pews?' he said.

Livinia Reedy gave her fiancé a death stare. 'Do you really think she'll be able to manage it?' she said through gritted teeth.

'You can tie a bow can't you, Caprice?' The man looked hopefully at the girl.

Caprice nodded. 'I've helped Mummy with events lots of times. Bows are my thing.'

'Well, I hope so. Because, truly, I don't have time to redo them,' Miss Reedy said stiffly. 'I've tied a couple already and there's a pile on the front pew. I've got to go and get the rest because *someone* forgot them.'

Mr Plumpton smiled at Caprice and then hurried off, visibly relieved to make his escape. Miss Reedy bustled away too, leaving Caprice to enter the chapel alone. The girl picked up a length of white organza and proceeded to tie it around the third pew. It was repetitive but enjoyable work. There was something lovely about making the bows just right, and when she'd finished the last one she stepped back and admired her handiwork.

Livinia Reedy was walking along the driveway, her arms laden with swathes of fabric, when she noticed a white van attempting to squeeze between a parked car and a post. There was a loud bang as the driver misjudged the distance and the post fell over with a thud. 'What a twit,' Livinia breathed.

'Excuse me, do you work here?' a young man called from the driver's seat.

Livinia did her best to pretend she hadn't heard him, hoping he'd go and bother someone else.

'Oi,' the fellow called out again.

Livinia threw a look to the heavens before turning to him. 'There are lots of volunteers who can assist you with where you need to be. I'm rather busy at the moment,' she said, then continued on her way.

But the white van puttered along beside her. 'Could you help me?' the fellow persisted. 'I've lost my dog and I think he might be here at the school.'

Livinia rolled her eyes. 'Please, there are hundreds of dogs here at the moment. How could I possibly help you find yours?'

'No, I meant this dog,' he said, thrusting a flyer in her face.

The woman peered at the poster and frowned. 'Look, wait there while I take these inside. I'll be back in a moment.'

'Okay,' the lad said.

'Honestly, I don't have time for this now. Where is everyone?' Livinia mumbled as she marched up the steps. She walked into the chapel and was immediately overcome. 'Oh, Caprice,' she sniffed. 'They're amazing.'

Caprice looked over to see the woman's face contort as if she were holding back a flood of tears. 'Are you all right, Miss Reedy?' she asked.

'Pull yourself together, woman,' Livinia berated herself. She scrunched her eyes and took a deep breath. 'Yes, I'm fine, thank you. Would you mind going on with these?' she asked, dumping the bundles of fabric in the girl's arms. 'I have to go and sort something out.'

Caprice nodded and watched as Miss Reedy rushed over to the white van idling outside. It was the most beaten-up florist van she'd ever seen. There was a young man in the driver's seat, his tattooed arm resting on the open window.

Chapter 37

By four o'clock on Saturday the dog show was wrapping up for the day, with patrons heading off to their accommodation. Alice-Miranda and Jacinta had been busy guiding people to various places around the showground all afternoon. Alice-Miranda had kept an eye out for Major Foxley but the man was nowhere to be seen and when she did manage to have a quick chat with Mrs Parker, the woman said he'd gone over to Fayle to check on the events there.

Millie trudged up the path to meet her friends. 'I'm exhausted and my feet hurt,' she moaned. 'What's your day been like?'

'Fun,' Jacinta nodded. She waved at Sloane, who was jogging over to her friends.

'How come you've got so much energy?' Millie said to the girl. 'Haven't you been on cleaning duty?'

Sloane grinned. 'Yup, but I got to ride around on the back of the trailer most of the time.'

'Wish I was on cleaning,' Millie said, wrinkling her nose.

'At least we're free tomorrow,' Jacinta said. 'I can't wait to see who takes out Best in Show and then in the afternoon we've got the wedding.'

Millie looked at her friend, who seemed deep in thought. 'Are you okay, Alice-Miranda?'

'Yes of course,' she said, much too quickly for Millie's liking.

'No, you're not,' Millie said. 'I know that look. Something's up.'

'It's just that I had a very strange encounter with Mayor Wiley earlier today,' the child said, biting her lip.

'That's not unusual. I've only *ever* had strange encounters with him. The man's a peacock – seriously, who wears their mayoral robes and chains to a dog show?' Millie said.

'What did he say?' Jacinta asked.

'He told me he was getting a dog,' Alice-Miranda said.

'I suppose being at a dog show might actually inspire you to want one,' Sloane reasoned.

Alice-Miranda shook her head. 'It wasn't that. He said that he was getting a cavoodle and that Major Foxley was organising it for him,' she explained. 'And then he pulled out a photograph of Fudge cut from one of our flyers.'

'What?' Millie gasped. 'He can't have Fudge!'

'That's the thing. I don't know if Major Foxley intended to give him Fudge or if he just gave him the picture because Fudge is the same sort of dog,' she frowned.

'Why did he have the picture, anyway?' Millie said.

'Didn't we give him a copy of the flyer when we saw him at Nosey's? Maybe Major Foxley breeds those sorts of dogs and he just happened to have it in his pocket or something,' Sloane said.

Alice-Miranda nodded. She remembered him looking at the flyer but couldn't recall if he'd kept it.

'It's strange that he didn't mention he breeds cavoodles, but that must be it. Major Foxley would have come forward straight away if Fudge belonged to him, and of course he wouldn't be taking our puppy to give to Mayor Wiley. What was I thinking?'

'Now that's settled, is anyone hungry?' Millie said. Her stomach was ready to eat itself.

'I think the churros van's still open – and they have them with chocolate sauce and ice-cream. What do you think?' Jacinta asked.

'Sounds good to me,' Sloane said, which was seconded by Alice-Miranda and Millie.

The girls linked arms and skipped away. Alice-Miranda dismissed her worries about Mayor Wiley and Major Foxley and decided to concentrate on chocolate churros instead.

Darius Loveday wandered into the Dankworths's kitchen and put the kettle on. As there was no one around, and Roberta had insisted that he make himself at home, he did just that. He had to, anyway, because she seemed to spend every waking minute with the dogs and Barry was in and out all the time.

A guttural growl, followed by an artillery of high-pitched barks, shot off behind him. He turned around to see Roberta's ridiculous poodle skittering left and right. This afternoon she was wearing a pink and white polka-dotted coat and matching booties on her feet. 'What's got into you?' he chuckled.

'Farrah, put a sock in it,' Barry barked, walking in through the back door. 'Sorry, Darius, we've not long come back from the show and she gets very excited around all those other dogs.'

'She wasn't the only one today,' Darius replied. 'Is Roberta home? I was hoping to interview her in the aftermath of the first day.'

Barry nodded. 'She's in the Poochie Palace, giving Citrine a bath.'

'Your wife's certainly one of the most dedicated dog owners I've ever come across,' Darius said. 'How do you think she'll take it if things don't go her way tomorrow?'

Barry scoffed. 'Oh, that's not going to happen. I can assure you of that.'

'You think she'll win?'

'Well, she deserves to,' Barry replied. He made himself a cup of tea and sat down at the kitchen table with their guest.

'Yes, but the fickle hand of fate rests with the judges,' Darius said, 'and there was a lot of support for Becca Finchley out there today.'

'But Citrine is magnificent, and so is Roberta,' Barry said.

'True, but she doesn't just have Siggy to worry about. There are five others in the hunt and that scottie is quite the card. He looks like a little old man the way he hurries about. The crowd was certainly on his side.'

'Look, if you want to talk to Roberta again on camera this evening, I'd really appreciate it if you don't mention the other competitors. She takes it all very personally,' Barry said.

Darius sipped his tea and tapped his foot on the floor. 'Barry, may I ask you something?'

'Of course,' the man replied.

'Have you ever heard whispers on the circuit of puppy farms belonging to people in this crowd?'

Barry frowned and shook his head. 'No, absolutely not. I can't imagine anyone who loves dogs would ever engage in that sort of hideousness. Anyway, I thought it was usually crossbreeders who sell to the pet shops through a middle man.'

'Mmm, it is . . . usually,' the man said, watching Barry closely.

'Why?' Barry asked. 'Have you had a tip-off?'

Darius Loveday took another long sip. 'No, just rumours. I thought television was a competitive industry until I entered the dog show world.' He stood up and emptied the dregs of his tea in the sink, then put the cup into the dishwasher. 'I'd better get the lads. They'll want to have an early night given the hysteria we're bound to encounter tomorrow.'

'See you later then,' Barry said.

He waited for the man to leave before walking over to the butler's pantry. Barry scanned the shelves until his eyes fell on exactly what he was looking for. He pulled it down from the shelf and carried it to the garage.

Chapter 38

'Right, everyone,' Mrs Howard said over the din in the sitting room at Grimthorpe House, 'I need you all to settle down and pay attention as we have a lot on tomorrow.' She waited for the girls to hush before continuing. 'Does everyone have their dresses for the wedding pressed and ready, hanging on the doorhandle of their wardrobe?'

There was a chorus of tired yeses. Sloane yawned, setting off a chain reaction around the room, which Mrs Howard didn't miss.

'Good. Now, put up your hand if you are on any sort of duty in the morning.' Several arms shot up in the air. Mrs Howard nodded. 'I don't care if there's a terrier tantrum or poodle pandemonium, you must be back here to get changed no later than three o'clock. Mrs Parker assures me that the Best in Show will be announced by then and that will give everyone enough time to get back from the show-ground and frock up to your sparkling best.'

'Mrs Howard, where's Fudge?' Millie asked. 'I was supposed to give him his dinner.' The little dog had slept at the house overnight but there had been no sign of him in the afternoon.

'There was a note, Millie. It said that the pup had been collected, so I assume that he's with Miss Grimm and Mr Grump,' Mrs Howard said. She had barely been able to read the scrawly writing and thought that whoever had come to get him must have been in a dreadful hurry. 'Anyway, it's probably just as well as he's more likely to get out with all the girls coming and going from the house. He hasn't had his full vaccinations yet and I wouldn't want him catching something with all these other hounds about.'

'Will he come to the wedding?' Sloane asked.

'I can't imagine so, dear,' the woman replied.

'But he'd be so adorable in the photographs,' the girl said. 'We could find him a big bow to wear.'

'Which he'd chew to bits,' Millie pointed out.

'We'll see. Now, I know it's early but I want everyone to have showers and be off to bed within the next half-hour,' Mrs Howard instructed. 'I don't need any tired and grumpy girls tomorrow.'

There was an audible groan around the room.

Alice-Miranda stood up and the rest of the girls followed suit. 'Goodnight, Mrs Howard,' the child said. 'I'm so excited about tomorrow.'

Mrs Howard smiled. 'I don't know if I'm excited or terrified but I'm sure it will be lovely in the end,' she agreed.

Damon cradled the pup on his lap as they tore along the lane, a cloud of dust billowing behind them. 'This one's a cute little fella,' he said. 'Nice and clean, not like the others, although I wish he'd sit still.' The pup wriggled, trying to free himself from the lad's grip.

'He's going to bring a pretty penny, isn't he?' Declan said. He clutched the steering wheel and dodged a pothole. 'Can you believe the price that woman has agreed to pay? We've been mugs to have worked so long getting paid a pittance. We should've thought about being our own bosses a long time ago.'

Damon snorted. 'Yeah, we've got more brains than that idiot we work for. The old fool couldn't even remember we'd changed the locks on the gate.'

'Good thing too, or we'd have been done for,' Declan said. 'I still wish we could get rid of this mutt tonight.'

'What if that pesky little girl and her friend saw us at the school?' Damon said, stroking the pup's head.

'No one saw us apart from that teacher and she was in such a tizz about her wedding I doubt she'll even remember giving him to us.' Declan crunched the gears and the van lurched forward. 'Besides, what could be more perfect than having thousands of people crawling all over the place with dogs?'

'So what's the plan now?' Damon asked.

'We'll head over to Pidlington first thing in the morning.'

Damon looked at the pup in his lap. 'Hey, Dec, I've just had a brilliant thought.'

'You're full of bright ideas lately, aren't you?' Declan turned left, past the 'Keep Out' signs and into the overgrown driveway. 'All right, don't keep me in suspense, genius.'

Chapter 39

Daniel Finchley had tossed and turned for most of the night. When sleep finally overtook his tired body, he'd dreamt about his father. They were building a tree house in the oak tree with the timber his dad had bought before the accident until, like a hologram, the man began to fade away. Daniel desperately tried to reach for him and tumbled out of the tree, freefalling into nothing and waking with a start.

He threw off the covers and pulled on his track-suit pants and an old T-shirt. Yesterday had been hard. He was happy that his mother and Mrs Bird had done so well, but Daniel had been reminded of his father at every turn. People were kind and wanted to offer their condolences; there were just too many of them. Daniel wiped his eyes. He could hear the patter of raindrops splashing against his window and decided to go for a run. The house wasn't big enough for him and his head full of memories.

Millie hopped out of bed and walked to the window. She drew back the curtain to reveal a grey sky, which was accompanied by the steady drumbeat of rain thrumming overhead. 'Poor Miss Reedy,' she said. 'Yesterday was such a gorgeous day and now it's raining cats and dogs.'

Alice-Miranda padded over to join her friend. 'You know, they say it's good luck to have rain on your wedding day.'

'Maybe a bit of drizzle,' Millie said, shaking her head. 'Not this.'

The girls got dressed, donned their rain jackets and boots and headed up to the dining room for breakfast. They were surprised to find Sloane was already there and even more surprised to see that she was sitting with Caprice.

Alice-Miranda smiled at the two girls and sat down. 'Good morning.'

'I'm not sure that Miss Reedy will think so,' Sloane replied, gesturing to the window.

Mr Grump and Miss Grimm entered the dining room together and walked towards the girls' table.

'Good morning,' the headmistress and her husband greeted the children. 'Did Fudge behave himself last night?'

Millie looked at her in alarm and Alice-Miranda's brow wrinkled. 'Isn't he with you?' they asked.

Ophelia shook her head. 'No, we left him in the boarding house. We were out at the dog show all day yesterday.'

'Mrs Howard said there was a note that he'd been picked up. She assumed that it was from you, Miss Grimm,' Alice-Miranda said.

'Oh, that's odd. It wasn't me. I wonder if one of the other staff members has him.' The woman looked around to see who was in the room. Over in the corner, Mr Plumpton was having a cup of tea. He looked to be muttering to himself as if he were rehearsing something. 'Excuse me, Josiah, have you seen Fudge?' Miss Grimm asked.

The man jumped, startled at the sound of her voice. 'I thought Miss Reedy would have told you – someone came to claim him yesterday. The young man had one of the girls' posters and a photograph with the pup, so she really had no choice other than to hand him over.'

'No!' Millie wailed. 'She can't have! We've just named him.'

'I'm sure that Livinia left a note but, with everything going on for the wedding, and the florist not arriving yesterday afternoon, it must have slipped her mind to tell you herself,' the man said apologetically. He glanced up at the dining-room clock. 'Sorry, I have to go. There's still lots to do.' He scurried over to the servery and deposited his teacup, then made a beeline for the door.

Miss Grimm's face fell. 'How disappointing.'

'I'll say,' her husband added. 'I was really starting to develop a soft spot for the little guy, even if he has destroyed two pairs of my shoes.'

Ophelia Grimm looked over at the girls, who were similarly crestfallen. 'Don't worry, we've done the right thing giving him back to his owners. It's not fair to keep something that isn't ours.'

'Can we get another puppy?' Millie asked.

Just as Miss Grimm opened her mouth to reply, Mrs Howard stampeded into the dining room, her cheeks flushed. 'Miss Grimm, a word please,' the woman puffed.

Ophelia spun around. 'Is something the matter?'

'I'm afraid I've just had a call from Mrs Parker,' the woman said, gasping for breath. 'The gutters at the village hall have overflown and flooded the whole place. She needs to move the events here.'

Ophelia Grimm's shoulders slumped. 'Oh, heavens, can't they go to Fayle?'

Mrs Howard shook her head. 'They have a full program and, besides, she's already sent word out. There are cars lined up along the driveway and out the front gate.'

Aldous Grump patted his wife's shoulder reassuringly. 'I'll go and find Charlie.'

'And I'll get over to the gymnasium,' Miss Grimm said. 'Today was always going to be tricky but, honestly, this is the last thing we need.'

'Wait until Livinia finds out,' Mrs Howard said as she and the headmistress rushed out the door.

Millie cradled her chin in her hands. 'I can't believe Fudge is gone,' she moped.

'Me either. I'm going to miss him,' Sloane said. 'I hope Miss Grimm lets us get another dog.' She glanced over and spotted a chew toy Miss Grimm had got for him, poking out from under a table.

'I think she will,' Alice-Miranda said. She looked at Caprice, who had remained silent on the subject. 'What do you think, Caprice?'

The girl looked up. 'Huh?'

'What do you think about Fudge?' Alice-Miranda repeated.

'I'm sorry he's gone,' the girl said softly. She bit her lip and frowned. 'You know something funny? Mr Plumpton said that the florist didn't come yesterday but I saw their van when I was helping Miss Reedy set up the chapel at lunchtime.'

Alice-Miranda flinched. 'What sort of van was it?'

'It was an old bomb with dents all over it,' Caprice said. 'I thought it was rather odd at the time.'

Alice-Miranda, Sloane and Millie exchanged curious glances.

'What are you all looking like that for?' Caprice asked.

Alice-Miranda leaned forward. 'Are you sure it was the florist?'

'Well, I thought so,' Caprice said, shrugging. 'Miss Reedy was having a meltdown about the florist not arriving and then later on I saw her talking to the man in the white van. She was in a flap about something, so I assumed it was them.'

'Did it have any writing on the side?' Millie asked.

Caprice shook her head.

'What did the man look like?' Alice-Miranda said.

Caprice looked at them, bewildered. 'There were two men. I didn't really see them up close but the one who was driving had a tattoo on his arm.'

'A tattoo!' Sloane exclaimed. 'What was it of?'

'A star,' Caprice said. 'It was pretty big, which is why I could see it when he was leaning out the van window.'

Alice-Miranda's eyes widened. 'That's the same man we saw in the village with that fellow. The one who said he didn't know anything about Fudge.'

'Do you think Fudge has been stolen?' Sloane gasped.

Alice-Miranda nodded. 'And I bet I know where they've taken him. Sloane, call Constable Derby and tell him what's happened – we'll be out on the road past Chesterfield Downs. Millie, come with me.'

The two girls pushed back their chairs and hurried out.

'Be careful!' Sloane called after them. She and Caprice looked at one another, wondering exactly where the girls were headed.

Chapter 40

Daniel jumped the stile and jogged alongside the fence that led down to the lane. He liked the feeling of the rain on his face, and every now and again he stuck out his tongue to slurp some drops. He ran on and on, counting his footfalls as he dodged puddles along the road. Soon, the wooden fencing morphed into barbed wire, large sections of it overwhelmed by thick, tangled shrubs and tall weeds. As he passed a locked gate, he heard the whine of an engine and the grating sound of worn brake pads on metal. Instinctively, he hid behind a bush. He looked back, thankful that his grey raincoat provided camouflage against the foliage.

Daniel saw a scrawny young man unlock the gate and a white van drive through – the same white van he'd seen tearing up and down the road many times before. But what were they doing coming out of the government land?

'Hurry up!' a gruff voice called out.

'Yeah, all right, keep your hair on,' yelled the lad who was closing the gate. An explosion of barks rang out from inside the van. 'Shut it, you lot!' he shouted, and thumped on the side panel before leaping into the passenger seat.

Daniel blinked, his mind racing. Millie had been right about the dogs. Was it possible the police had missed something?

The van pulled out onto the road and sped away. Daniel waited until it was far enough out of sight and then hurried back to the gate. He climbed over it and ran up the track, which wound its way across the field, down over a creek and then up into the woods. He pushed on from one small rise to another until the foliage cleared and he could see several sheds that looked like long cylinders cut in half. He remembered his father telling him once that that sort of building was called a Nissan hut; they looked as if they were made of concrete and half-buried in the mountain.

The rain was coming down even heavier now as Daniel raced towards the closest shed. There was a huge padlock hanging loose on the door and he could hear something scratching to get out. Daniel turned the handle and pushed. The door scraped across the concrete floor and a pungent stench smacked him in the face. Daniel retched as a bundle of caramel curls leapt up at him. He grabbed the dog in his arms and cuddled him close, then peered into the darkness. 'Who are you?' he said as the pup licked his face. 'And what is this place?'

Cages upon cages were stacked against the walls. Daniel walked further into the shed, holding the pup in his arms. And then he saw her.

'Molly!' the boy exclaimed. The dog flinched and lifted her head. 'What have they done to you?'

Daniel set the pup down on the ground and unlatched the cage, reaching in to touch the cavalier King Charles spaniel. The skin under her belly hung loose and her teats were cracked and raw. The pup nudged his head past Daniel and whimpered, its mother whining in reply.

'Let's get you out of here.' Daniel looked around for something to carry her in. She was far too weak to walk. He lifted her out of the cage and she stared into his eyes. 'It's okay, girl, I'm taking you home.'

*

Alice-Miranda and Millie had the ponies tacked-up and ready to go in record time. The school was crawling with thousands of people and it seemed as though there were that many dogs as well.

'We'd better go cross country,' Millie said as she spied the line of cars clogging the front driveway.

They took a left out of the stables and headed for the field and the right of way that cut the school in half. The girls urged their ponies into a trot, then a canter, and soon reached the main road. They crossed into the lane that led to Chesterfield Downs. The rain pelted their backs as they rode as fast as they dared past the emerald fields of Her Majesty's property and Becca Finchley's cottage.

'How much further to the army land?' Alice-Miranda called to Millie.

'I don't remember but, now that I think about it, we should be able to tell by the barbed wire.' They rode on for at least ten more minutes and, just as Millie said, the fencing changed. 'Keep your eyes open for a gate,' she called.

Half a mile further, Alice-Miranda pointed to a break in the wire. 'Look!'

Sure enough, there was a gate partially hidden by thick overgrowth. It was open and the girls raced through, urging Bony and Chops along the muddy track. They rode on for quite a while before slowing to a walk.

'I don't know if we've thought this through properly,' Millie said, suddenly plagued by second thoughts.

'What do you mean?' Alice-Miranda replied.

'If those guys have gone to all that trouble to steal Fudge, I don't think they'll want to give him back,' Millie said.

'No, probably not. But you can't just go around taking dogs that don't belong to you,' Alice-Miranda replied, wondering if Millie was right.

The girls rounded a corner and the timber cleared, revealing three concrete sheds built into the side of the hill. Parked in front of one of them was the battered white van. The two fellows she had encountered outside Mr Munz's shop were just getting out of it.

'Quick, over there.' Millie pointed to the left of the first shed.

The girls slipped down to the ground and led their ponies to a cluster of thick trees, where they tied them to a low branch. They crept back towards the van, taking care to stay out of sight.

'You're such an idiot! How did you *not* put the pup in the van?' the taller of the two men yelled.

'I thought you had!' the scrawny lad snapped. 'I was concentrating on getting the rest of them – except that old one.'

'So much for your bright idea of taking the lot of them – then you forget the one we've actually got a buyer for.'

'I'll get buyers for all of them – you wait and see, Dec. When we're rich, you'll be eating your words.'

The first fellow shook his head. 'You're a bigger moron than I first thought.'

The girls inched closer. The rain had eased off to a steady drizzle. Alice-Miranda looked at Millie and put a finger to her lips. She motioned to the van, and they hurried over to it. It had two windows high up in the back and muffled whimpers were coming from inside.

'What do we do now?' Millie whispered.

Alice-Miranda peered around at the lads, who were about to enter one of the sheds. 'We wait,' she said, her lips set in a grim line.

'Hey! What's the door doing open? Did you do that too? Now the pup'll be gone, you idiot,' one of the men shouted.

They stalked into the darkness.

'Who the heck are you?' the taller of the two silhouettes demanded. 'And what are you doing with that dog?'

Alice-Miranda and Millie looked at one another in surprise. 'There's someone else in there,' Millie whispered.

Alice-Miranda motioned for Millie to follow her. She dashed to the open door and squinted into the shed, her eyes adjusting to the dim light. 'It's Daniel,' Alice-Miranda gasped. She wondered what he was doing up there.

Millie's eyes widened as she spotted the familiar bundle of caramel curls skittering around the boy's legs. 'And there's Fudge.'

Daniel's heart was racing. His mind was too. 'I . . . I was just out running and I heard the dogs barking,' he said.

'Didn't you see the signs on the fence?' the shorter fellow demanded. 'This is *private* property.'

'Hey, I've seen you before,' the first bloke said, his eyes narrowing. 'You're that Finchley kid.'

The shorter lad shook his head. 'Cripes, what are we going to do with him now?'

'Just let me go home and I won't tell anyone,' Daniel begged.

The taller man snorted. 'As if.'

'We've got to help him,' Millie said, tugging on Alice-Miranda's sleeve.

Alice-Miranda shook her head. 'Wait, let's see what they're planning first.'

The brothers looked at one another and the shorter one motioned to Molly's cage.

'Righto, get in there,' the taller fellow ordered, pointing at it. 'Both of you.'

Daniel felt as if his feet were buried in concrete.

'Go!' the shorter lad ordered. 'Now!'

Daniel walked to the cage and put Molly in first. She whimpered and cried but settled down once the boy climbed in with her. The pup rushed to Daniel but the taller lad snatched him up. The shorter fellow snapped a lock onto the cage door.

'You're never going to get away with this!' Daniel shouted. 'You're going to jail.'

'We're not going to jail,' the taller lad scoffed. 'And I'd pipe down if I were you. I can't imagine the boss will be quite as understanding as we are. I mean, we could have done away with you good and proper.'

'Puppy farms are illegal, you know. You can't keep dogs like this. It's immoral!' Daniel yelled at them.

'Puppy farm?' Millie mouthed, her mind reeling. 'What monsters.'

Alice-Miranda nodded. 'Those poor animals.'

'Who's your boss?' Daniel shouted.

'Why should we tell you?' the shorter lad snapped. 'Though, it would be a nice surprise.'

His brother grinned a yellow smile. 'More like a shock.'

'Come on, Declan, let's go or we'll be in some *major* trouble,' the shorter man chuckled. 'Get it? Major trouble? I'm a genius.'

Alice-Miranda gasped and looked over at Millie, the pair reading each other's minds. They jumped into action and pushed against the shed door, which scraped like fingernails down a chalkboard.

'What the?' The taller of the two lads rushed towards the entrance. Suddenly, the pup wriggled free from his captor and leapt to the ground. He raced through the narrow opening to freedom just as the door clanged shut. Millie quickly slammed the bolt across. Alice-Miranda grabbed the padlock and secured it.

'Fudge!' Millie picked up the pup and cradled him close. The pup licked the tip of her nose.

'Sit tight, Daniel,' Alice-Miranda called. 'We're getting help!'

'We can get out of here, you know,' one of the men yelled, banging against the door.

'I don't think so,' Millie shouted back. She'd checked either side of the shed. There were no windows and the back half of the building was wedged into the hillside.

'Alice-Miranda, I think the van's full of dogs,' the boy shouted.

'Got it!' the child replied, and rushed over to the vehicle. Sure enough, there were cages of the creatures as well as two boxes of tiny writhing puppies.

Millie almost threw up at the sight of them. 'What should we do?' she said, looking around. 'We can't leave them in the van.'

Alice-Miranda thought for a moment, then ran to the next shed and pulled open the door. An awful smell of damp dirt hit her, but at least it didn't reek of animal waste and fear. Millie put Fudge on the ground, then picked up a box of pups from the back of the van, and carried them carefully to the shed. Alice-Miranda followed with the other one. They returned to the van and opened the cages inside. The adult dogs, though cautious, followed the pair to the shed.

'Sorry, guys, but someone will be back to get you soon,' Millie promised as she closed the shed door.

Fudge danced around at Alice-Miranda's feet. 'You're coming with us,' the girl said, bending down to pick him up. She stuffed the pup down the front of her sport's shirt and zipped her jacket.

'Good thinking,' Millie said as the two girls raced over to their ponies and took off down the hill.

Chapter 41

Becca Finchley glanced at the kitchen clock as Vera brushed Siggy for the tenth time that morning.

'I'm sorry, dear, but we have to go if we're to make it in time,' the older woman said, patting Becca on the forearm.

'Can we give him another ten minutes?' she asked.

Vera Bird shook her head. 'Afraid not.'

Becca had woken up early and had been surprised to find Daniel gone. She was used to his early morning runs but she hadn't expected he would head out this morning – not when they had the show. Now, two hours later, she was beginning to worry. She wondered if he couldn't face going back again today. There had been so many memories for both of them.

'Why don't we drive over to the school and, once we're sorted, I can come back and pick him up?' Vera suggested. 'We can leave a note so he knows that's what's happening.'

Becca nodded. 'That's probably the best idea.' She wheeled herself to the sideboard and hastily scribbled him a message, then folded the paper in half and propped it up on the middle of the kitchen table.

'I've got the dog bag packed in the car,' Vera said. 'I added another spray bottle too. I noticed Siggy's coat was a bit dry yesterday, so I've got a Listerine mix.'

'You've been doing your homework. That's an old trick,' Becca said as she rolled herself out the back door to Mrs Bird's car.

Vera put Siggy into the dog carrier on the back seat, which was strapped in safely. 'Well, dear, this is it. I wonder if we can do it again,' Vera said, shutting the door.

Becca frowned. 'Do it again?'

'Oh, I meant I wonder if *you* can win Best in Show again,' the woman corrected herself.

Becca took one last look across the field, hoping to see Daniel jump over the style, but he was still nowhere to be seen. She sighed and wheeled herself around to the passenger door.

'Good afternoon, ladies and gentlemen, girls and boys, what a wonderful day,' the announcer's voice blared through the speakers.

Ophelia Grimm didn't quite agree with his assessment. Charlie Weatherly had already pulled two bogged cars from the bottom of the oval and the school was beginning to resemble a pigsty. The rain had eased off for about half an hour but it was now coming down heavier than ever and Ophelia had just heard from her husband that there was some imminent flooding of the local creeks and rivers. All she could hope for now was that the crowd would be gone by half past three as Myrtle Parker had promised.

Vera Bird and Becca Finchley had arrived half an hour ago, having sat in traffic outside the school for the best part of forty-five minutes. They were now inside the gymnasium, which smelt like a rather nasty combination of wet socks and damp fur.

'I'm afraid I haven't got time to go back and get Daniel now,' Vera said, glancing at her watch.

Becca nodded. 'I don't know why he had to go out this morning. He was supposed to help me present the Finchley Award too.'

Vera looked past the woman's shoulder and caught sight of Major Foxley ambling over to them. She quickly turned away and began busying herself with Siggy. 'Becca, dear, I think I'll take her for a walk. She needs to loosen up a bit and I'll give her coat a spray.'

'Good morning, Becca,' the man said. 'All set for a big day?' The brass buttons on his double-breasted jacket gleamed.

'Hello Alistair. What a shame – you just missed my neighbour, Mrs Bird,' Becca said, gesturing to the woman hurrying away. 'I couldn't have done any of this without her. Her sister used to show dogs, and breed them too.'

'Really? And what was her name?' he asked. He squinted at the old lady, a cloudy memory scratching at the back of his mind.

Becca hesitated, her forehead puckering. 'Isn't that funny? I've never thought to ask her that,' she said.

'And where's your boy?' the man asked.

'Daniel wasn't feeling well,' she lied.

'Oh, what a pity,' the man said, patting her on the arm. 'I do hope you're still planning to present the Finchley Award for Excellence. Your husband would be so proud.'

Becca smiled. 'Yes, of course.'

At the other end of the sports hall, Roberta Dankworth's stomach was in knots. She had located a power point and was now fluffing Citrine's coat with her supercharged hair dryer. 'This wet weather is wreaking havoc on your fringe, baby girl,' she mumbled, wondering if there was time for another round of hot rollers.

Barry ran over and passed his wife a spray bottle. 'Here you are, darling,' he said. 'Sorry I took so long.'

'Where have you been?' she hissed. Ever since they'd arrived Barry had kept disappearing and, quite frankly, she was fed up. She snatched the bottle and furiously pumped it all over Citrine's coat, then pulled out a large round brush and started up the hair dryer again.

'How are you feeling today, Roberta?' a voice shouted over the wail of the hair dryer.

'How do you think I feel?' she snapped. She looked up and realised that it was Darius Loveday and his crew. Her angry face instantly melted into a smile and she flicked her hair. 'I mean, it's a bit tricky with the weather and the last-minute change of venue but we're excited about the competition. Aren't we, baby girl?' She kissed Citrine on the nose and grinned at the camera.

'Ladies and gentlemen,' the announcer boomed, 'it gives me great pleasure to announce that the Best in Show will be starting in ten minutes' time, so take your seats and get ready to cheer for the prettiest pooches at this year's Chudleigh's Dog Show!'

Alice-Miranda and Millie turned into the driveway and trotted as fast as they dared. Fudge had stopped squirming long ago and Alice-Miranda wondered if the rhythm of Bony's movement had put the little fellow to sleep.

'Hey!' Sloane called out, waving to them. She and Caprice had been keeping watch for the past hour.

'We called Constable Derby. He said that he'd go and have a look as soon as he got back from another job over at Downsfordvale.'

'Thanks, but I need to talk to him right away,' Alice-Miranda said, slipping down from the saddle. 'Can you take Bony?' she said to Millie as she unzipped her jacket and reached under her shirt.

'Fudge!' Sloane and Caprice gasped in unison at the sight of the puppy. 'How did you get him back?' Sloane asked.

'Did they just hand him over?' Caprice weighed in.

The child shook her head. 'Not exactly – we'll tell you about it later. I need to call Constable Derby.'

'Do you want me to look after him?' Caprice asked, stepping forward.

'Yes, please.' Alice-Miranda smiled and passed her the puppy.

'I'll meet you back at the gym as soon as I put these two away,' Millie said, gesturing to Bony and Chops.

'I can give you a hand,' Caprice offered.

Millie nodded.

'I'll come with you then, Alice-Miranda,' Sloane said.

As the girls took off towards the school office, Alice-Miranda relayed everything that had happened to a wide-eyed Sloane. There was no one about but it didn't take long for them to locate Constable Derby's number. The man was already on his way back to town and couldn't believe his ears when Alice-Miranda told him what was going on.

'What's he going to do?' Sloane asked once the girl hung up the phone.

'He's coming straight here but he'll call for back-up from Downsfordvale to go and get Daniel and arrest those villains,' Alice-Miranda replied. In the meantime, we need to find Mrs Finchley and tell her what's happened.'

Sloane chased her friend across the quadrangle, heading for the gymnasium.

Chapter 42

Alice-Miranda and Sloane tore along the path and raced inside. The stands were packed to the brim and it looked as if the contestants were lining up for the final event. 'There she is,' Alice-Miranda said, spotting Becca Finchley off to the side.

Meanwhile, Vera Bird had just sprayed Siggy with the water bottle when a terrible smell rose up and thwacked her in the nostrils. 'Siggy, was that you?' she accused the dog, who stared at her with doleful eyes.

Vera pulled a brush out of her doggy bag and ran it down Siggy's back. Instead of giving it a beautiful sheen, her coat suddenly looked dank and greasy.

'What on earth?' Vera unwound the lid of her spray bottle and sniffed. 'Fish oil!' the woman exclaimed. 'How did that happen?'

'Oh, pooh, what's that dreadful smell?' yelped the woman beside them. Her Scottish terrier sneezed and turned around to escape the stench.

Vera gulped. It was too late to do anything about it – the dogs were being called onto the arena. She took a deep breath and pranced out from under the archway, with Siggy striding alongside her.

Edith Parbury, the judge for the division, wrinkled her nose as they went past.

Barry Dankworth watched on from his front-row seat. He was clutching Farrah Fawcett, who Roberta had insisted on bringing along as their lucky charm. The little poodle was hopping around on his knees. She sniffed Barry's hand and pulled her head away sharply.

'Mrs Finchley!' Alice-Miranda called from the barrier. She and Sloane were waving madly to get the woman's attention.

Becca turned around and looked in the direction of the girls. 'Hello Alice-Miranda,' she called back, pushing her chair towards them.

'Mrs Finchley, Daniel's all right,' the child began, then kicked herself for being so insensitive.

The colour drained from the woman's face. 'What do you mean he's all right? Did something happen? Where is he?'

'It's a long story but we've found your dogs.'

'What are you talking about?' Becca said. She looked from one girl to the other in bewilderment. 'Where are they?'

'In the old army bunkers on the property next door to you. They've been right under your nose the entire time. I'm afraid you'll be quite shocked when you see them,' the child said.

'Why? What's the matter?' Becca felt sick to her stomach. She would have collapsed if she weren't already sitting down.

'It's a puppy farm,' Alice-Miranda said.

Tears filled the woman's eyes. 'My poor babies,' she sobbed.

'The police are heading out there now to arrest the men responsible and to free Daniel,' the child explained.

'Oh my goodness, he's up there with them?' Becca said, clasping her hand over her mouth.

Millie and Caprice raced into the hall with Jacinta, who had been on her way to watch the final event when she ran into them. Caprice was holding Fudge tightly in her arms.

Becca glanced over to the ring, where Mrs Bird was leading Siggy around.

'What's happened to her fur?' Sloane said. The dog's coat had completely lost its sheen and she was looking more like an oily teenager than a beauty queen.

Edith Parbury ran her hand over Siggy's back and blanched as if she were going to be sick. 'Madame, this dog stinks!' she gagged.

'It looks as if there is a problem with little Siggy,' the commentator said, and the entire audience seemed to lean forward in their seats.

'Someone has replaced my water bottle,' Vera protested. 'We've been sabotaged!'

'Aha!' Alistair Foxley stood up from his chair in front of the commentary booth. 'I know where I've seen that woman before. You're not Vera Bird. You're Phyllis Mould, the most despicable woman to have ever graced the dog show circuit.'

Vera Bird looked up like a deer in headlights and began to shake all over. 'N-no, I'm not,' her voice trembled.

At that moment Becca felt as if her whole world was caving in again. 'Phyllis Mould?' she echoed. 'You can't be. I heard that story from my husband – she was a dreadful woman – but you're nothing like that.'

'I'll bet that she sabotaged Siggy on purpose, because it was your father-in-law, Becca, who banned her for life for cheating,' Alistair Foxley declared, looking very pleased with himself.

Barry Dankworth's jaw dropped. This was better than anything he could have hoped for.

'Becca, please, it's not true,' Vera began. 'I love Siggy. I would never have . . .'

From the corner of the arena, Darius Lovejoy held up his hand. 'No, it wasn't Mrs Bird or Mrs Mould or whatever her name is,' the man said, striding into the show ring. The cameraman and sound technician scampered after him. When he was sure he had everyone's attention, Darius spun around and pointed at the front row. 'It was Barry Dankworth!'

A gasp went up around the arena.

'What? I didn't do anything!' the man shouted. Farrah jumped down from the man's lap and raced into the arena, leaping onto Citrine's back.

'Barry! What's he talking about?' Roberta thundered.

The man gulped.

'Don't try to deny it, Dankworth,' Darius said. 'I planted a camera in your house. I've got it all on tape.'

Barry looked at Roberta and instantly gave up pretending. 'I did it for you, Roberta. It was always for you. I know how much you wanted to win and you said that the only competition was Siggy. I'm sorry, Becca, but you don't know what it's like living with her if things don't go the right way.' The audience gasped as Barry confessed all. Reg Parker was sitting in the stands, shaking his head. He knew Roberta was tricky, but poor Barry must have been desperate to have gone this far.

Alice-Miranda turned around to see Constable Derby flying through the door. 'He's over there!' she said, pointing across the arena.

The policeman nodded and ran over to Becca Finchley. 'Daniel's safe,' the man assured her. 'He's with some of my colleagues and Dr Davidson is up there now. He's going to take all of the dogs back to his surgery.'

'Thank you.' Tears streamed from the woman's eyes and she reached out to grab Alice-Miranda's arm.

'Come with me, you two,' Constable Derby said, then strode into the show ring with Alice-Miranda and Millie by his side.

'What's going on?' Miss Grimm said. She was with her husband and most of the staff in the stands. It seemed that pretty much the entire school had turned out to watch the last of the events but were being treated to something completely unexpected.

The police officer looked at Barry Dankworth and shook his head.

'I'm sorry,' Barry wept. 'I don't know what I was thinking. I just love Roberta so much and I know how hard she works. It didn't seem fair to have it all taken away from her.'

'Mr Dankworth, you've done a disgraceful thing, and I'm sure that you will be dealt with by the relevant authorities, but we're not here for you,' Constable Derby explained.

There was another gasp from the audience.

'Well, who are you here for?' the commentator blared, completely forgetting that he was live on air.

'That's him,' Alice-Miranda said as she pointed at Major Foxley.

'What are you pointing at me for, you little upstart? Don't you know who I am?' the man roared.

'Yes, you're Major Alistair Foxley,' Constable Derby said.

Darius Loveday stepped forward. 'I think you mean *Private* Alistair Foxley,' he said, and the crowd drew a collective breath.

'That's absurd. What's the meaning of all this?' the man shouted, his handsome face blotched with red. He began to limp sideways, his eyes scanning for the nearest exit.

'I've been doing some digging these past few months after a tip-off that someone very high up in the dog-breeding world was involved in some underhand activities. Our investigations have unearthed several interesting facts, one of which is Alistair Foxley's alleged military rank.'

'This is detestable,' Alistair Foxley snapped. 'I'm suing the lot of you for defamation.'

'After Constable Derby arrests you,' Alice-Miranda declared.

The man took a step back. 'What for?'

'It's a long list,' Millie said, glaring at him.

'Cruelty to animals, for one thing,' Alice-Miranda said.

'Illegal puppy farming,' Millie continued.

'And dog theft,' Constable Derby added, stalking towards the man with a pair of handcuffs.

'You have no proof,' Alistair Foxley spat.

Constable Derby raised his eyebrows. 'What about the confessions of Declan and Damon O'Malley?'

Becca Finchley could hardly believe her ears. The man was a monster.

Alistair Foxley gulped and set off, limping across the arena as fast as he could. All of a sudden, Farrah Fawcett leapt off Citrine's back and rushed at the man, yapping and snarling like a beast possessed. She nipped at his heels as he tried in vain to dodge the feisty poodle.

'Stop that! Get away from me, you curly-haired rat!' Alistair Foxley roared. He raised his cane in the air but, before he had time to strike, he was laid flat by Citrine. The Afghan hound pinned him to the ground, baring her teeth, and this time she definitely wasn't smiling.

Constable Derby ran across the arena.

'Arrest that man!' Myrtle Parker shouted, horrified that her show had descended into chaos.

Citrine stood aside as the constable pulled the man to his feet before handcuffing him. The crowd jeered and dogs barked as Alistair Foxley was marched from the building. It took several minutes for things to calm down.

'Well, ladies and gentlemen, girls and boys, that was certainly . . . unexpected,' the commentator said, recovering from the interruption. He looked over at Myrtle Parker, who was madly jabbing at her clipboard. 'But I believe we still have to award our Best in Show?' he said, shrugging his shoulders at her.

Edith Parbury looked at them uncertainly, then cleared her throat. 'I would like to announce the winner of this year's Best in Show.' The woman walked over to Roberta Dankworth. 'I don't believe you had anything to do with your husband's brainless act, Mrs Dankworth, and what a fool that man is because, my dear, I'd like to declare Nobel Citrine Best in Show for the second year running.'

Roberta burst into tears and hugged the woman. Citrine flicked her fringe and grinned as her owner was handed an enormous silver trophy.

The crowd clapped and cheered while Roberta, Citrine and Farrah Fawcett posed for the cameras.

Chapter 43

Alice-Miranda looked at the clock. 'The wedding!' she cried.

'Oh my goodness, we're late!' Miss Grimm stood up and beckoned to the girls and staff. 'We need to get to the chapel or Miss Reedy and Mr Plumpton will think we've abandoned them.'

'What about our clothes?' Jacinta called out.

Most of the girls were in their school tracksuits and splattered with mud.

'We'll just have to go as we are and get changed after the ceremony,' the headmistress said as she led the charge down from the stands.

'Can you take Fudge, Miss Grimm?' Caprice said, passing the pup to the startled headmistress.

'Where did he come from?' She cradled the pup, who barked excitedly. 'Never mind, you can tell me later. Come on, everyone! Hurry!' she ordered, not realising her clarion call had got the whole audience on the move.

A woman with a hyperactive shih tzu turned to the fellow beside her. 'Where are we going?'

'Beats me, but that lady looks to be in charge and I wouldn't want to mess with her,' he replied.

'Bridezilla Reedy is going to go nuts,' Millie said as the girls bolted towards the chapel.

It seemed that everyone at the dog show was following them and before long there were people and dogs clamouring to get into the building.

Alice-Miranda and the girls raced upstairs to the organ balcony, where the Winchester-Fayle Singers were warming up.

Mr Lipp stared at the group in horror. 'What's all this?'

'Nice of you to dress up, ladies,' Lucas joked, smiling at the girls. He and the lads looked immaculate in their black suits.

'What happened to you?' Sep whispered.

Millie rolled her eyes. 'Long story.'

Father Colin walked from the vestry at the side of the chapel. He looked out into the congregation and jumped. Mr Plumpton followed the man and was just as surprised to see the ragtag guests, many of whom were four-legged. 'Are we in the right place?' he whispered to the groom.

Josiah looked at his watch and at Miss Grimm, who appeared to be holding a puppy that looked just like Fudge. She smiled back at him as if there wasn't a problem in the world. His heart thumped. Surely this menagerie would send his bride-to-be fleeing. 'Well, it's the right time and the right place, but I suspect we might have the wrong guests,' the man squeaked. Just as he was about to go and speak with Miss Grimm, the sun came out and the silhouette of a tall woman appeared in the doorway.

'Is that an angel?' George Figworth gasped.

The entire congregation turned around as Mr Trout began to play the wedding march. Light streamed through the stained-glass windows, creating dappled colours on the floor and illuminating the organza bows and floral arrangements which Miss Reedy had been up since the crack of dawn creating.

'Is that seriously Miss Reedy?' Millie leaned over and whispered to Alice-Miranda.

Alice-Miranda's brown eyes twinkled and a smile spread across her face as the woman began her walk down the aisle, her eyes fixed straight ahead on her groom. 'Of course it is. Doesn't she look beautiful?' the tiny child whispered back.

Millie nodded. 'Plumpy looks like he's about to pass out.'

The English teacher was wearing a floor-length fitted lace gown with elegant long sleeves. Her hair was pulled back into a loose chignon at the nape of her neck, softening her face. Mr Plumpton was resplendent in a grey morning suit. Although the man had taken off his top hat for the ceremony, it would no doubt give him some much-needed extra height for their official photographs.

Upstairs, Caprice was doing her best to ignore a little scratch tickling her throat.

Mr Plumpton stood there, nervously waiting for his bride to realise that the congregation wasn't quite what she'd expected, but she hadn't taken her eyes off him the whole time.

'Livinia, you're breathtaking,' Josiah said, taking the woman's arm.

'You too,' she whispered back.

Mr Plumpton nodded at Father Colin, who quickly got on with it. 'If there is anyone here who knows of any reason why this couple may not be wed, speak now or forever hold your peace,' the minister announced loudly.

Caprice coughed, no longer able to hold it in, drawing an audible gasp from the crowd. 'What? I've got a tickle,' she hissed, narrowing her eyes at the heads that had swivelled around to glare at her.

Father Colin looked at the girl, then cleared his throat. 'Right then.' He waited another few seconds before continuing.

'Look – Plumpy's got a tear in his eye.' Sloane nudged Jacinta, who had just grabbed a tissue from her own pocket. The girl turned to her friend. 'Are you crying too?'

'No, it's dust,' Jacinta mumbled, quickly dabbing at her face.

Sloane grinned. 'Yeah, sure.'

The happy couple completed their vows and Father Colin looked out at the congregation, then back at the bride and groom. 'It gives me great pleasure to now pronounce you husband and wife.' The man nodded at Josiah Plumpton. 'You may kiss your bride.'

The children craned their necks to see Mr Plumpton lean across and peck Miss Reedy's smooth cheek.

'That's not a kiss!' Sloane exclaimed, rather more loudly than she'd meant to. A titter of giggles echoed through the chapel.

'Give her a proper smooch, Mr P,' Figgy called from the choir stalls. 'You've waited long enough.'

Miss Grimm glared at the lad before the congregation dissolved into fits of laughter. The Science teacher turned to the crowd and then looked back at his blushing bride before he planted a kiss on Miss Reedy's cherry-red lips.

'Oh, Mr Plumpton!' Miss Reedy gasped.

'Yes, Mrs Plumpton?' the man replied with a wink, his nose glowing like a beacon.

The congregation went wild, clapping and cheering, and were quickly accompanied by a cacophony of barks and howls. Fudge wriggled out of Miss Grimm's arms and skittered to the altar, dancing around at Miss Reedy's feet. Mr Plumpton bent down and picked him up. It was then that his bride registered her bedraggled guests and a rather large number of blow-ins.

For a second she felt quite dazed. 'What's all this?' she said.

'We didn't think you'd mind, love,' a man with an Alaskan malamute said. 'We were just over at the show and then that woman up the front there told us to hurry up and get over here.'

'The headmistress. She's the *headmistress*,' someone said, interrupting him.

'Well, I love a good wedding as much as the next person,' the man said.

'Me too, and you look beautiful,' a woman clutching a dachshund called out.

A man with a stumpy bulldog wolf-whistled and the entire congregation rose to their feet. Miss Reedy's face split into the widest of grins as Mr Plumpton raised their hands in victory, while Fudge nestled into the crook of his other arm. As the jubilant newlyweds turned to leave, Mr Lipp nodded at Mr Trout and the choir. Caprice Radford and Figgy stepped forward and the music began.

Mr Plumpton stared up at them. 'What's that?'

'Your special request,' Mr Lipp called back.

Mr Plumpton frowned. 'But I asked for "Can You Feel the Love Tonight?"'

'No, you didn't,' Mr Lipp insisted. 'You asked for this.'

Cornelius Trout huffed and stopped playing.

'Oh, Livinia, I'm so sorry. There's been a misunderstanding,' Mr Plumpton sighed.

The woman beamed at him. 'Josiah, don't be silly. I know I'll love it no matter what.' Any trace of bridezilla had well and truly disappeared.

'All right then,' Josiah said, and gave the man the thumbs up. Within seconds the children had burst into a rousing rendition of 'Hakuna Matata'. Josiah looked at his bride. 'No worries.'

'For the rest of my days,' she said, and leaned in to kiss his cheek.

Mr and Mrs Plumpton (and Fudge too) wiggled their way down the aisle and out into the sunshine, where a photographer snapped away, capturing every joyous moment.

And just in case you're wondering . . .

Alistair Foxley was a self-aggrandised war hero, who had completely invented his military rank and achievements to create a fake history. He concocted his wealthy background to impress others. His knowledge of dogs had stemmed from his mother, who had also run a down-at-heel breeding operation. The man detested the stinking beasts that provided his income but he loved the glamour and glitz of the shows. Being out of sight and out of mind, the puppy farm had never bothered him at all.

As Chairman of Chudleigh's Dog Show, Private Alistair Foxley had easy access to the animals. He had been building up his enterprise to be one of the largest in the country and what he'd needed more than anything was breeding stock. Alistair had taken over the abandoned military-owned land years ago, having known about it from his time there as a young man. It was a terrible coincidence that the Finchleys had purchased the property next door and, when Alistair Foxley learned of this, he saw a golden opportunity. Cavoodles were all the fashion, and Becca Finchley had both poodles and cavaliers. Little did he know he would have them handed to him on a plate when the couple was involved in a life-altering motor accident.

Foxley had suspected that the pup on the flyer was one of his own but the O'Malley lads vowed that it wasn't. He'd gone to investigate for himself but had been prevented by the locked gate. It was just luck that he still had the picture on him when he ran into Mayor Wiley and thought he could sell him another of his cavoodles. After all, in the grand scheme of things, the loss of one pup was nothing, really. Alistair Foxley was sentenced to twenty years in prison for his long list of crimes.

Mayor Wiley was thrilled when Becca promised to sell him one of her puppies once her breeding operation was up and running again.

Declan and Damon O'Malley were given five-year jail terms for their roles in the operation. Two dunderhead brothers hoping to get rich quick had been lured to work for the man by the promise of fast money. They came unstuck when they wanted their fast money to become lightning cash.

Vera Bird, known to some as Phyllis Mould, had been a breeder of champions until her obsessive competitiveness did her in and she'd been caught sabotaging her rivals at a Chudleigh's thirty years before. Heartbroken and appalled by her own behaviour, Vera stopped breeding. By the time her last dog died, her love of canines had been replaced by a love of television shopping and speculating on the stock market, which funded her addiction.

She'd called in on the new neighbours not long after they'd moved in and was mortified to learn that they were Finchleys. Becca's father-in-law, Emerson, had been the man who had banned her for life and the thought that his son might remember her had caused her to stay away – at least until the accident.

Just thinking of what she'd done still made her burn with shame.

When it all came out at the dog show, Vera confessed the whole sordid tale to Becca and Daniel and even invited them up for tea, where they realised the extent of her addictive disorder. Becca is helping Vera to get her life back on track and there have been thousands of dollars' worth of donations to the local canine charities of her unopened goods. In turn, Mrs Bird is helping Becca and Daniel with the dogs, who have all been nursed back to health following their horrific ordeal.

Daniel has kept up his running – not because he's running away from life but because he's decided he wants to be a cross-country champion. His mother is continuing her recovery and there have been signs that she may one day walk again.

Barry Dankworth's crime was one of passion and stupidity. He was banned by the Kennel Club from attending any dog shows for the next two years, after which he could apply for reconsideration. Roberta was furious that his idiocy had almost ruined her reputation, but winning Chudleigh's Best in Show and starring in *Dog Days* had gone some way to appeasing her anger – that and the ever increasing lists of jobs she presented to him. Barry begged forgiveness from Roberta, who told him she'd think about it.

For all its controversy, this year's Chudleigh's was hailed a great success, not least of all for exposing the darker side of the canine industry and bringing one of its most evil breeders to justice. Myrtle Parker was interviewed by every news station in the country and claimed (to the chagrin of her fellow Show Society committee members) that she had suspected there was something not quite right about Alistair Foxley from the moment she'd met him. He was simply far too charming to be real. Reginald Parker was proud of the way his wife had pulled the event together and told her so. But when an offer for the village to host an upcoming science-fiction convention appeared in the post, Reg decided that it would be best dealt with in the rubbish bin.

Mr Plumpton and Ms Reedy (she decided that, after years of being Miss Reedy, she'd find it too hard to change her surname) boarded a plane bound for South America for their honeymoon. Contrary to popular thinking, they were not attending a once-in-a-lifetime event. When Miss Reedy asked what the surprise was, her husband told her that he'd concocted the whole story so they could have time off during the term. After all, it was much cheaper to travel when it wasn't school holidays and he'd found a particularly excellent deal. They did go on a jungle safari, though, and one night, on an expedition led by world-renowned ornithologist, Bongo Dodge-Hollows, they spotted an exotic new species of bird with the most curious banded feet. Miss Reedy suggested that it be named the bandy-footed bongo bird in his honour.

Alice-Miranda and Millie never did get to deliver the Fanger's Chocolate to the Fayle sisters. It wasn't until weeks after the drama of the fire and the dog show that Alice-Miranda remembered them. When she found a little pile of shiny wrappers in the corner of Bonaparte's stable, she had a pretty good idea of where they'd ended up.

Fudge, meanwhile, has made himself right at home. He likes to share himself around, though, and finds a new bed to sleep on pretty much every night of the week. Much to Millie's annoyance, he does seem especially partial to Caprice. Mr Grump has lost seven pairs of shoes to date but he really doesn't mind.

Cast of characters

Winchesterfield-Downsfordvale Academy for Proper Young Ladies staff

Miss Ophelia Grimm	Headmistress
Aldous Grump	Miss Grimm's husband
Mrs Louella Derby	Personal secretary to the headmistress
Miss Livinia Reedy	English teacher
Mr Josiah Plumpton	Science teacher
Howie (Mrs Howard)	Housemistress
Mr Cornelius Trout	Music teacher
Miss Benitha Wall	PE teacher
Miss Verity Tweedle	Art teacher
Mrs Doreen Smith	Cook
Charlie Weatherly (Mr Charles)	Gardener

Winchesterfield-Downsfordvale students

Alice-Miranda Highton-Smith-Kennington-Jones	
Millicent Jane McLoughlin-McTavish-McNoughton-McGill	Alice-Miranda's best friend and room mate
Jacinta Headlington-Bear	Friend

Sloane Sykes	Friend
Caprice Radford	Friend of sorts
Constance Biggins, Mimi Theopolis, Anna, Ella, Mia, Paige	Friends
Sofia Ridout	Head Prefect

Fayle School for Boys staff and students

Professor Wallace Winterbottom	Headmaster
Mrs Deidre Winterbottom	Professor Winterbottom's wife
Parsley	Professor Winterbottom's West Highland terrier
Mr Harold Lipp	English and Drama teacher
Lucas Nixon	Alice-Miranda's cousin
Septimus Sykes	Lucas's best friend and brother of Sloane
George 'Figgy' Figworth	Student

Villagers

Myrtle Parker	Show Society President and village busybody
Reginald Parker	Myrtle's husband
Newton	Myrtle's garden gnome
Ambrosia Headlington-Bear	Jacinta's mother
Silas Wiley	Mayor of Downsfordvale
Nancy Mereweather	Secretary to Mayor Wiley
Constable Derby	Local policeman, married to Louella Derby
Herman Munz	Owner of the local shop
Marta Munz	Herman's wife
Evelyn Pepper	Racehorse trainer and manager
Indira Singh	Owner of the local curry house
Dr Davidson	Vet
Father Colin	Minister

Others

Bonaparte	Alice-Miranda's pony
Chops	Millie's pony
Roberta Dankworth	Dog breeder and owner of Nobel Kennels
Barry Dankworth	Owner of Haute Hound, married to Roberta
Citrine	One of Roberta's six Afghan hounds, Chudleigh's reigning champion
Farrah Fawcett	Roberta's anxious poodle
Sapphire	One of Roberta's hounds-in-training
Becca Finchley	Breeder of cavalier King Charles spaniels and toy poodles
Daniel Finchley	Becca's son
Siggy	Becca's last remaining cavalier King Charles spaniel and previous Chudleigh's champion
Vera Bird	Becca Finchley's neighbour
Major Alistair Foxley	Chairman of Chudleigh's Dog Show
Declan O'Malley	Village lad
Damon O'Malley	Village lad and Declan's younger brother
Darius Loveday	Host of *Dog Days*
Malorie Sugsworth	Chudleigh's hound expert
Edith Parbury	Chudleigh's judge
Fudge	Runaway cavoodle
Molly	Fudge's mother
Kate	Paramedic

About the Author

Jacqueline Harvey taught for many years in girls' boarding schools. She is the author of the bestselling Alice-Miranda series and the Clementine Rose series, and was awarded Honour Book in the 2006 Australian CBC Awards for her picture book *The Sound of the Sea*. She now writes full-time and is working on more Alice-Miranda and Clementine Rose adventures.

www.jacquelineharvey.com.au

Jacqueline Supports

Jacqueline Harvey is a passionate educator who enjoys sharing her love of reading and writing with children and adults alike. She is an ambassador for Dymocks Children's Charities and Room to Read. Find out more at www.dcc.gofundraise.com.au and www.roomtoread.org/australia.

Want to know how it all began?
Read on for a sample of
Alice-Miranda at School

Chapter 1

Alice-Miranda Highton-Smith-Kennington-Jones waved goodbye to her parents at the gate.

'Goodbye, Mummy. Please try to be brave.' Her mother sobbed loudly in reply. 'Enjoy your golf, Daddy. I'll see you at the end of term.' Her father sniffled into his handkerchief.

Before they had time to wave her goodbye, Alice-Miranda skipped back down the hedge-lined path into her new home.

Winchesterfield-Downsfordvale Academy for

Proper Young Ladies had a tradition dating back two and a half centuries. Alice-Miranda's mother, aunt, grandmother, great-grandmother and so on had all gone there. But none had been so young or so willing.

It had come as quite a shock to Alice-Miranda's parents to learn that she had telephoned the school to see if she could start early – she was, after all, only seven and one-quarter years old, and not due to start for another year. But after two years at her current school, Ellery Prep, she felt ready for bigger things. Besides, Alice-Miranda had always been different from other children. She loved her parents dearly and they loved her, but boarding school appealed to her sense of adventure.

'It's much better this way,' Alice-Miranda had smiled. 'You both work so hard and you have far more important things to do than run after me. This way I can do all my activities at school. Imagine, Mummy – no more waiting around while I'm at ballet or piano or riding lessons.'

'But darling, I don't mind a bit,' her mother protested.

'I know you don't,' Alice-Miranda had agreed, 'but you should think about my being away as a holiday. And then at the end there's all the excitement of coming home, except that it's me coming home to you.' She'd hugged her mother and stroked her father's brow as she handed them a gigantic box of tissues. Although they didn't want her to go, they knew there was no point arguing. Once Alice-Miranda made up her mind there was no turning back.

Her teacher, Miss Critchley, hadn't seemed the least surprised by Alice-Miranda's plans.

'Of course, we'll all miss her terribly,' Miss Critchley had explained to her parents. 'But that daughter of yours is more than up to it. I can't imagine there's any reason to stop her.'

And so Alice-Miranda went.

Winchesterfield-Downsfordvale sat upon three thousand emerald-coloured acres. A tapestry of Georgian buildings dotted the campus, with Winchesterfield Manor the jewel in the crown. Along its labyrinth of corridors hung huge portraits of past headmistresses, with serious stares and old-fashioned clothes. The trophy cabinets glittered with treasure and the foyer was lined with priceless antiques. There was not a thing out of place. But from the moment Alice-Miranda entered the grounds she had a strange feeling that something was missing – and she was usually right about her strange feelings.

The headmistress, Miss Grimm, had not come out of her study to meet her. The school's secretary, Miss Higgins, had met Alice-Miranda and her parents at the gate, looking rather surprised to see them.

'I'm terribly sorry, Mr and Mrs Highton-Smith-Kennington-Jones,' Miss Higgins had explained. 'There must have been a mix-up with the dates – Alice-Miranda is a day early.'

Her parents had said that it was no bother and they would come back again tomorrow. But Miss Higgins was appalled to cause such inconvenience and offered to take care of Alice-Miranda until the house mistress arrived.

It was Miss Higgins who had interviewed Alice-Miranda some weeks ago, when she first contacted the school. At that meeting, Alice-Miranda had thought her quite lovely, with her kindly eyes and pretty smile. But today she couldn't help but notice that Miss Higgins seemed a little flustered and talked as though she was in a race.

Miss Higgins showed Alice-Miranda to her room and suggested she take a stroll around the school. 'I'll come and find you and take you to see Cook about some lunch in a little while.'

Alice-Miranda unpacked her case, folded her clothes and put them neatly away into one of the tall chests of drawers. The room contained two single beds on opposite walls, matching chests and bedside tables. In a tidy alcove, two timber desks, each with a black swivel chair, stood side by side. The furniture was what her mother might have called functional. Not beautiful, but all very useful. The room's only hint of elegance came from the fourteen-foot ceiling with ornate cornices and the polished timber floor.

Alice-Miranda was delighted to find an envelope addressed to 'Miss Alice-Miranda Highton-Smith-Kennington-Jones' propped against her pillow.

'How lovely – my own special letter,' Alice-Miranda said out loud. She looked at the slightly tatty brown bear in her open suitcase. 'Isn't that sweet, Brummel?'

She slid her finger under the opening and pulled out a very grand-looking note on official school paper. It read:

Winchesterfield-Downsfordvale Academy for Proper Young Ladies

📖

Dear Miss Highton-Smith-Kennington-Jones,

Welcome to Winchesterfield-Downsfordvale Academy for Proper Young Ladies. It is expected that you will work extremely hard at all times and strive to achieve your very best. You must obey without question all of the school rules, of which there is a copy attached to this letter. Furthermore you must ensure that your behaviour is such that it always brings credit to you, your family and this establishment.

Yours sincerely,
Miss Ophelia Grimm
Headmistress

Winchesterfield-Downsfordvale Academy for Proper Young Ladies
School Rules

1. Hair ribbons in regulation colours and a width of $3/4$ of an inch will be tied with double overhand bows.
2. Shoes will be polished twice a day with boot polish and brushes.
3. Shoelaces will be washed each week by hand.
4. Head lice are banned.
5. All times tables to 20 must be learned by heart by the age of 9.
6. Bareback horseriding in the quadrangle is not permitted.
7. All girls will learn to play golf, croquet and bridge.
8. Liquorice will not be consumed after 5 pm.
9. Unless invited by the Headmistress, parents will not enter school buildings.
10. Homesickness will not be tolerated.

Alice-Miranda put the letter down and cuddled the little bear. 'Oh, Brummel, I can't wait to meet Miss Grimm – she sounds like she's very interested in her students.'

Alice-Miranda folded the letter and placed it in the top drawer. She would memorise the school rules later. She popped her favourite photos of Mummy and Daddy on her bedside table and positioned the bear carefully on her bed.

'You be a brave boy, Brummel.' She ruffled his furry head. 'I'm off to explore and when I get back I'll tell you all about it.'